GESAR OF LING

Gesar of Ling

···················· A BARDIC TALE ····················

FROM THE SNOW LAND OF TIBET

Retold by David Shapiro

Edited by Jane Hawes

BALBOA
PRESS

A DIVISION OF HAY HOUSE

Design by Gopa & Ted2, Inc.
Cover art by Greg Smith

Balboa Press books may be ordered through booksellers or by contacting:

Balboa Press
A Division of Hay House
1663 Liberty Drive
Bloomington, IN 47403
www.balboapress.com
1 (877) 407-4847

This is a retelling of the mythic story of Tibet and is not
intended to provide specific instructions of any kind.

Print information available on the last page.

ISBN: 978-1-9822-2513-1 (sc)
ISBN: 978-1-9822-2515-5 (hc)
ISBN: 978-1-9822-2514-8 (e)

Library of Congress Control Number: 2019904104

Balboa Press rev. date: 04/22/2019

This book is dedicated to the people of Tibet.

Table of Contents

Acknowledgments

THE CORPUS OF THIS WORK bears the strong imprint of a number of contributors. Without the original translation begun by Robin Kornman, completed with Lama Chönam and Sangye Khandro, and then extensively reworked by Jane Hawes, this work could never have been contemplated, no less completed. The original spark for Robin to dedicate so much of his too short life to the epic came from Chögyam Trungpa, Rinpoche, who was also my main teacher. However, my personal inspiration to work on the Gesar epic came largely from the excitement and commitment that Lama Chönam and my wife, Jane Hawes, had to the completion of the text that Shambhala then published. After my initial attempts to rewrite that work, a number of people read and made helpful suggestions and offered encouragement.

My daughter Hazel Shapiro and my good friend Tom Light were early readers and offered enthusiasm and much support. Hazel also read the final text with a detailed eye, and I am grateful for her clear seeing. Stephanie Lain gave helpful suggestions all along the way. But Ellen Broyles, along with her master's in French, her love of the language of English, and her aggressive and diligent marking pen, propelled this text forward. Jane Hawes went over the final work line by line by line, and without her love and devotion, neither would this work have been completed nor my life be worth one of those proverbial tinker's damns.

I would also like to acknowledge *Treasury of Lives (https://treasury oflives.org)* for the kind permission to use the two maps of Tibet that are included and were produced with the expertise of the cartographer Karl Ryavec, Professor of World Heritage, University of California, Merced.

Foreword by Lama Chönam

I AM SO PLEASED that my good friend and student David Shapiro has brought forward this volume. I was born and raised in the Golok region, in the northeastern part of Tibet, and it was here that the legend of Gesar likely arose, revealed as terma (spiritual treasure written down based on pure vision) and developed through the authentic oral traditions of bards and storytellers. Asian scholars believe that this is the longest epic that exists in the world. Its interwovenness with the Tibetan culture and history cannot be overstated.

The extemporaneous style of the narrative is sometimes in verse, sometimes in prose, and sometimes a mingling of the two, and studded with ancient proverbs that have become part of the fabric of everyday dialogue in Tibet and particularly in Golok. The proverbs abound in both spiritual and worldly examples, lessons, and advice. My grandmother had a proverb for every occasion, and not uncommonly did they come from the epic. In my village we often heard tales from the epic song performed by itinerant bards and, in my own large family, it was my responsibility on many nights to read from the various stories of Gesar. The Gesar narrative was part and parcel of a childhood in Tibet and its stories are still performed throughout Golok as dramas and operas.

Just as other mythic tales demonstrate the values of a given society, the Gesar epic displays those of Tibet. For example, the term karma, which has been adopted into common English usage and is perhaps often misunderstood or grasped only superficially, is illustrated in the Gesar text from a more nuanced view that probes the complexity of thought, intention, and action. This plays out in a rich web of forces that produce the circumstances in which we live and result in the choices that bring us forward. It is a far cry from an eye for an eye and its converse, that a good deed will necessarily be rewarded.

As is mentioned in the Introduction, there are approximately 120 volumes of Gesar stories. These first three span the time from his birth until, as a young man, he becomes the king of Tibet. Most of the latter volumes describe the various battles that he has with the enemies of Tibet and in their graphic telling might strike our modern ears as harsh. Nonetheless, they represent this land and its culture as it was, as well as the importance of loyalty, honesty, integrity, and compassion.

Many scholars, far more learned and eloquent than I, have written commentaries and given explanations regarding the classic world epic of King Gesar. Although I am unqualified to offer any new academic perspective, my intention in this foreword is to impart to the reader a taste of my experience as a nomadic child born and raised in the land where this remarkable legacy is still felt.

In Golok, the epic shines like a mirror reflecting a time past but still alive in the sights and sounds of the high plateaus, in the ruins of the heroes' castles, in the same mountains, rivers, and meadows where they lived, and in the customs of the people. The Golok dialect is full of the same vocabulary, proverbs, parables, and phrases that were used in Gesar's time. Therefore, it is natural for me to share this with you, the readers, since this is what shaped my early life in Golok and is as familiar to me as everyday speech.

The book presented here is based on the same three volumes that I translated and worked on with Robin Kornman, Sangye Khandro, and David's wife Jane Hawes, and which was published by Shambhala Publications in 2012 as The Epic of King

Gesar of Ling. Robin, Sangye, and I worked together on this translation for several months a year from 1994 to 2000, with every intention to celebrate the publication of this work as a team of colleagues. However, just as the Buddhist teachings strongly remind us, all things are transient and, sadly, Robin passed away from cancer in July of 2007 and his life's work was published posthumously with Jane's help.

King Gesar

The main character in the epic is the Lord of Ling, King Gesar, who was not an ordinary human being but rather a manifestation of the enlightened activity of all the buddhas, brought forth by the strength of their great compassion at a time of despair in the land of Tibet. At the request of an enlightened buddha, Amitabha, Gesar emanated from the pure land to the world of humans, bringing vast benefit. Out of his compassion for all beings, Gesar manifests the energy of the bodhisattva protectors of the three families, Manjushri, Avalokiteshvara, and Vajrapani, who themselves are embodiments of the Buddha's wisdom, compassion, and power. This same energy exists today and will arise in the future to overcome the evils that stem from ego-centered passion, aggression, and ignorance (our own included).

Scholars hold that King Gesar was born in Golok or in neighboring Kham, in the Earth Tiger year of the first Rabjung (the sixty-year cycle used in the Tibetan calendar), the year 1038 CE. Gesar lived until the age of eighty-eight (Tibetan reckoning counts gestation in the womb as the first year of life when calculating age) and passed away in 1125 CE, on a peak near the great mountain Magyal Pomra in Golok.

The stories of Gesar are exciting in their own right as fine tales, but to understand them as they are intended, it is crucial to keep in mind that King Gesar's every word and deed was an expression of his ultimate wisdom, compassion, and power. Gesar was an enlightened being, sent by the buddhas and bodhisattvas at a time of crisis and terror to bring peace, not only to the land of Ling, but to the hearts and minds of humanity worldwide. This is particularly important to recall when considering the many stories of conflicts and battles. The wars Gesar waged were not holy wars to overpower or convert countries of other faiths. He was not fighting to conquer others because of their color, race, religion, or politics.

GODS AND DEMONS

Throughout the epic one encounters the terms drala, werma, and windhorse, as well as references to various gods and demons. It can be difficult to understand these terms, and discern whether they represent certain kinds of energy, formless beings, good or bad luck by other names, or perhaps something else altogether.

Drala and werma are ancient designations that gained primacy with the Gesar epic and represent protector principles of Gesar and the people of Ling. Drala can sometimes be understood as the powerful and overwhelming energy behind great accomplishment. As for werma, there are said to be thirteen principal werma, represented by thirteen animals. For example, in the second volume of the epic, when Gesar's uncle Trothung hires a magician to kill Joru, Joru invokes drala and werma, following which they all manifest as inconceivable legions of protectors to overwhelm the magician.

The drala and werma protect not only Gesar, but also every human who embodies dignity and goodness. According to ancient Tibetan beliefs there are drala that accompany each ordinary human birth. These drala are referred to as siblings because they are born of the mother simultaneously with the child. These spirit beings are formless aspects of one's mind, and their power and number vary according to each individual.

There are many categories of guardian spirits, including those for the house, castle, farmland, domestic animals, entranceways, paths, ornaments, clothes, food, companions, family lineages, and prosperity.

Finally, the epic is steeped in the notion of lungta, or windhorse. Windhorse is the supreme steed, carrying wish-fulfilling jewels, and able to travel freely without obstacle. The windhorse represents the energy of success and four mighty animals symbolize the power of windhorse: the mythic garuda bird and the dragon roam the heavens, and the snow lion and the tiger are earth-bound. The red tiger represents bravery; the white snow lion, magnificence; the green garuda, uplifted energy; and the blue dragon represents renown.

THE LEGACY OF GESAR

In Tibet, there are some who see Gesar as an enlightened being and a wisdom deity, while others are simply inspired by his story, taking him and his warriors as ordinary role models—little boys want to be Gesar and girls want to be Queen Drukmo. The thread of these stories has naturally passed down through generations, its traditions remaining strong in Golok and other regions of Tibet. However, it remains to be seen if the propagation of its cultural wisdom will persist. Many in the younger generation have had little opportunity to encounter the legacy of Gesar, and hence are unaware of its relevance in a modern context.

Now, while the Gesar epic is still a living tradition, there exists the opportunity to apply this ancient wisdom concerning basic human goodness to the complexities of modern worldly life.

These noble qualities are developed between human beings, through direct and personal heart connections. Through earnest cultivation of these qualities, without pretense or hypocrisy, there is the chance for each of us to become like the heroes and heroines of Gesar's time. As a result, the peace and prosperity that would fill our world could be a rebirth of the glory of the land of Ling, reawakening the inner wisdom of this current millennium and spanning the continents of this world.

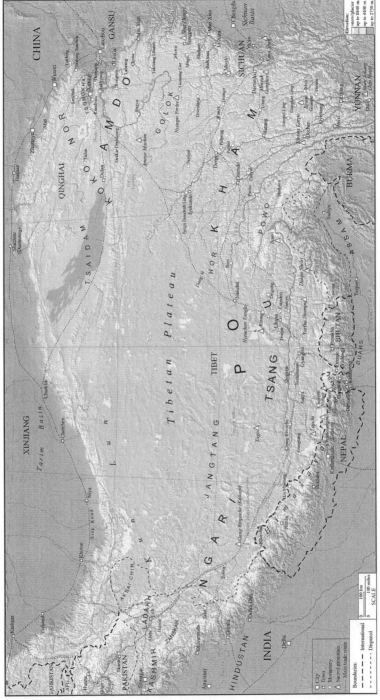

Copyright © 2015 Treasury of Lives

Elevation
snow/glacier
up to 5845 m.
up to 4480 m.
up to 2750 m.

CHINA

GANSU

QINGHAI

KOKONOR

TSONGKHA

AMDO

GOLOK

SICHUAN

Sichuan
Basin

Chengdu

XINJIANG

Tarim Basin

K u n l u n

Silk Road

TSAIDAM

KHAM

HOR

Tibetan Plateau

PO

POWO

U

JANGTANG

TIBET

TSANG

NGARI

H i m a l a y a

NEPAL

Kathmandu

BHUTAN

DUARS

BURMA

ASSAM

INDIA

Delhi

HINDUSTAN

PAKISTAN

KASHMIR

LADAKH

AKSAI CHIN

Amritsar

AFG.

TAJIKISTAN

Boundaries:
International
Disputed

□ City
□ Town
◇ Monastery
△ Sacred mountain
⋯⋯ Main trade-route

SCALE
0   100 km
0   100 miles

TIBETAN PLATEAU

AMDO

Introduction

GESAR OF LING IN EPIC LITERATURE

T HE *GESAR OF LING* epic is the national epic for the country of Tibet and its people. Ling, where much of the action in the text takes place was a kingdom in northeastern Tibet, likely including portions of land between Amdo and Kham, though this remains to this day somewhat controversial. This area can be seen on the map pages. The later tales of the epic also occur in these lands. Scholars generally accept that it is the longest single piece of literature currently in the world canon, encompassing 120 volumes and 20 million words. A number of different accounts of the epic span from Persia through Tibet, and into China and India. The version presented here is the one most commonly referred to when the epic is studied in the present day. Gyurmed Thubten Jamyang Dragpa, a disciple of the great Mipham Jampel Gyepe Dorje (1846–1912), compiled it in the late nineteenth century.

Just as was true for *The Iliad* and *The Odyssey*, many early versions of the Gesar epic were sung by bards, having been composed orally, and then passed down from singer to singer. Just as the tales we know as the Homeric epics were written down hundreds of years after their initial composition, likewise the epic of Gesar of Ling was sung and composed for centuries before the present versions were rendered into text.

All epics share certain characteristics. There are nine generally accepted characteristics of the epic form, which include such things as humanity's interactions with deities, long lists and speeches, and a heroine or hero who manifests the virtue

1

of a civilization. The first recorded epic of which we are aware is that of Gilgamesh, thought to be a Sumerian ruler circa 2700 BCE, which tells a somewhat convoluted and gruesome story that displays both the good and bad of those Sumerian times. The oldest written copy of the *Epic of Gilgamesh* comes from a library compiled in the seventh century BCE. In a similar way, we can see that, for most epics, there is an oral tradition that exists for some time prior to its being set in stone, velum, papyrus, or paper.

To the inhabitants of a land, epics impart a harmonious view of their culture and an understanding of their place in the world. Whether it is *The Iliad*, the *Epic of Gilgamesh*, the Arthurian legend of the Lady of the Lake, the *Mahabharata*, or the great tales of Scandinavia, Native America, or Africa, these stories impart cultural knowledge vital to their respective people. While the times and places may vary across the globe and the millennia, the basic characteristics of what epics *do* and how they do it are fairly constant.

For instance, the Gesar epic contains information needed in order to inform native Tibetans of their cultural heritage. While we in the West may think of nomadic people as somehow simple, the epic shows their civilization to be rich, profound, colorful, and sophisticated. The culture of Tibet that is described in the epic represents the Tibet of the Medieval Period, and hence some coarseness persists that may seem harsh to our modern ears. An active attempt was made to bring the heart of the culture forward without either sanitizing or simplifying and to present to current readers a story to which they could relate.

It describes how knowledge and wisdom, in this case with some Buddhist trappings but actually universal, can be transmitted. It is an example of how the best qualities of being human, such as loyalty, compassion, and virtue, will triumph over evil, deception, and self-interest. This describes how an unsullied mind, awake and aware, frees one from the taint of confusion and ignorance and aids in one's own journey to insight.

While the use of proverbs is common in other epics, the Gesar epic stands out for the breadth and depth of its proverbs. Their importance to the Tibetan people as well as nomadic people in general cannot be overstated. The proverbs represent the major method by which the cultural, philosophical, and religious knowledge of Tibet is transmitted. All the proverbs are arguments by analogy. For instance, to imply that one must act at the proper time, a proverb might state, *If the rain has not moistened the crops, then what is the point of placing seeds there?*

Each of the proverbs may be understood on many levels, and all are vital to the culture and to this day are woven into debate and discussion. While the meaning of some of the proverbs is quite obvious, others are more challenging and require the readers' intellect to bend a bit, such as, *Sons and nephews without fathers and uncles may be strong, but they are like a tigress wandering an empty plain. The people use such a tigress as a target for their stones.*

It is hoped that, while reading the epic, the colorful nature of the original language will not be lost and that the liberal use of proverbs will act as a further window into these people and this time.

Notes Regarding the Text

The work that led to the text you have in your hands was begun in 1991 when Dr. Robin Kornman began to research the Gesar epic. At the time, Kornman was a student of the great Tibetan Buddhist teacher, Chögyam Trungpa, Rinpoche, and had just completed his doctorate in linguistic study at Princeton

University. Using the early translation of the first volume that he had done for his doctoral thesis, Robin went on to continue his study and translation work until his death in 2007.

Chögyam Trungpa's lineage descends directly from the Mukpo clan, of which Gesar was a member. Although Robin started the work alone, in 1995 he began an active collaboration with Lama Chönam and Sangye Khandro. Over the next six years, together the threesome completed a rough draft translation of the first three volumes. Robin also began teaching Tibetan to a small number of students, one of whom was Jane Hawes, who went on to become an important contributor to his translation and the editor of this text.

Lama Chönam was born in 1964 in the Golok region of northeastern Tibet. He entered the Wayen Monastery at the age of fourteen, where he studied and received teachings from many important lamas in Tibet. Lama Chönam left Tibet in 1990 to fulfill his hope of meeting His Holiness the Dalai Lama and making a pilgrimage in India and Nepal before returning home. After accomplishing that, he was invited to visit the United States, which has become his new home.

Like many Tibetans, Lama Chönam has had a lifelong interest in the epic of Gesar. As a child, he heard the epic from the bards of his native land, and when he grew older, he read the stories to his family. In 1999, he and Sangye Khandro founded the Light of Berotsana Translation Group.

Sangye Khandro, born Nanci Gustafson, traveled to India in 1971 to meet His Holiness the Dalai Lama and study Tibetan Buddhism. She arrived in Dharamsala, India, shortly after The Library of Tibetan Works and Archives had opened its doors to Western students. For the next seven years, she traveled and studied extensively in India and Nepal, becoming adept in the teachings as well as preparing herself to become one of the foremost translators of spoken Tibetan. She has authored many texts, often in collaboration with Lama Chönam.

Jane Hawes had become a student of Chögyam Trungpa, Rinpoche, in 1976. A practicing physician, she began to study Tibetan with Kornman in the mid-2000s, collaborating with him on a number of translations but devoting most of her time to working with him on the epic. In 2009, Jane joined the Light of Berotsana Translation Group.

The book that resulted from this collaboration, *The Epic of Gesar of Ling: Gesar's Magical Birth, Early Years, and Coronation as King*, was published by Shambhala Publications in 2012. The current text is taken from that and placed in a format and language that strives to be more readily accessible to a contemporary audience, one not necessarily trained or knowledgeable regarding Tibetan or Buddhist texts. Much, though not all, of the technical jargon has been eliminated and the storyline adjusted. All that is good in the text comes from others. The mistakes are mine alone.

Regarding the transliteration of Tibetan names and places, all possible attempts have been made to remove the sometimes confusing diacritical markings that attend Tibetan transliteration. However, in order to be certain of some important pronunciations, it was felt necessary to retain some, hence the é that has the long *a* sound. In pronouncing *ph*, *ch*, or *th*, the *h* is nearly silent in Tibetan and the sound is closer to an aspirated *pa*, *ca*, and *ta*, respectively, as in *pack*, *chrome*, and *top*.

King Gesar of Ling

ๆ๑ ๑ ๑ ๑

His Early Years
WHEREIN WE SET THE SCENE

I T WAS A dark era in the Land of Snow. After thousands
of years of nomads herding the animals that grazed the
grasslands and planting the barley that grows so abun-
dantly in the highlands, trouble was in the air. The land had
been divided among several clans, and now the greed and
desires of the kings had undermined the peace of this great
northern kingdom. From this chaos a new king was born, one
who would come to be renowned and beloved by all of Tibet.

This is his story, the tale of King Gesar, the telling of his
extraordinary birth, childhood, adolescence, and how he came
to be the king of that ancestral great Tibetan plateau known as
Ling. It is a wondrous tale with many captivating characters
whose exploits are both harrowing and magnificent. Like other
great tales, there is a timelessness about this story that marks it
as one of the world's great epics—one that encompasses some
twenty million words in one hundred and twenty volumes, the
first three of which will be retold here.

Across eight centuries, the story was not confined to the written word. Rather it was told in song by wandering minstrels
and visionary bards who memorized thousands of lines and
scores of melodies. In Tibet, the Land of Snow, there were—and
still are—hundreds of such bards. Journeying there today, you
would hear this story told, sung much as it once was. This tale

is more than simply the retelling of deeds by people long dead; in truth, the very telling of the epic invokes the richness of culture and a display of the complexity of human life as a whole and, as great literature invariably does, changes forever those told and those telling.

Our story begins in the ninth century CE (the 800s). At this time, the land known now as Tibet was an area largely isolated from the world around it. It was a fabled land that had begun to awaken from eons of isolation, an isolation that had not been interrupted by a Caesar or an Alexander, but would be, in the not too distant future, by a Great Khan. Aside from a few centuries of contact with China, Tibet was alone in its lofty perch.

In northeastern Tibet where most of our story will unfold, there are many natural wonders, including caves and valleys as well as the magnificent headwaters of three of Asia's great rivers: the Yellow, the Yangtze, and the Mekong. Tibet is bordered by the Himalayas, the majestic result of tectonic movements that still shape our world as the Indian Subcontinent continues its geologic collision with Asia. It is truly a cosmic landscape that is closer to the heavens than any other land on earth.

∽ᘐ∽ᘐ∽ᘐ∽ᘐ∽ᘐ

So it was that in the midst of these dark times, early in the ninth century, the Tibetan king Trisong Detsen asked Padmasambhava, a great Indian Buddhist teacher and meditation master, to help his people pass from the ancient, ancestral religion of Bon to Buddhism. In Bon there was a pantheon of native spirits, gods, and demons that needed to be quelled or pacified.

Through the depth and strength of his profound meditation practice, Padmasambhava came close to accomplishing this task, but to have been completely successful, he would have had to bind and overpower these beings, not twice, but three times. Had he done that, it is said that Tibet would have entered a long period of happiness and prosperity. However, he was distracted by horrific demon ministers who, employing powerful and dark incantations, prevented him from carrying out the third of the necessary bindings. Following this, the chance for peace slipped away. War broke out. Foreign borderland warriors, kings, and demons wandered into central Tibet, and many of the rightful kings fell from power.

CHAPTER 1

In a lovely bedchamber within a lovely fortress,
King Chipon sleeps. He dreams
A dream that bodes of great things to come,
And a great assembly is planned.

WHILE IN THIS LAND of Tibet there was considerable strife, there were also pockets of prosperity thriving under the rule of strong and just chieftains. In one such area lived a wise king, Chipon Rongtsa Tragen [Elder Chief of the Tiller Clan], who lived within a fortressed castle. The king was an elder statesman—past his youthful prime but still a sharp thinker and skillful tactician. His beard and hair were a smoky white, and his discerning, ebony eyes were creased by fine, sprightly wrinkles at their corners.

When the wind blew, as it often did in the Tibetan highlands, his hair would flow behind him. His shoulders and chest were broad, and he still had well-muscled arms and thighs. He was quick to smile, spoke softly in a low voice with melodious tones, and offered thoughtful advice. He had no use for fools or small talk, but he was generally pleasant to both his fellow warriors and attendants. Moreover, he was one of the Thirty Mighty Warriors.

As Chipon slept in his Lotus Sunrise chamber, he had a dream in which, just as the sun rose over Magyal Pomra, the great mountain of northeastern Tibet, the rays of the sun illuminated the entirety of Tibet. In the midst of those rays, a golden vajra[1] descended onto the peak of another mountain in this same part of Tibet, known as Ling, where our story takes place.

On the broad plain below, the gods of the hunt were gathering. Miraculously, at midday, constellations sparkled over the mountain pass with great ropes of colored light extending to Mapham Lake where Chipon's youngest brother, King Senglon [Lion Minister], stood holding a parasol of white silk with a rainbow-like fringe of red and green. It was an immense parasol stretching thousands of miles: from Persia in the west to China in the east, south to India, and to Hor, the lands just north of the Tibetan plateau.

Then from the southwestern sky came a lama, a great teacher, astride a white lion. A large, white hat shaped like a lotus flower sat firmly on his head. He had a vajra in his right hand and an ornamental spear, a khatvanga, in his left. On the blade of the khatvanga were impaled three human heads: one fresh, one a fortnight old, and one fully dried. A rather striking, naked woman, whose skin was deep red, accompanied him.

Though unclothed, she wore intricately etched bone ornaments crafted from skulls and long bones on her upper arms, wrists, and ankles. A thin bone skirt and necklace encircled her body, clanking whenever she moved. These two beings, speaking in unison, said to Chipon, "Great chief, sleep not, but awake. At the first light of dawn, the royal parasol of the sun rises over the great mountain—if you wish the sun's rays to benefit Ling, no good will come from an old man's foolish sleep. Listen, and do as we say." Then in his dream they sang.

Listen, chief of the great tribe of Ling.

---

1. The Sanskrit term for the ritual item that represents the skillful means of compassion. The Tibetan term is *dorje* and literally means "thunderbolt" or "diamondlike." It is pictured at the end of each chapter.

If you do not know the measure of your own sleep,
The slumber of your ignorance will be inexhaustible.[2]
The omens are not bad; they are good.
On the eighth day of the second month of summer,
Gather all your citizens
From the mighty kingdoms abroad,
Down to the fathers and uncles of the local clans.
At daybreak as the sky lightens,
Have them meet on the great plain of the Land of Snow.
Perform feast offerings and render praise to the local
    spirits.
Burn sandalwood and juniper,
And with the best of woods, erect thirteen smoke-
    offering altars,
Hoist thirteen grand flags,
And lay out an abundance of precious alms.
When it is time to enjoy the feast offering that grants power,
It is best for the host not to drool.
In the same way, on the day when you set out these
    festive dishes,
Do not be slack in your preparations.
If you have understood, your heart should be light.
If not, all our efforts have been in vain.

Their song finished, the lama and the red woman dissolved into the western sky like snow on hot coals, and Chipon startled awake and shouted out to his attendants. Such a loud and

---

2. The many traditional Tibetan proverbs that grace this story are placed in *italics*. For the most part, they are self-explanatory. Also of note is that the song ends with a couplet that, as you will see in many of the songs that follow, is essentially a disclaimer, suggesting it is up to the listener to grasp the meaning of the song.

fearsome voice was so unusual for the king that his attendants became frightened, wondering what could be the matter.

What's more, Chipon then cried out an old Tibetan curse that translates as, *Go eat your father's flesh.* The two servants put aside their fear, swallowed hard, entered his chamber, and stopped short, taken aback to see Chipon, who as king was typically unaccustomed to dressing himself, fully dressed. They were also surprised because usually he spent a few hours every morning meditating and reciting prayers, and here he was, dressed and ready for action. This behavior did not make them any less uneasy, and they murmured a few proverbs to gain some perspective. *When the avalanche falls down the white snow mountain and the snow lion seeks its prey on the plains, it is certain that wild game will be restless. When dark fog banks roll down the slopes of the glaciers and the gentle showers of rain wish to fall, it is certain that the sky will be overcast. When the dear chief arises early from his throne, it is certain that the servants will be on edge.*

These proverbs did very little to mellow their anxiety, and as they stood there, still fearful, they heard Chipon call out, "This morning I had a remarkable and subtle dream, perhaps the most impressive dream a king has had in the history of our people. I will need help to interpret the dream. We should call the powerful teacher, Thangtong Gyalpo [King of the Empty Plain]."

But immediately he reconsidered. "Now that I take into account the importance and clarity of the dream, I think it best to skip the tedious interpretations these lamas are so prone to make and simply divulge my dream."

And that is just what he did, telling his servants, "I will send letters to Gyalwé Lhundrub [Spontaneously Accomplished Victor] and Kyalo Tonpa Gyaltsen [Teacher Victory Banner]. Now, please brew some tea and bring it here."

Lhundrub was a relatively young but wise chieftain of one

of the six districts of Middle Ling. He was a brave and powerful warrior who eventually became a loyal friend to Gesar. His valor was displayed as he fought in many important battles. Eventually, in a later story, he will die while attempting to rescue Gesar's future wife, Drukmo.

Kyalo Tonpa, also a warrior, was a district leader in Ling as well as Drukmo's father. Wise and reputed to be the richest man in Tibet, Tonpa was beloved by his people, and in all things, he was fair and kind. Though somewhat older, he had broad shoulders and a strong, imposing brow. His black beard, speckled with gray, extended below his chin to a triangular point. Despite his size, he had delicate hands and was renowned as much for his elegant calligraphy as for his wealth.

It was a great relief to the servants to hear that this was what all the fuss was about, and they set about to comply with the king's wishes. Off they went to brew the royal tea, returning with a gleaming copper teapot, fragrant with the steeping leaves.

As was customary, Chipon offered the first portion of the tea to the gods, showing thanks for his auspicious dream and asking them to allow his speech to flow. Chipon, while a proud man, was not very confident of his songs and voice, but he warbled a melodic chant of offering.

Right as he was singing the last notes, just outside his window, a beautiful and powerful turquoise dragon roared, veritably shaking the heavens. Chipon was overjoyed, taking this as further proof of the auspiciousness of his dream. And he settled down to enjoy his tea. Then finally, he got around to writing the letters, the first one to Lhundrub:

> To Lhundrub, the honorable great chieftain who, through the power of his merit, has achieved a great station. You, who from your ocean of virtue ripens to

fruition like the golden sun, know that I rejoice! Here in the ocean of the land of Ling, we have seen the birth of a lotus, an auspicious dream. If you wish to share the petals of this amazing prophecy, be timely in arranging your compassionate attendance. This letter is a trifle, but the mounted courier will explicate.

Then another to Kyalo Tonpa:

To Tonpa Gyaltsen, whose virtues are manifest. From the milky ocean of that unceasing virtue, the timely ripening of your excellence is the moon and stars. I was visited by a one hundred-petaled flower of a dream. Your moonlight will help me to release the prophecy; pray do not miss this fortunate moment. This letter is a trifle, but the mounted courier will explicate.

In addition to these two letters, inspired by his dream, letters were sent to all the people of Ling, hinting at the prophecy and commanding them to come to the main gathering place, Nyida Khatrod [Conjoined Sun and Moon], on the morning of the fifteenth day. In Tibet, this is a day of great significance. As the first day of the month is always the new moon, the fifteenth would be the day on which the full moon falls, and it is considered to be auspicious.

Chipon wondered whom else he might invite to this grand gathering where he planned to disclose and describe his prophecy. In particular, there was the great sage Thangtong, whom Chipon had first thought of contacting right after his dream. Now the king realized that Thangtong's attendance was imperative. But this teacher was a wanderer, constantly moving, with no fixed address.

Just as Chipon was contemplating the gathering, Thangtong

himself was off in a deserted cave, dreaming, and in his dream, he was visited by Padmasambhava, who in a clear and strong voice said to him, "It would be excellent if you went to the land of Ling. That would bring great joy and benefit to beings and possibly peace to this war-torn land."

Awakening at once and immediately understanding the importance of this undertaking, Thangtong headed off as instructed. At this time, he had been living in a cave for some months, meditating and studying scripture. He had grown thin and wiry, and his dark eyes now glinted like polished coal. His short black goatee and mustache blended into his dark complexion, leathered and creviced from exposure to the altitude's strong sun and wind. His voice was melodic, and everyone listened attentively whenever he taught. It was on the tenth day, five days before the gathering, that he arrived at Chipon's castle gate and sang this song.

> My view is vast and unbiased,
> My meditation experience stable and still,
> And my conduct, free from the contrivances of hope
>   and fear.
> You are known far and wide by the name of Chipon,
> Trustworthy elder of the world.
> Imperial chief of this great district,
> Through your accumulated merit, you were born as
>   a king.
> Where can greater authentic presence be found?
> This illusory empty armor of the body
> Is impermanent. Since flesh and bones will separate,
> How can the fissures of skin be worse than that?
> I have spoken only out of my empty confusion,
> But since life is impermanent and the time of death
>   uncertain,

It is pointless to procrastinate when action is necessary.
You, great chief, take this to heart.

These words warmed Chipon's heart to the guru, and Chipon sang a song praising and welcoming him, requesting that he stay and teach. Chipon offered a khata, a ceremonial scarf, an unusual act for a king. Having been entreated with such urgency, Thangtong, though a wanderer at heart and accustomed only to an isolated cave, agreed to stay.

Meanwhile, Lhundrub was having his own dream—curiously much like Chipon's dream. In Lhundrub's dream, an impressive man with armor, helmet, horse, and complexion, all of gold, said to Lhundrub, "I am the main local deity of this great mountain, known as the great spirit-zodor, Magyal Pomra, and I say to you: do not sleep. Quickly arise and ready yourself. The fortune and future of the six tribes of Ling depend on you. Go now and prepare a great reception with lavish and extensive offerings."

Lhundrub had no choice but to fulfill the calling of such a powerful dream, and the very next day he performed a juniper smoke offering and conducted a great feast, gathering his people in a grand banquet hall. Just as the festivities were occurring, Chipon's messenger arrived with the sealed letter.

As these things are done, the messenger first sang a song of praise and then gave a detailed account of Chipon's dream, which closely paralleled Lhundrub's own prophetic dream. When he had examined the letter, struck by the similarity of the dreams and feeling great respect for Chipon, he spoke a few proverbs describing his fellow warrior. *Although the sun is warm, it is difficult for him to be overheated. Although the wind is frigid, it is hard for him to be chilled. Unless words are of meaning, they do not escape his mouth. Unless there is a point to his actions, he holds his seat.*

Lhundrub had his best steed, Gawa Trazur [Bright Blaze], saddled, and he departed for Nyida Khatrod, accompanied by eight attendants.

At the same time and in the same way, Kyalo Tonpa had his own dream and received a letter from Chipon. Even though he was older and a bit rickety, as soon as the messenger told him of Chipon's dream, he set off on horseback to meet the others.

Then on the thirteenth day of the month, two days before the full moon, the great lama Thangtong, the chieftains Lhundrub and Kyalo Tonpa, along with Chipon, who had initiated the meeting, came together at a great banquet hall. After eating and drinking, King Chipon presented them all with khatas, each one of which had a name such as One Thousand Lotus Fringed.

Then Chipon addressed the other three. He told them much of what they already knew, about the dreams and the prophecy as well as the auspicious alignment of the constellations and the planets. He was very optimistic that all the signs portended that great things were about to unfold. He also detailed plans for the upcoming countrywide gathering with its grand feast and celebration to help these good omens become a reality. Thangtong concurred with this song interpreting Chipon's dream.

> Listen, lords of Ling.
> You hold the lineages of clarity and power.
> Thus your dreams are not delusions.
> The sun rising from the peak of Magyal Mountain
> And the light rays that reveal the land of Ling
> Are a sign that the sun of wisdom and compassion
> Will enrich this land of Tibet.
> That a golden vajra emanated from that
> And descended on the peak of that majestic mountain

Is a sign that a divine being will take birth.
That a cord of light extends into Mapham Lake
Is a sign that this being's mother will emerge from
    the nagas.
The silk umbrella held in the hand of Senglon
Is a sign that Senglon will be his earthly father.
There are many great signs in the dreams.
Therefore do not blunder, but quickly act.
Try your best and do not fail.
Prepare now to convene the assembly of Ling.
Hereafter, from today onward,
Whatever you wish, will be.

Two days later, the great Full Moon Gathering took place. From all over Tibet and its neighboring lands, citizens, ministers, and kings came to hear of the dream prophecy and to make plans. Many great minds discussed the significance of the dreams and their promising predictions for Tibet.

After the burning of much juniper and the offering of objects and prayers, all those assembled joined in a celebratory feast, after which they rested in the belief that good fortune was sure to follow. Though what that was exactly and what was to be done were a little unclear even to the very brightest of the participants.

CHAPTER 2

In order to aid Tibet,
A divine creature meets a great teacher.
Plans and promises are made,
And all appears congenial.

A T THAT TIME, life in Tibet and in most of Eurasia was tenuous and oppressed by suffering. Famine and diseases such as plague were widespread. Unable to bear the sight of such misery, the Noble Bodhisattva[3] Avalokiteshvara supplicated the Buddha Amitabha, who was known for his compassion.

Avalokiteshvara asked Amitabha for his help in ending the suffering in Tibet. Amitabha replied by revealing the following family tree: a divine son would be born to two celestial beings, Odden Kar [White Luminosity] and his wife, Manda Lhadzé [Celestial Flower]. This son would in turn have a son with his wife, and the son would be named Dondrub [Accomplisher of Benefit]. If Dondrub's mindstream could be developed and transferred into a human being, the world would greatly benefit.

Amitabha continued, telling Avalokiteshvara, "You will need help with this. You must start by going to the continent of

---

3. A bodhisattva is a great being who has put off his or her own enlightenment in order to benefit all sentient beings. Avalokiteshvara is generally held to be the greatest of the bodhisattvas. The reader can find Avalokiteshvara as well as the other characters of the story in the Name Glossary.

Chamara and supplicate Padma Totreng [Lotus Skull Garland,[4] one of the wrathful forms of Padmasambhava]."

Avalokiteshvara took Amitabha's advice. Using only the mind energy of his perfect meditation, Avalokiteshvara traveled to Chamara. There he found a fearsome land filled with rakshasas, fierce, evil cannibal creatures, horrifying to behold. They were said to be so terrifying that ordinary humans could not bear the sight of them, and even Yama, the Lord of Death, shunned that land.

Avalokiteshvara had turned himself into a demon tiger cub with a stunning crown inlaid with pearl. He was the size of a small mountain lion, and his thick fur was black with patches of crimson red. His eyes were an even deeper red and glowed with his inner warmth. His muscled body was long and sinewy with a jet-black tail, and a halo of glimmering white light surrounded him.

He arrived at the eastern gate of Padma Totreng's fortress, where a seven-headed rakshasa demon minister standing eighteen feet tall met him. Each of the seven frightful heads looked down, and the demon minister snatched up the cub on the spot, holding him at arm's length in front of his main head. His large eyes were bloodshot and his breath foul. Spittle sprayed from his mouth when he spoke.

For a few moments, he just stared at the demon cub. Unused to visitors, he was rather surprised by the cub and asked him for what reason he had bothered to come all the way to this terrible place. In fact, he was so taken aback that he uttered a few proverbs—a practice quite common in Tibetan storytell-

---

4. While it may seem a trifle strange, the wearing of ritual bone ornaments such as skulls was reasonably commonplace. In general, bone ornaments are used to reduce one's attachment to one's body and, more subtly, one's sense of self.

ing. *Lacking great matters in mind, there would be no reason to come here. Unless you have been possessed by an evil spirit, why would you drown in a river? Only a serious crime could put a wealthy man in jail.*

The rakshasa demon minister went on to tell the cub what a fierce and frightening place he had come to, one where death and devastation are doled out like candy and where far more ferocious demon cubs have met their end. And then he inquired again as to why he had come. The demon cub answered that he came to see and speak only with the minister's master, Padma Totreng.

After some back and forth concerning the fierce disposition of this master and despite all the warnings that the rakshasa could muster, the adamant demon cub was finally allowed to enter Padma Totreng's chambers.

Padmasambhava had many forms depending upon what was required of him, and Padma Totreng was one of his wrathful forms. At one point, the king of Zahor had perceived Padmasambhava as both evil and mischievous and therefore had sentenced him to death, having him bound and thrown upon a great cemetery pyre. There his body burned for three days, and when the fire finally extinguished, Padmasambhava had risen up in the form of Padma Totreng. Mighty, tall, dark blue, and wrathful was he.

He had a golden vajra in his right hand, a skull cup filled with blood in his left, and a khatvanga in the crook of his left arm. After he arose from the cemetery ash, he moved to the island of Chamara, the abode of evil humans and cannibal demons, and there he became their king. This was the being now sought out by Avalokiteshvara in the guise of the demon cub.

The demon cub and Padma Totreng *do* meet, in a tantalizing, mystical way. Again through the power of his deep meditation, Avalokiteshvara had transformed from the demon cub

into an eight-petaled golden lotus, which was spinning with
Avalokiteshvara's mantra

OM MANI PADME HUNG HRIH AH
written on the petals in Tibetan

ཨོཾ་མ་ཎི་པདྨེ་ཧཱུྃ་ཧྲཱིཿཨཿ

The rakshasa minister, who had been guarding the doorway,
was taken aback by the transformation of the demon cub. And
without any further challenges, he brought the lotus flower
into his master's chamber. Padma Totreng already realized
why Avalokiteshvara had come to see him, and he agreed that
helping to lead Tibet back from the brink of disaster, warfare,
and poverty would indeed be a worthy goal.

Padmasambhava understood that he would need to instruct
Dondrub,[5] and so it was that he traveled to the celestial realm in
order to empower Dondrub's mindstream. With his abhisheka,[6]
Dondrub received the name Topa Gawa [Joyful to Hear] and
proceeded to give a complex discourse on the nature of mind
and enlightenment and how to strive toward compassion.

Soon after, Padmasambhava invited many great teachers to
bless the child with their own unique powers, wisdom, and
understanding. In this way, Topa Gawa quickly matured into
an extraordinary being.

Then Padmasambhava set about discussing the terms under
which Topa Gawa would become an earthly human—experi-
encing the heartbreak of suffering and impermanence as well
as the great joy inherent in human existence—all in an attempt
to bring peace to Tibet. Despite any misgivings he may have

---

5. A reminder to the reader: Dondrub is the celestial being spoken of by Amitabha, and destined ultimately to become Gesar.
6. In Buddhism, the process of maturing one's mind is done with the guidance of a teacher or guru and culminates in an initiation ceremony called an
abhisheka.

had, Topa Gawa understood the importance of Padmasambhava's request and took this mission to heart.

Furthermore, he was fully aware of the great turmoil that plagued the land. In addition, he knew the difficulties that faced him, and in order to improve his chance of success, Topa Gawa suspected that he would need a number of things to help him in his quest.

In the course of their discussion, Padmasambhava sang a song that clarified the importance of the undertaking. His song entreated the child but, beyond that, asked for help from a vast array of protectors, gods, and local spirits.[7] Topa Gawa responded with a few proverbs. *The complex scam of this world is all to put food on the plate. When a boy is born, he benefits himself by working for others. When a horse is swift, he is victorious in the race. When a weapon is sharp, it cuts meat and bone. This deed you would have me do is a great burden, like a heavy tax laid upon a beggar's son.*

Topa Gawa was now ready to list his requirements to take on the troubled land of Tibet, which was overrun with all manner of gruesome creatures and peopled by humans run amok with aggression, pride, jealous desire, and, notably, their own insular ignorance of the same. The land was glorious with its immense plains and titanic mountain peaks beneath the mirroring blue

---

7. Regarding these gods, protectors, and local spirits, there were many of them, arranged in eight categories of which the nagas, or serpent spirits, are but one. Every stream, valley, mountain, tree, and animal was possessed by one or more spirit beings. It is said that, as people built roads and moved into areas bringing modern civilization, the spirit beings retreated to more rural abodes, where they can still be found. There is a story of a road being built in 1974 near Kathmandu in Nepal. As the road construction approached a large stream, the villagers saw that two large snakes that had dwelled there had vanished. Fearing the worst, they entreated the construction overseers to abandon the project. They did not, and a few weeks later, the stream dried up, and the water never returned. The villagers are sure it was the loss of their naga protectors.

sky, but defiled by the misery and strife of its inhabitants. Topa Gawa listed his concerns and desires in this short song.

> The song begins with Ala.
> Thala leads the melody.
> I will work for the benefit of beings in the land of Tibet
> And tame the difficult to tame.
> No doubt there will be great hardship,
> But I will strive only for the benefit of others.
> Nevertheless, unless my arrow of compassion
> Relies upon the bow of skillful means,
> The target will be hard to hit.
> Self-awareness that fulfills all wishes
> Is not attached to illusory wealth.
> I need a father born of nobility
> And a mother descended from the nagas.
> Although I am unattached to worldly desire,
> I need a wife who is a wisdom dakini
> And who is free from faults.
> I need a land that is endowed with splendor and glory
> And subjects who are faithful and courageous,
> Displaying valor as we tame the hordes of demons.
> I will need a horse, a warrior's armor and weapons,
> And a resourceful enemy to hone my skills and keep
>   me sharp.
> If you cannot grant your blessings for this,
> Although it is easy for me to make promises,
> It will be difficult to fully accomplish the benefit of others.
> Therefore Padmasambhava, do not be idle; grant my
>   requests.

Topa Gawa's requirements were legion—a father born of noble stock, either a king or a king's heir, and then a mother who is the daughter of a naga king. The nagas are a class of deity associated with all things water, similar to mythic water beings from other lands, mermaids and mermen, for instance. Nagas were generally shown to have human upper bodies, blue scales, and serpentlike lower bodies. The women, known as nagi or nagini, had lustrous, long turquoise hair. They were also known to possess miraculous waterproof shoes known by the curious name, Mind's Amusement. The function of these shoes remains a mystery to this day. Topa requested a wife who was a full-blooded and, no doubt, very beautiful dakini.[8] He then went on to ask for a land that was adorned with riches and naturally abundant, along with a group of loyal subjects that will aid and accompany him on his journeys and trials.

Lastly, he asked for the general accoutrements that any warrior would want: a great steed and a supply of both armor and weapons. Finally, he requested a secret understanding with Padmasambhava that he would have an adversary in his Uncle Trothung, who would test him at every turn.

Padmasambhava, thinking through these suggestions and beginning to consider how best to fulfill Topa Gawa's requirements, entered a state of meditative absorption. First, in his mind's eye, he scoured the great land of Tibet, surveying the cities and provinces and their peoples. He considered their good and not-so-good points, including the geography of the mountains and rivers as well as the demeanor of the various clans that resided in one place or another. Eventually he settled on an area of northeastern Tibet with breathtaking mountains and rushing rivers as well as people of great strength of character.

---

8. Dakinis are female deities that represent space and insight itself and who are born to bring benefit to all beings. They can be alternately tricky, playful, seductive, motherly, or wrathful.

King Senglon, from the ancient lineage of Masang, was chosen as the child's father and the daughter of the naga king Tsugna Rinchen as his mother. He was promised a miraculous horse, a god among horses, a beautiful being that could speak wisely in the human tongue, and he was supplied with armor and weaponry. All this Padmasambhava related to Topa Gawa, who listened carefully and considered well Padmasambhava's words, and then he gave his assent by reciting the following proverbs. *If the hordes of enemies were not a dense crowd, how could we distinguish the heroes? If we are unable to distinguish the heroes, how can we know honor? If the plain is not smooth, the racehorse cannot run the course. If the racehorse is unable to run the course, how can we determine which is fastest?*

So saying and in effect girding up his courage to undertake the task before him, Topa Gawa sang a grand song of aspiration to Padmasambhava, who, pleased with his day's work, heard it in a state of smiling contentment.

I am Topa Gawa.
That lion cub on the peak of the snow mountains—
If its claws do not slash and cut,
Its six powers are of little benefit.
That roaring dragon dwelling amidst the southern clouds—
If its harmonious roar does not pervade the entire kingdom,
The wishing-fulfilling jewel held in its claws is of little benefit.
If a tempered iron chisel cannot carve a stone,
Then a chisel of pure gold will not do the trick.
The true colors of a heroic boy are revealed by his enemies.
The true colors of a young girl are revealed by her confidence.
Therefore, I will accomplish what you command.
The time has come for me to tame the evil ones.

Come what may, I will accept.
Teach me that I understand the complexity
Of this world realm and its bizarre inhabitants,
And then in accord with your wishes,
I will accomplish your commands.

Thus he sang, and Padmasambhava rested contentedly but knew that there were difficulties ahead for the troubled land of Tibet.

CHAPTER 3

It came to pass that two tongues were placed
Firmly in the cheeks of two holy men.
The naga royalty gave up their daughter,
And Topa Gawa's blissful reverie was nearly over.

S PINNING HIS MIND this way and that, Padmasambhava focused his attention to the naga princess, the youngest daughter of the naga king, and considered what he would have to do in order to have her become Gesar's mother. Sitting quite still, he stroked his chin and thought about what would make the nagas give up a princess.

After considering a number of even more dastardly schemes, he came up with the idea of secretly poisoning Lake Manasarovar,[9] the very home of the nagas. This was, of course, only a part of his sly plan, which required not only the poisoning of the lake, but also conniving in such a way that the nagas would believe that he, Padmasambhava, was the only one who could save them from this calamity. A thin smile lined his face, and his eyes glinted mischievously. Once again he stroked his chin.

Then he recited a number of magical incantations over certain substances and next cast them into the lake. The poison

---

9. This is one of the world's largest high-altitude freshwater lakes. It is at a 15,000-foot elevation and has a surface area of 160 square miles and maximum depth of 300 feet. It is spectacular to behold, deep blue in color with the holy mountain of Kailash visible to the north. It lies in southern Tibet approximately 600 miles east of Lhasa. The lake is sacred to Hindus and Jains as well as to Buddhists.

acted swiftly and powerfully, and soon sickness overcame the naga tribe. Some became lame, others went blind or deaf, and a few had terrible abdominal pain or ghastly, foul-smelling ulcerous sores. Each person's illness was unique. Not surprisingly, the simultaneous occurrence of these various illnesses caused widespread panic.

Every day more and more, nagas were affected by the epidemic until throughout the kingdom no family was spared. A great council convened wherein the king, his ministers, and many of the naga people gathered together to debate what to do. With loud voices and harsh tones, the nagas complained to their leaders and beseeched them for help and guidance. Within their songs, speeches, and complaints were a few lines of proverbs: *A healthy body, full of vitality will never be appreciated until it is pained and sick. A happy life, full of leisure, will never be appreciated until the moment of death. Unless our own mouths water from hunger, we never appreciate a poor man's need to hoard.*

The king, realizing the severity of the epidemic and the ensuing difficulties of his people, recalled a few proverbs and followed with a short song.

> *If there is no place to roost, the bird does not land.*
> *Without the bird's sudden flight, a horse has no cause to bolt.*
> *If the horse does not bolt, why would the rider's head crack?*
> We of the naga race are thought to have clairvoyant
>   powers.
> How could we be this blind?
> Let all diviners perform divinations
> And every astrologer draw up their charts.
> In the highland pass of Marshod
> Dwells Dorje Ngangkar [White Vajra],
> A master of divination and prophetic rites
> And great friend of the nagas.

Promptly we should request his help.
Accomplish at least this, naga subjects!

Therefore, they sent a naga child by the name of Nangwa Ziden [Majestic Appearance] to seek out Dorje Ngangkar, who was widely known for his divination skills, and bring him to the king.

In the meantime, Padmasambhava had had a chat with that same diviner, Dorje Ngangkar, in which Padma told the sooth-sayer to advise the nagas that they must ask him, Padmasam-bhava, to come to their aid. Knowing the power and completely enlightened nature of this great teacher, Dorje Ngangkar prom-ised to do what was requested.

Just moments later, the naga child arrived at Dorje Ngang-kar's dwelling. Dorje Ngangkar was a stooped and elderly wise man with white hair that flowed to his shoulders and a wispy white beard. He dressed in fine wool spun from yaks and dyed to a milky white. Out from underneath all this whiteness, his complexion was dark and ruddy with a deeply furrowed brow overhanging his pensive hazel eyes. His face gave the impres-sion of frowning and smiling at the same time as if in response to the cosmic irony with which we all live.

There was a depth to his countenance that caused the minds of those who encountered him to stop, if even for just a moment. Without a trace of self-importance, he was an impos-ing elder. The child, whose wisdom allowed him to grasp what he beheld, approached and gave him a one-eyed crystal jewel and a greeting.

"Master of the divination ceremonies of the phenomenal world, with clairvoyant power you possess the divine eye that knows all. We of the pure kingdom of the nagas have been struck by scores of dread diseases, many of which were pre-viously unknown to us. Why did this happen? What have we done wrong? We do not know what will help us or what medicines will cure us. My sovereign, the glorious king of the nagas, Tsugna Rinchen, has sent me here with these tidings in order to invite and beg you, the famous and renowned diviner, Dorje Ngangkar, to come to our land and aid us in our time of terrible disease and devastation. Please listen attentively, and accept our invitation."

The great soothsayer agreed to come and provide aid in this time of the nagas' need. In light of what he had just promised Padmasambhava, Dorje Ngangkar knew that he would have to be very clever in order to convince the nagas to invite Padma, the Lotus Born One. He began by loading the backs of fifty mules with 360 divination threads, 1,500 divination sticks, 150 divination stones, 32 divining arrows, a 3,600-square divination board, and a weighty ancient and precious divination text.

As soon as he had gathered his divination tools, the elder and the child set out and soon reached the naga land and came before the king. Arriving before the assembly and the king sets Dorje Ngangkar to remember these proverbs: *A clever man who spins a web of lies, without reviewing his tricky thoughts three times over, cannot dupe the wise. A great white vulture with wings of wind, without circling at height three times, cannot home in on its prey.*

Then he related to all assembled how difficult and dangerous this divination was likely to be. Many items would need to be arranged, the diviner craftily suggested, in order to increase the odds that the revelation he gave would be perfection itself and thus lead these poor people from their most sorrowful state.

He continued in a great booming voice, "In order to do divinations for the king of the nagas, for the illness of the naga population at large, and for important affairs in general, the offerings must be abundant. The following must be prepared: a large precious cloth placed on a stainless white divination

ground; thirteen golden, grooved divination arrows; fifty varieties of precious jewels; the collarbone of a white vulture; the
right leg of a white ewe; and an untarnished crystal mirror.
With these things in place, I will be able to banish ambiguity
and clearly proclaim what you need to do to end this horrible
epidemic."

Not having any choice, the nagas arranged all the necessary
materials before him. Then Dorje Ngangkar placed the stainless white divination cloth in front. It was ornamented with the
thirteen golden, grooved divination arrows. The collarbone of
the white vulture and the right leg of a white ewe were then
ceremonially placed upon it. He fastened the untarnished crystal mirror and upon that spread the fifty varieties of precious
jewels.

Finally on the white cloth, he arranged the 3,600-square
divination board, the 1,500 divination sticks, the 360 knotted
threads, as well as the 32 divination arrows. His movements
were made with both a practiced elegance and a speed most
beguiling. The naga audience was entranced as he rubbed his
hands together, pressing hard and concentrating deeply, making a long, serious face as though yearning for a powerful and
clear revelation. Then with a great flourish, he gazed with glis-
tening eyes up toward the heavens and related his vision to the
assembly.

> *So!* From the upper glorious spirit castle,
> Supreme divination master of the phenomenal world,
> Guide the divination I make here today.
> Dark fog obscures the divination.
> Hidden turmoil obstructs the divination.
> Clear the obstruction of delusion that fosters stupidity
>   and dullness.
> Clear the veil that is like clouds from above.

Clear the veil that is like fog from below.
Uncovered, it will be clearer than a radiant, luminous
    crystal.

I perform this illuminating divination today
Because the kingdom of the pure nagas
Is oppressed by impure obscurations.
To begin with, how has this occurred?
Secondly, what are the conditions?
Finally, what can be done to remedy this?
Clearly reveal all answers; hide and obscure nothing!
[Concentrating most intently and looking down, he
    continued.]
Oh! This divination is disturbing—
These bad omens seem impossible and the diseases
    incurable.
In the kingdom of the nagas,
This first came about from the land of humans
When the king of Tibet, Trisong Detsen,
Invited Padmasambhava and erected the temple Samye.
Though the Tibetans embraced him,
The nagas resisted his teachings,
And this broke the Lotus Born One's heart.
If remedies are not performed soon,
The kingdom of the nagas will surely be destroyed.
The cure must come from the land of Tibet
Where Guru Padmasambhava still resides.
If you are unable to invite this master to come here,
Then remedy and hope are beyond your reach.
According to the tradition of the ancient Tibetan sayings:
When it comes to life itself, do not be stingy with possessions.
When it comes to possessions, do not be careless.
Naga king and great assembly, bear this in mind.

As soon as these words were heard, the naga king Tsugna Rinchen exclaimed his joy and loaded up thirteen mules with precious gems for the diviner, who was then escorted back to his homeland, with none of the nagas any the wiser. Though some of the more skeptical nagas thought there was a fleeting glint of amusement in the diviner's eye.

However, Tsugna now had a dilemma. None of the naga nobles had ever even met Padmasambhava and therefore were reluctant to request the aid of the Lotus Born One. There was silence in the face of the naga king's entreaty until a fearless child, Yerpé Trin-ga [Cloud Lover of Yerpa], said, "I will call on the great master and try to get him to come. It will be easier to send a child such as myself, and I am happy to go."

The naga citizenry was relieved, if a bit embarrassed that a child bore this weighty task. With a wish-granting lapis lazuli vase and a magical cooling jewel that prevents the spread of fire, Yerpé Trin-ga left.

Padmasambhava of course knew he was coming, but when the child arrived at his cave, he feigned ignorance. Without hesitation, the child beseeched him with a short song.

> Lord Lotus Born, I bow down to you.
> Please cleanse all impure obscurations.
> Of course you know all about a person like me.
> I am a naga boy-child
> Sent by the naga king Tsugna Rinchen,
> A courier, a mere messenger.
> This inexhaustible wish-fulfilling lapis vase
> And cooling fire-preventing jewel
> Are the offerings our king has sent.
> We of the pure kingdom of nagas
> Have been stricken by disease and fouled by pollution,
> And untold incurable illnesses have arisen.

The prognosticator Dorje Ngangkar from Marshod
Received negative divinations and disturbing predictions.
He counseled that you are the sole remedy for our ills,
And so it is that I request your help
To avoid the devastation that otherwise will be the
  nagas' fate.
Forgive my boldness, but this is how it is.
Please make haste and come.
Whatever load you lay upon us, we shall carry.
Whatever you propose, we will completely embrace.
This request comes from all the nagas.
Lord Guru, you are our only hope.

  In order not to appear too eager, Padmasambhava dissembled by singing a few proverbs and a short song.

The guru who pursues material gain,
Scurrying around here and there, meets with sin.
A selfish man
Full of activities meets with conflict.
A rich man, nonetheless full of discontent,
Carrying his many wares to market, encounters enemies.
Now then, naga child, listen here.
The mere title "guru" does not make one a guru.
Just saying "others' benefit" does not make it so.
It is through realization that the mind is set free.
Attachment and ego-clinging must be cut.
Not seeing one's own faults, yet proclaiming those of
  others,
Being biased about religion and individuals—
Exactly thus we cling to this false self.
Seeking food, clothing, patrons, and fame—
There is no greater demon than that.

I, a lowly little monk, asleep in my rat hole,
Have no expectation of receiving great wealth from
    the nagas,
Yet I feel obliged to go.
Although I have no interest in ordinary material wealth,
It falls to you to fulfill whatever I request.
If you agree to this, then this guru will go.
If a great mountain is invited as the guest,
There must be a great plain to be its host.
For without that, why should the great mountain move?
If a broad river is to pass through a narrow channel,
There must be a golden canal to be its conduit.
For without that, the river cannot flow.
Naga child, keep this in mind.

Yerpé Trin-ga answered proverbially.

If the young warrior with his brand-new weapons
Does not get the great buck's rack,
His flashy gear is superfluous.
If the maidens carrying ornate pails
Do not get the pure mountain water,
Their silver ladles are of no value.

And so, after a bit more begging, the charade was concluded with Padmasambhava sending the boy back to the naga land, saying that he would shortly follow.

Yerpé Trin-ga returned to the naga king to report, "This guru Master Padma may be as famous as the turquoise dragon, but he is as feeble and unlucky as a flame in the wind. In name he may be great as a pristine snow leopard, but if you get near him, you see that he is just a mangy dog. Frankly he seems like a dull-witted, somewhat plodding monk, but I guess that, if he can cure the nagas' diseases, we had best put up with him. On the other hand, as the proverbs say, *Do not debate a stupid man. Do not play with nettles. Do not bargain with a stubborn man.*"

Yerpé Trin-ga continued, "Although I did not have time to get to know him, he insisted that I make impossible and impractical promises. When he spoke formally, he spoke what sounded like good philosophy, but underneath the conversation, he was like a merchant selling spoiled meat. Kind King Tsugna, if he fails to benefit us, you will have many more complaints, but on the other hand, since it was the great diviner who recommended him, you have no choice. In times of need, one must act decisively. At this point, it seems that we have placed our trust in Padma's hands, and I assured him that his wishes would be granted."

When the naga king asked if there were any specific articles Padma required, the boy replied, "No, all he did was quote proverbs about inviting great mountains and guiding swollen rivers. Though he did mention that the diseases that have afflicted us are dangerous."

The nagas discussed all of this amongst themselves. Understanding the seriousness of the diseases that had spread so quickly, they agreed that it was time to act. While they were concerned about what Padmasambhava might ask in return, they saw no way around this dilemma. The general consensus among the naga people was that they needed to prepare to pay Padmasambhava, and they reconciled to giving up their riches.

Just moments later, through his magical powers, Padmasambhava arrived at the upper treasure gate of Lake Manasarovar. To the north was the great peak of Mount Kailash, which, though sixty miles away, loomed large and snow-covered, an intense white shroud over the great expanse of the cobalt blue lake. The sky was such a deep blue that it seemed to meld seamlessly into the water.

On its shores, Padmasambhava saw ailing nagas writhing on the ground, clutching their sides, and groaning in pain. The young had not been spared nor the old left in peace. They were blind, mute, or worse and covered with grotesque ulcerous sores, shivering, and their tails were shriveling. They cried out in collective desperation.

In one of the great naga castles, Lapis Turquoise Peak, the naga prince Legpa Charbeb [Excellent Rainfall] convulsed continuously in lonely suffering. It was there that they brought Padmasambhava and asked him to be seated on a golden throne. The naga king Tsugna Rinchen, shaking with well-deserved angst, brought a red pearl plate loaded with varieties of luscious ripe fruits and served a special ceremonial tea.

He said, "Gracious One, sole protector in this and future lifetimes, welcome! Are you exhausted from your journey? If not, Gracious Teacher, listen as I offer this song, which is an account of what has happened here." And here is a bit of what he sang.

> Just as the sun in the lofty firmament
> Nourishes the lotus in the mud,
> We in the realms of nagas and animals
> Ask you to nourish us with your compassion.
> Here in our pure naga kingdom,
> Dreadful diseases have struck our people,
> And the sores and tumors on their limbs multiply.
> Although we have not ceased to make offerings,
> They have been to no avail.
> Just before midnight several days ago,
> Pestilential vapors descended into the heart of the
>   naga land.
> Horrifying bad omens ensued, and from that time on,
> The pure land of the nagas has been afflicted with
>   pollution,

And numerous incurable diseases have arisen.
The prognosticator Dorje Ngangkar warned us, saying,
"If you do not persuade Padmasambhava to help,
The country of the nagas will be no more."
If you do not dig with a hard rock,
You will not reach the treasure that is deeply buried.
Without climbing the steep face of the mountain,
The hunter cannot eat the mountain goat's meat.
Without handing over your precious treasure for ransom,
You cannot buy back your cherished life.

Tsugna finished by telling Padmasambhava that the diviner had admonished them not to be attached to their wealth and that they were willing to pay whatever was requested. The Lotus Born One then restated how difficult and dangerous his task was and that, when it was successfully completed, he would point his finger at whatever he felt would be sufficient payment.

Quoting the proverbs, Padmasambhava went on to confirm that they must be sure to pay his fee, whatever it may be. *Whatever makes a beggar's mouth water—whatever a poor man's stomach can take—that is what may be required.*

The naga king and his ministers were each thinking to themselves that this was exactly as the messenger boy had reported, and recalling their beloved proverbs, they regarded Padma as a man who *grabbed the tongue before the head was cooked*[10] *or scooped out the noodles before slurping the broth.*

Swallowing hard, the king again promised to pay whatever was asked. Thus reassured, Padmasambhava set out his requirements for the healing ceremony. He asked for as many

---

10. The tongue of the slain animal when cooked with the rest of the head is revered as the best part.

medicinal plants as possible, pure water, and all the healing medicines they might have, as well as yellow gold, creamy silver, red copper, blue turquoise, and clear crystal. He went on to also request a vase encrusted with five gems and adorned with sprigs of kusha grass, a mighty lion, a wish-fulfilling cow, a nourishing dri (female yak), a fertile sheep, the milk of a long-lived goat, a white divination board, a rare clockwise-swirling conch, a divine white offering cake with blown petals, and a triple-notched divination arrow. Padma said that he needed to have all of these by the following morning for a ceremony to be held on the Turquoise Plain. All nagas ailing or in any way unwell were to be brought there.

All the ceremonial items were arranged as requested, and the sick and crippled were escorted, carried, or dragged to the site. Some needed stretchers; others were blind and needed to be led. Meanwhile, Padmasambhava had constructed an elaborate mandala with the ritual items that he had requested.

Now he incanted many complex and artful magic formulae. He blessed the mandala with mantras and the Turquoise Plain itself with many types of incense smoke, milk from five different animals, and great plumes of medicinal smoke from the plants and herbs. He chanted in a deep and melodious voice.

OM AH HUM
I supplicate the Three Rare and Supreme Jewels of
   Refuge.
The illness of the five poisons, whose essence is
   ignorance,
Is cured by the medicine of the wisdom of self-awareness.
Outwardly, there are three: wind, phlegm, and bile.
Inwardly there are three: heat, cold, and agitation.
Secretly, three as well: passion, aggression, and delusion.
When they arise, they arise from the expanse of the mind,

And when they dissolve, they dissolve into the expanse of
   space.
The outer four elements are the father of poisons;
The inner four elements are the mother of poisons.
The Three Rare and Supreme Ones are free from poisons.
By the truth of these authentic words,
The three poisons dissolve into the four elements.
This wisdom water, the essence of the buddhas,
Cleanses the five poisons of the five castes of nagas.
May the unclean and impure become pure.
Wash, wash, wash them clean.
Cleanse, cleanse, cleanse the corruption of broken vows.
Oust, oust, oust the obscurations of the demonic forces.
Move, move, move near us, O essence of long life.
May the nagas within their watery kingdom
Be free from sickness and gain bodies of gods,
Be free from old age and gain the body of youth.
May they be sheltered by the protecting deities.
From this day onward,
May all nagas be liberated from disease,
May human and animal diseases be prevented,
And may the entire naga realm be established in
   well-being.
May all be happy and at their ease.

Thus he chanted and prayed. As he had finished his purifi-
cation and smoke offering, all the ailing nagas were instantly
cured of their diseases. More than just cured, they were better
than they had ever been before. The crippled danced—even
those who previously could not dance. The mute and previously tone-deaf broke into song, the blind saw the outer and
inner beauty of our world, and the deaf heard both cosmic
and earthly melodies. Henceforth, all the nagas became more

radiantly splendid than ever before, and the naga king Tsugna Rinchen was understandably overjoyed with this turn of events.

Naturally, the inhabitants of the naga lands were ecstatic. But then, immediately and predictably, they started to worry at what price their joy had been bought. This led to a great deal of speculation and anxiety, but they decided to be proactive and gather their riches together. In their minds, this would somehow lessen the bill that was coming their way soon.

They each contributed gold, silver, and jewels and began to present these to Padmasambhava. Though Padmasambhava, you may recall, was interested only in the naga princess, and his pleasant air quickly became one of indignation and ire. The nagas looked on apprehensively as his countenance darkened. It was said that his face turned as dark as gathering storm clouds, while his nostrils flared like great frothing waves.

Glaring, he had some choice proverbs for these nagas. *Not repaying the master's kindness, the guard dog steals the butter. The hunter profits by the stag's rack, but the stag dies. Your proffered recompense is no better than rubbing oil into a rock. If you remove the bridge once you have crossed a river, it will be pointless to look back to see if there is a boat.*

He then reminded them in no uncertain terms that he was the guru who had power to kill or cure and that he had no particular interest in their jewels. Having promised to give to Padma whatever he requested, the nagas were quite concerned.

Padma then requested to speak with the naga queen, Lady Demkar Lhamo [Undulating White Goddess]. She was the wife of the naga king and mother of their three daughters. The nagas' first thought was that Padmasambhava planned to kill the princesses but, paralyzed by their own terror, they obediently brought the queen to him.

The guru said to Demkar Lhamo, "Your family's offering to

repay my great kindness is certainly a poor excuse for a gift. There is not a thing that they have brought that I want. Multi-colored precious stones, yellow sand, all of this, what would I want with it? I cannot eat it. I cannot wear it. If I were to wear it, these jewels would only weigh me down and bring me to an early grave. On the other hand, I have heard that you have several lovely daughters. I want you to bring them here."

The naga queen was mortified that the guru would make such a demand, and her face flushed in embarrassment for him. Not wanting to appear as stricken as she was, she merely stammered and slowly backed away.

She turned to the crowd and awkwardly repeated what the guru had commanded. She paced back and forth, weaving among the ranks of the nagas. Finally and with much dread, she scribbled a note and placed it before the naga king, who slapped his hands and thought, *Alas, how unfortunate! Just as our messenger boy thought, that stupid guru is intent on disgracing himself.*

He announced the contents of the note and submitted that the offering to Padmasambhava would be the naga maiden of his choice. Despite the terror written on their queen's face, piti-fully, the nagas sighed with relief, as their own pain and loss of wealth now promised to be much less if the payment turned out to be one, or even all three, of the naga princesses.

The nagas decided to bring seven young noble girls as well as the three princesses. In this way, they wanted to ensure that Padmasambhava would find someone to his liking and not reconsider, taking their precious wealth instead.

Regarding the princesses, the eldest daughter, Godchung Karmo [Little White Vulture], had already been promised to the son of the yaksha queen. The yakshas were ghostlike nature spirits, notoriously poor at dealing with disappointment, and the nagas were concerned should the beautiful Godchung be his choice.

The middle daughter, Khatsar Lumo-tso [Joking Nagini Lake], was promised to a Chinese dignitary. This match too the nagas were fearful of disrupting. The youngest daughter's somewhat unusual name was Lenyu Khatam Do-to [Mute Stone Hammer], and the nagas were certain that Padmasambhava would not choose her.

All seven of the other girls, highborn every one, were quite lovely, clothed in silken brocade. They were standing straight as bamboo shoots in the spring, with glowing skin and fine figures. The king's youngest daughter was also known by her dakini name as Metok Lhadzé [Divine Flower] and stood out as not nearly as lovely as any of the others.

With a heavy heart, the naga king Tsugna Rinchen said to his three daughters and the other young noble ladies, "Because of the great kindness of Padmasambhava, we have been cured of this terrible pandemic, and we are beholden to him. We have promised him whatever he asks for. Even though we have offered eighty mule packs of jewels, fifteen liters of gold dust, and other precious items, he has said that we must offer him one of you. Now as it turns out, my eldest and middle daughters have already been promised. But as the proverbs say, *Just as one turns to the warmth of the sun, whoever shows great kindness must be rewarded.* What can we do but return his kindness? So you all must go to him, and we have no choice but to abide by his selection."

There was much commotion as the nagas gossiped amongst themselves and wondered whom Padmasambhava would select. There were also many snide, nasty comments aimed in the guru's direction. Finally the girls arrived before the guru, tentative but composed, counting on each other for support.

The guru rolled his head from one side to the other, his sharp rooster eyes darting around. When he saw Metok Lhadzé, he said, "Of the last two girls in the line, the final one is resilient and humble, and though you may not think her the most divine in appearance, she manifests genuine spirit. I may be but a wizened old man, but my heart and mind are drawn to her."

Then—reminiscent of the proverbs that say, *If something is outrageous enough, even staid old monks will laugh,* or, *if you are too full, you will vomit into your own bowl*—without a moment's hesitation, everyone there doubled over, old women's chests heaved, men cried out, and even the youngest babies swooned from their continuous laughter. Their sides ached from belly laughs; their eyes stung with each guffaw. As the proverb says, *It is not hard to make a choice, but it is a shame to have made the wrong choice.*

They clearly thought a foolhardy choice had been made. The king was struck mute in surprise until the guru said, "Well, are you going to offer her to me or not?"

And the king replied, "Of course, as it is said, *The small boat is already in the water. The arrow is in the bow. The foot is in the stirrup.*"

Then Guru Padma rattled off a list of further items he required. These included the special tent called Yudra Ting Gung-gu [Turquoise Yak-Hair Tent in Nine Partitions] and the naga's sacred twelve-volume *One Hundred Thousand Verse Wisdom Sutra*.[11] Padmasambhava also chose a female yak, the dri with three turquoise horns, from among the livestock of the nagas; the wish-fulfilling jewels that dispel poverty and thirst; and the Small Maroon Golden Urn that produces an endless

---

11. This is a sacred text that had been given to the nagas by Nagarjuna, a great Buddhist philosopher who lived in India around 150–250 CE. It is more commonly known as *The Prajnaparamita Sutra*.

supply of food. It was quite a list, but as he had worked so hard at this hoax, he did not want to risk being exposed as a fraud by not asking for ample payment.

All the nagas returned to their homes, driven by their large sighs of relief, and the naga princess Metok Lhadzé sang this song to her parents, the king and queen.

> You in the golden throne above,
> My dear father, Tsugna Rinchen,
> There is no birth without a father and mother.
> And more rare than that is a father with a loving
>   mind.
> The idiot race of red-faced, meat-eating Tibetans
> Does not clearly distinguish between dirty and clean.
> More than death, I fear going to such a land,
> But my duty is inscribed upon my skull.
> Despair pervades my thoughts, and my heart aches.
> Nonetheless this is my parents' just command,
> And as it repays their gift of my life,
> So it is that my mind's tumult abates.
> *A traveler on a long journey should pack well, hauling*
> *   his wealth.*
> *Without provisions, one would be a beggar in the borderlands.*
> *The arrow shot at long range should be bedecked with feathers.*
> *Featherless, it is merely a notched bamboo stick missing*
> *   its mark.*
> *The bride sent far away should be bedecked with gifts.*
> *Destitute, she is only a barefoot stray and prey to all.*
> Warm clothing and pleasing speech,
> Loving counsel, and kind advice,
> All these I need from you.
> Although this maiden girl's mind is grieving,
> I would not oppose the command of my loving parents.

I will never forget the kindness of you, my parents,
And I will keep you in my heart.
Do not forget me, your daughter.
Please hold me close.
If I am in need, I will think of you.
If I am not in need, then happiness is my own merit.
You, my parents, please keep this in your hearts.

After she sang, Tsugna Rinchen said to Padma, "Our naga kingdom has been reestablished in well-being. To repay your kindness in having cured the nagas of illness, we have no choice but to offer our daughter. As the proverb says, *The maiden girl does not remain in her family home. The vulture does not stay in its nest to die. A woman's fate is to abandon her parents' home. A young tiger's honor is to fall in battle.*"

And to his daughter, he said, "You are my own flesh and bones and beloved to me, but I would cut off my own head before going against my word. I cannot disregard the vow I made to Padmasambhava. Of course, you will go laden with your dowry of jewels, clothing, and all that has been requested since you are my cherished daughter, and your groom's home, so far away, will now be yours."

The following morning, the king had assembled the requested items and, along with the queen and a retinue of ministers, bid his daughter and Padma off with a song.

I am the naga king Tsugna Rinchen.
No one else governs here.
Listen, Guru Padmasambhava.
We invited your skillful means to cure us.
As your heart overflows with compassion,
You came gladly and looked upon us.
In order to repay your kindness,

I offered an abundance of jewels,
But you were not pleased with illusory wealth.
Since you desire my naga daughter, who am I to argue?
I offer her to you in accordance with your wishes.
May it come about that Tibet flourishes
And that the human world benefits.
May all aspirations be fulfilled!
If you understand the song, keep it in your heart.
If you do not understand, there is no way to explain it.

Thus he sang, and for reasons he did not quite understand, feelings of warmth and connection with Padmasambhava overcame the usually unemotional king as a tear dropped silently from his right eye. He stood silently, his heart torn by the fatherly despair of giving away his daughter and his kingly dedication to his people's future. Padmasambhava was confident that, although there had been some temporary suffering, everything had worked out for the best, and he expressed his assurances by reciting from the old proverbs. *If a guru is happy, the strength of his teachings will increase. If a daughter's dowry is grand, a father's reputation is enhanced. If an attendant's food is rich, their exertion will be all the more.*

So it was that Padma had blessed the nagas and put an end to their suffering and pain. Illness abated, drought and sandstorms were eliminated, and the intellect of the entire naga nation was elevated as deception, illusion, and ignorance could no longer gain purchase on their minds. Although the parting was difficult and emotional, the king escorted Padma and his daughter out of that watery country.

Then after a while, Padmasambhava thought to himself, *I had better find a home for this princess and someone to protect her until she can become Gesar's mother.* Turning to the naga princess, he sang.

I am Padmasambhava,
And you, of course, are Metok Lhadzé.
Listen, as here is my question.
I have no reason to remain with you,
And you must choose a land to inhabit,
A king, a leader, and a family.
Whatever your choice, I will make it so.
You will stay there for three years,
And then I will send the keeper of the prophecy to you.
Now, speak up clearly.

Thus he sang. She stood as though suspended in time, bewildered and speechless, as all along she too had thought that Padma's intention was to make her his wife or consort.

After some moments, Padmasambhava went on. "If you have no suggestions, I know just how to figure out where you should go." He took off his ceremonial three-pointed hat—a large ceremonial, jewel-encrusted hat that was encircled by masses of rainbow light rays—and flung it far up into the sky.

It sailed off and landed on the roof of the tent of Ralo Tonpa,[12] the king of the Gog Clan. King Ralo Tonpa saw the hat flying toward him and thought, *This must be a great omen. But of what?*

Some say that the hat chanted melodiously and continuously as its jewels sparkled in the bright Tibetan sun. Reverently, Ralo Tonpa picked up the hat and placed it on his shrine as an object of devotion. That very night, he had a prophetic dream in which a man dressed in white and surrounded by rays of light gave him a vase filled with nectar and said, "Early tomorrow morning, go and see who has arrived at your doorstep, and whatever is asked of you, do without hesitation. Thereby,

12. He is not to be confused with Drukmo's father, the chieftain Kyalo Tonpa Gyaltsen who had received one of the letters from Chipon about his prophetic dream.

your entire clan will prosper. Failing your duty would bring sorrow to many."

When Ralo Tonpa awoke, vaguely remembering the dream and rubbing the sleep out of his eyes, he dressed and went to see if anyone would be at the door. As he opened it, Padmasambhava, clad in white and wearing a lotus hat, arrived at his doorstep, accompanied by an incredibly beautiful girl leading a dri laden with her belongings.

Through the selflessness with which she had given up her former life, Metok's inner beauty, warmth, compassion, wisdom, and insight now manifested in her outer appearance.

Ralo Tonpa thought this was most certainly last night's prediction, and he said, "Greetings, well-accomplished yogi and consort. Where have you been, and where are you going? What are the provisions that you carry on the back of this dri? Is there anything I can aid you with? Come in and sit down. Let us have some tea and talk."

The guru replied, "Ah yes, I have come from the barbarous continent of Chamara, and to there I will return to meditate and to keep the vicious rakshasas and spirit demons in check. But first, I have come here to see you, Ralo Tonpa." Padmasambhava gazed at him with eyes that had known great joy as well as deep suffering, and the great compassion of this teacher overcame Ralo Tonpa.

Recalling last night's dream, he became filled with devotion toward the guru. He offered tea, liquor, and tsampa,[13] and with respect and devotion, he requested blessings and teachings.

Padmasambhava replied, "Listen, Ralo Tonpa Gyaltsen, the main reason that we have come here is that I need your help, as does this lovely maiden who accompanies me. In short, this

13. Tsampa is a traditional Tibetan staple of roasted barley flour. It is often mixed with butter and sweetened.

nagini princess, whose name is Metok, needs a home for three years, a safe home where she can be sheltered and her belongings protected. You are to keep her as you would your own precious daughter. She is not to wed, and her possessions, many of which are quite valuable, are not to be either bartered or sold. If you fulfill all this, your inner realization will blaze forth, and your wealth will expand. The entire district of Gog will prosper and know peace."[14]

Then Ralo Tonpa, up to the challenge put forth by the guru, hitched up his chuba[15] and, projecting strength, nobility, and courage, said, "As the proverbs state, *The merit of the colorful meadow entices the rain. The merit of the third month of spring seduces the cuckoo. The merit of the irrigation ditches in the fields gathers the southern clouds.* Just so, the merit of Ralo Tonpa will safeguard and support this uninvited nagini maiden. I will do all you ask. I will keep her secure, protected, and unmarried, and her possessions will not be sold to others but remain hers. All this I promise. Thank you for your trust and for this task."

Thus he spoke, and Padma replied, "So be it. As for me, once again as in the proverbs, *If I were to entrust my possessions, it would be to an upright soul. If I were to entrust my child, it would be to someone with a loving mind. If I were to entrust my wealth, it would be to a person of integrity.*" Then he added, "The happiness and sorrow of this girl depend on you. I have nothing else to say." He dissolved into a ray of white light and departed toward the southwestern sky.

The naga maiden remained in the land of Gog for two years and five months. Finally the celestial clock ticked forward, and

14. See Song Appendix, Song #1.
15. A chuba is an ankle-length coat bound at the waist that is the traditional dress for the nomadic men and women of Tibet. "Hitching up your chuba," while not a proverb, is a common way of referring to shoring up one's strength or courage.

time ripened. And it was in a distant space, one of pure thought and energy, that the spirit child Topa Gawa blissfully resided.

Within this bliss, he came to know that the time had come for him to accomplish the benefit of beings and that he would soon pass from that divine realm into the human realm of desire and action. A broad smile adorned his face as he thought of the adventures that might follow.

CHAPTER 4

Gog and Ling skirmish, and in the fight,
Chipon's son is killed.
The revenging army finds a dri and a princess,
And Gogmo finds a husband.

ESPITE THE encouraging words from Padmasambhava, while Gogmo [Metok's new name, literally
meaning "woman from Gog"] is living with Ralo
Tonpa as his daughter and he is protecting the gifts given to her
by her father, things are not going at all well in the land of Gog.
In fact, they had become embroiled in a series of increasingly
aggressive skirmishes with the bordering country of Ling. Ling
and its neighbor situated to the north and west, Gog, were both
sending raiding parties of armed warriors across their previously agreed upon border.

After one such raid, during which Gog had captured many
yak, dri, and goats, the men of Ling had retaliated with a harsh
and well-planned attack. During the battle, in which the warriors from Ling eventually prevailed, Chipon's son, Lenpa Chogyal [Simple-Minded Dharma King], was killed. This enraged
the Ling warriors, who quickly avenged his death, setting the
stage for what was about to occur.

Chipon's brother, Senglon, was a willowy man, not as tall as
some of his fellow warriors but strong, intelligent, and kindly.
He was already famed for his arrow divinations, a form of
fortune-telling common in Ling. He had fine features with a
thin, straight nose and a thin salt-and-pepper beard that was

only slightly trimmed and reached to the base of his neck. It is said that he glowed with inner strength and was possessed of a voice and words so sweet that none would tire of listening to him.

His first wife, the daughter of the Chinese emperor, had born him a singular son named Gyatsha Zhalkar [Chinese Nephew], who himself grew strong and true, with broad shoulders and a sure honesty. He possessed a discerning, though emotionally tinged, sharpness of mind, and he was a fearless warrior and capable swordsman. He had large, dark eyes, long black hair, and a broad forehead. His ears were peaked, and it was said his hearing was so acute that he could hear whispers at a hundred paces. As he grew, he became more and more valued as a fierce but loyal warrior and a good-hearted fellow. It was also said that women were not in any way averse to his charms.

During these last skirmishes and raids with Gog, Gyatsha was off in China, staying at the palace of his grandfather, the emperor. When he returned from China, he was incensed at the death of his cousin, and despite the pleadings of his father and his Uncle Chipon, who both felt that adequate revenge had already been visited upon Gog, Gyatsha went off on his own and organized a small army. He intended to go into Gog to bring down further havoc and revenge. To his father he sang,

> My older cousin Lenpa Chogyal,
> When I think of him now, my heart grows angry.
> This elder cousin was lost to Gog,
> And I will be his final avenger.
> I will not tarry, but head for the land of Upper Gog.
> First, to take revenge,
> Second, to drink the blood of my enemy,
> And third, to see to it that the land of Gog is no more.

If you understand this speech, may it be sweet to your
ears.

If not, there is no way to explain it.

Chipon, brighten up; the revenge that should have been is
in my hands.

As soon as he had finished, Gyatsha decided to set out for
Gog with the little army he had already assembled, and though
Chipon thought that this was unwise, he could not convince
Gyatsha of the foolishness of his plan. Nonetheless, Chipon
sang his own song aimed at the young and still brash Gyatsha.

I cannot help but sing this song,

Lest my grave be despoiled by the spit of my fellow
warriors.

Relax; listen to what I say,

And let these words pour into your youthful mind.

Last year, we clashed with Gog over land and wealth,

And as we reached neither treaty nor accord,

A war was fought between Gog and Ling.

Though for the most part we prevailed

And destroyed the eighteen father tribes of Gog,

The benefit was little, as Lenpa Chogyal was slain.

But now Ling has already had its revenge

As the lives of many men were taken

And Gog has become a land of widows.

But unbeknownst to me, our revenging warriors left
bounty behind.

Riches of Gog, not to mention

Tsugna Rinchen's daughter, the nagini princess, remain.

Knowing I am without a son does not make me sad

Because you, my nephew Gyatsha, are alive and well.

I have no thought to seek further revenge.
I swear this is true on the scriptures of our elders.
Let me speak candidly.
As you understood, we left riches in Gog:
First, the daughter of the naga king Tsugna,
Second, the dri with prosperity horns,
Third, the little blue nine-partitioned tent,
And fourth, the volumes of *The One Hundred Thousand
    Verses*.
It is best to go shoulder to shoulder with Zigphen
As this is your first raid, Gyatsha.
And perhaps even without fighting you may be
    victorious.
If you understand these words, they're sweet to your ear.
If not, there is no way to explain it.

The uncles and nephews discussed Chipon's thoughtful words. And the very next morning, messengers were sent throughout Ling as the leaders had decided that they would send an overwhelming force of seventy thousand trained warriors to Gog. Three days later, at the crack of dawn, the troops had gathered and were ready to begin the expedition.

In the meantime, Gyatsha's other uncle, and brother to Senglon and Chipon, Trothung, was making devious plans. Trothung was the enemy that Topa Gawa asked for when listing what he would need to succeed.

These days Trothung appeared elderly, the wiriness of his youthful warrior days was now bent, and his face was framed with thinning hair and a patchy beard. His mind had formed from a steely spirit, but had been honed by anger and jealousy and was swollen with arrogance. Although he was an adept meditator, his mind was racked with the twin poisons of delusion and self-hatred.

Trothung was thinking, *Gyatsha Zhalkar is quite the warrior. If he leads these seventy thousand men into Gog, then the land of Gog will be no more. It will be annihilated. Gyatsha will become legendary throughout Tibet, and the naga princess as well as the Gog wealth will be his spoils. Even though some of the captured Gog treasures might become the general property of Ling, it seems unlikely that any wealth would fall to me. Perhaps I could at least secure the princess for myself.*

Settling on a plan, his thoughts continued, *I'll do the Gog King Ralo the great service of sending him a message, forewarning him in secret of the intentions of Gyatsha and the Ling warriors. In exchange, I will ask for the naga princess and anticipate that I might be granted some of the wealth of the nagas. Even if this plan fails, the princess' father is the wealthy naga King Tsugna, and if I save her, he surely will reward me.*

Penning the letter, Trothung attached it to the neck of a golden arrow and let the arrow fly.

> This epistle is respectfully presented to Ralo Tonpa Gyaltsenof Gog from Trothung, Chief of the Tag-rong Clan. Gyatsha Zhalkar is seeking vengeance for the death last year of Chipon's son Lenpa Chogyal. Leading seven armies of ten thousand mighty warriors each, he is about to attack you the day after tomorrow. Fighting them off is beyond hope.Rapid flight is your only recourse. Now I have done you a great favor. Do not forget this.

The arrow magically arrived at Ralo Tonpa's feet. He quickly read the letter and immediately sent messengers throughout the land of Gog. The entire nomadic country of Gog, including its army, packed up its tents and belongings and set off from their homeland. That very night they started their escape and headed south toward the Ma Valley, which bordered the country of Hor.

However, the mules and yaks were unable to bear the weight of the turquoise tent and *The One Hundred Thousand Verse Sutra*, so the Gog warriors struggled to lift them onto the back of Gogmo's precious dri, already laden with the other naga riches.

In the midst of the confusion and chaos of their escape, this dri, carrying all the treasure, turned around and around and wandered back in the direction opposite the retreating people of Gog. Dri are known to be as stubborn as mules, and they weigh nearly three times as much and can be difficult to guide. The naga princess Gogmo alone saw the dri take off, and not wanting to lose her treasure, she dismounted, leading her horse and tracking the dri on foot.

She was unable to overtake the dri, but her horse got loose, and not wanting to follow the dri, the horse headed back to find his retreating companions. Although Gogmo called back to the rapidly receding people of Gog, no one could hear her. Alone and increasingly distraught, she followed after the dri along the banks of the Ma River,[16] coursing through a great valley bounded on all sides by majestic mountain peaks.

No matter what she did, whether she went quickly or slowly, she could not quite catch up with the dri, although when she stopped, the dri halted as well. Continually falling short of catching it, she wandered on and on wherever the dri went, getting farther and farther from her countrymen and more and more lost.

As day broke over Gog, the Ling army, with its armor and weapons flashing, could be seen approaching and entering the territory. But the battle these warriors had hoped for was not to be, as the Gog soldiers and the people had fled the night before. The land of Gog was empty. It became clear to the army

16. The Ma River is now known as the Yellow River. Its headwaters are in northeastern Tibet.

that the entire country had escaped, leaving nary a trace for these blood-hungry soldiers. Halting their search, they met to discuss what to do next. The young warriors in particular were not happy, and many groused that they should all head back home to their families and cozy tents.

Chipon spoke up. "It seems we have come all this way for treasure, and wherever we Ling soldiers go, we can never return empty-handed, or we will lose our glory and pride. So let's have Senglon do a divination and base our decision to stay or go on that."

Senglon performed an arrow divination, the results of which he duly reported in song.

> If we travel as long as the time it takes to have
>   a tea break,
> We will behold great beauty,
> And a treasure beyond imagining will be ours.
> With no fighting, it will fall easily into our hands.
> Without the need to slide our swords from their sheaths
> Or nock an arrow into its bow,
> Victory will be achieved by our unexpected
>   good karma.

Inwardly sneering, Trothung thought to himself that this was unlikely to be the case as the treasure of the Gog had probably disappeared with the Gog king and his people. He figured he could accuse Senglon of an inaccurate prediction but thought better of this and, pretending magnanimity, he made a big show of offering any spoils that they might find to Senglon as a gift for his divination, all the while certain that he wasn't giving up anything at all.

After the divination, they made the customary offering of juniper smoke as a way of purifying the space and giving thanks to the local deities. As the ceremony was winding down, the naga princess suddenly appeared.

She had been chasing continuously after the dri and had finally collapsed, fatigued and delirious. She had passed beyond understanding what was real and what was not and had had a prophetic dream.

In the dream, a young boy wearing billowy, blue silken pajamas appeared with a beautiful turquoise pail full of fresh milk, along with the message that the princess' eldest sister was commanding her to go yet again after the dri. By so doing, she would be blessed and great benefit would come to all beings. She had awoken from the dream and had again started after the dri that now led her squarely into the midst of the Ling army. The soldiers were awestruck by her ravishing beauty and collectively thought, *Her beauty is wondrous beyond imagining. Her radiant complexion is like a pure white lotus blooming in a lake, and her twinkling eyes are like honeybees buzzing on the shore of that lake. Her straight body is like summer bamboo as its leaves flutter in the wind. Her body looks as soft as Chinese silk, and her long flowing hair, like combed silk threads, shines as if the strands had been painted with liquid glass.*

Gogmo was a proud as well as beautiful princess, regal of bearing, thoughtful, and appreciative of the steadfast Gog king and people who had treated her with such kindness. She resolved to not give them up, but at the same time, she saw that her destiny was now in the hands of the people of Ling and that there was no reason to hold back her story.

So thinking, she told them her story in a song that resembled the tremulous melody of the cuckoo.[17] She told them that she was the youngest daughter of the naga king Tsugna Rinchen and was given by the great teacher Padmasambhava to the

17. See Song Appendix, Song #2.

good but temporary care of Ralo Tonpa of Gog with whom she had lived for nearly three years as his daughter.

She denied knowing where the people and army of Gog had gone and told of how she had become first separated from them and then completely lost while attempting to capture her dri loaded with the precious belongings that she had brought from her homeland. She also related the dream that she had had as well as her belief that somehow she was fated to meet up with the Ling army and perhaps had even been brought there by her dri.

Everyone was rather impressed with her song and quoted proverbs. The young warriors were upset that they had no one to fight and no glory to win, but Chipon noted that the princess along with the treasure-laden dri were bounty enough and had been won without a fight, thus doubly powerful, invoking the ancient wisdom that a victory won without a battle was the greatest victory possible.

Trothung was sorely disappointed as the princess was now heading to Senglon rather than to himself. He was so angry that he appealed to the great mediator of Ling, an older fellow who was often called upon to arbitrate disputes, but he just quoted Trothung back to himself and added a few proverbs, opining that the princess must, by Trothung's own words, go to Senglon. He added a proverb, *A slip of the tongue cannot be recanted by a horse. An arrow released by the thumb cannot be drawn back by the hand.*

The arbiter further suggested that, while the princess should go to Senglon, the scriptures and the wondrous tent should become the general wealth of Ling. Senglon agreed.

Though deprived of battle and glory, inwardly many of the warriors were relieved, and with its newfound spoils in hand, the army returned to Ling from Gog, and Senglon welcomed Gogmo into his home. Now it must be noted that Senglon was already very much married to Gyaza Lhakar Dronma [Chinese Divine White Torch]. She was the daughter of the Chinese emperor and Gyatsha's mother, and Gyatsha had been visiting the emperor when he found out that his cousin had been killed in Gog.

At that time, Gyaza was Senglon's only wife, though at the time it was not unusual for men to have several wives or, for that matter, women to have several husbands. Gyaza was herself a beauty with flowing black hair, large eyes, and a lovely, round face. She was well-spoken, had a gracious demeanor, and doted on her son and all the children of Ling. On the other hand, she was beginning to feel her age and was not without jealousy.

As soon as Gogmo entered the tent, everyone could see her great beauty and generous manner. Wherever she went, there was an elegance that came with her, like the scent of incense pervading a room. With her straight spine, clear black eyes, long black hair, and soft voice, all who met her were entranced. All that would be, except for Gyaza who could only, and reasonably enough, see a rival.

As a result, Chipon had some work to do to keep peace within his brother Senglon's family. He declaimed that Senglon would keep his current marriage arrangement with his primary wife and that the nagini princess would sleep in her own tent. Since the azure tent that she had brought with her had been given over to Ling, Senglon would provide a tent for her to live in, and furthermore, she would have no say over Senglon's wealth or property. She would however be able to keep her precious dri, and Gyaza could supply her with what provisions she thought fair.

To Gyaza's credit, it should be noted that she gave Gogmo a mare, a dzomo (a non-fertile cross between a domestic cow and a yak), another dri, and an ewe. Gogmo, the nagini princess, had a small tent and a little pen that was called Yang Rawa Gozhi [Four-Gated Prosperity Corral] situated close behind the dwelling of Senglon and Gyaza.

The princess prospered there and won over the people of Ling, who began to call her Gogza Lhamo [Goddess Wife from Gog], or just Gogmo. It turned out that her dri had an inexhaustible supply of milk, and soon this saying became familiar throughout the land, *The white dri of prosperity has one hundred and three udders, but only Gogmo can milk it, and only the turquoise pail can contain the milk.*

She had been living in her tent for a number of months when one night a radiant guru appeared in a dream and told her to move her tent a fair bit farther away to a somewhat more secluded place in front of a frog-shaped boulder. Senglon helped her move the tent, and there she stayed. Gyatsha, Senglon's son, became quite close and friendly with Gogmo, and they bonded like long-separated siblings surprisingly reunited after a wondrous struggle.

CHAPTER 5

Gogmo has a wondrous dream,
And Joru has a miraculous birth.
His death is plotted by Trothung,
And much dark magic comes to naught.

ONE DAY GOGMO was strolling down by the edge of a nearby lake. The water was cool and refreshing, and its gentle waves slapped at the shore. It was surrounded by green meadows awash with flowers of so many colors that one was overcome by the pastoral loveliness. On three sides, majestic snow-covered mountain peaks surrounded the lake, and a beautiful plateau adorned with wildflowers stretched to the east.

This wondrous scene set Gogmo to think sadly of her homeland, her family, and all the friends and relatives she was so sorely missing. In this rather dark and tearful mood, as her sadness turned bitter, she sang this song in the melody known as River Slowly Flowing.

Helpless but to sing a few songs,
I must sing or do nothing at all.
I am the nagini princess, now known as Gogmo.
Dear blue lake, graced by a pleasing splashing sound,
Perhaps you are a messenger of the naga king Tsugna.
Listen, for I have something to tell you.
The meaning of my life is a charade.
I might as well be a barren woman's spawn.

I am a stray dog bereft in the wilderness,
My family left behind in the depths of the ocean.
Do you understand this, Golden King of the Waters?
When the dear chieftain dispenses law, he is full of
    clever words.
He says he has the happiness of the people at heart.
He says that craving the wealth of others is not
    permitted.
He insists that the dishonest will be punished by
    the law.
But his words do not fit his actions.
For the rich, penalties are just an illusion.
If the secret payoff is substantial,
You will see how an evil person escapes the law.
My father Tsugna can say whatever he wants.
He said that all three sisters were equally precious
And that he would come to me from any distance
And see to my happiness.
Empty words are all you have for me.
Father Tsugna, you have forgotten me these three years.
Now for the honest truth in the words of my song—
If you can see me, O guru, grant me your blessings.
If you can see me, O parents, give your support.
Not for an instant have I wavered from my task
Nor transgressed the words of my parents or my guru.
Please, someone attend to my sadness.

Crumpled, she was sitting there as rivulets of tears flowed down her fine face when suddenly her father, the naga king Tsugna Rinchen, appeared before her, rising up splendorous from the middle of the lake. Sharp and clear as the midday sun, he stood before her.

"Daughter, do not be distraught. It is not that the guru and

I don't see you. My heart too breaks from the shared sorrow of our separation. I have come with my earnest advice and support." And he offered this song to his youngest daughter.

> The song is Ala Ala Ala.
> Thala leads the melody.
> This place is the spring of the nagas,
> And I am Tsugna Rinchen.
> *Though both the sun and moon appear in the azure firmament,*
> *The blue sky does not favor one over the other,*
> *For the sun and moon each have their own karmic mandate.*
> *Though the mountains and meadows coexist on the dense earth,*
> *The colors in the meadows transform from summer to autumn,*
> *While the snowy crags of the mountains know not a seasonal*
>   *change.*
> *It is not that the dense earth shows favoritism to the meadows,*
> *But rather that the mountains and meadows have their own*
>   *karmic mandate.*
> I, naga Tsugna, have three daughters.
> The guru bid me send him the youngest
> And left the middle and eldest at home.
> I had no choice in the matter.
> That, my daughter, was your karma
> And it was not ours to change.
> I was required to give whatever dowry was mandated.
> You think that what you have is not happiness,
> That you are wretched, wandering miserably in this
>   foreign land.
> But it is you who have immersed yourself in suffering
> And your mind's attitude that is miserable.
> Take this jewel, which will fulfill your every desire,
> As it is the wish-fulfilling jewel.
> As for me, know that my thoughts are always with you.

From the depths of your current sorrow,
Your happiness soon will blossom
Like the abundant wildflowers upon this very plain.
If you understand my words, they are sweet to
    your ears.
If not, there is no way to explain.
You must keep this in your mind.

Having sung, he gave her a glittering jewel, and just as suddenly as he had arrived, he slipped back into his watery realm. Following the vision of her beloved father and his inspirational song, Gogmo's sad mood lifted, and she felt as though her body was full of light and energy. This feeling intensified until she fell into a swoon and lost consciousness, dreaming about a billowing white cloud that approached from the southwest and filled the space around her.

Riding upon that divine cloud was Padmasambhava. Just as she felt herself losing hold of the gossamer threads of reality, blanking toward a deep, black void, the great guru placed a golden five-pointed vajra on the top of her head and sang this song of prophecy.

Listen, fortunate one.
Bliss, suffering, and equanimity, these three,
If understood, are the self-appearance of emptiness.
The mind that dwells on enemies, friends, and those
    who are neither,
When seen to be as foolish as a kitten chasing a string,
    liberates one's life.
Know well that the mental pattern of confused thought
Has the solidity of a rainbow in the sky,
Seemingly real, but as fleeting as any illusion.
You may be separated from your father,

But I will not be separate from you for a moment.
Whatever thoughts occur in your mind are the nature
    of phenomena,
And whatever you do is perfection in action.
Therefore, tomorrow morning
It will come to pass that a magical child
Will enter your womb.
He will be the slayer who tames the dark side.
He will be the general and the lord of the black-haired
    Tibetans
And the twelve kingdoms of Ling
Will come to have him as their leader.
Your son will have a sublime, beautiful, and indestructi-
    ble body.
For him a mother's usual worry is unnecessary.
The first butter to his palate will be the long-life nectar
    given by me,
And his first drink will be served by your father,
    Tsugna.
Yours will be the first response to his enlightened
    speech,
And his first food will be offered by the spirit Magyal
    Pomra.
Do not forget my words,
Nagini, keep this treasure always in your mind.

Gogmo awoke from her sleep. Bliss and warmth suffused her body as a light coat of cool sweat enveloped her. Her troubled mind was calmed, and she remained lying there, tearful, but with joy, happiness, and a deep sense of peace and satisfaction with what she could now see as the true purpose of her life.

That night, while sleeping next to her husband, Senglon, Gogmo fell into a dream of a handsome and charming golden man in golden armor who came and, lying naked by her side, made tender and passionate love with her. Again bliss and warmth overcame her body, and she felt such longing that she could not bear to awaken from her dream lover.

The next morning just before dawn, she dreamed that a five-pointed vajra was blazing above the crown of her head with splendid light rays and rainbows. After spinning there for a few moments, it dissolved through the top of her head, and as she dreamed, once again great warmth suffused her body. For many days after all this, she disregarded food and was oblivious to cleanliness or clothing.

Of great concern to Senglon and his entire encampment, her bliss-ridden mind and mental distraction persisted for nine months and eight days. After a few months, it had become clear that she was pregnant. Those who dwelled near her heard songs and, often, spontaneous laughter coming from her little tent, particularly during the darkest hours of the cold Tibetan nights.

As her pregnancy was nearing its end, strangely, some of the warriors and their wives began to have their own dreams. Gyatsha dreamed that in Gogmo's tent there was a precious throne upon which was a golden vajra, blessed by Padmasambhava and blazing with light, while Chipon and many others also had dreams filled with various, sometimes mysterious but always auspicious, omens.

It was on the fifteenth day of the twelfth month of the Tiger Year that a great ease overcame her. Her body felt so light that it nearly rose up into the air, utterly loose and relaxed. Her mind loosened its grip on this and that, and as the sun rose, there appeared a translucent man, rosy white as a conch with the head of a great white bird, holding a spear with a white silken pennant and saying, "Gogmo, I am your firstborn son, Dungkhyung Karpo [White Conch Garuda]. I am a drala and therefore will not achieve the benefit of a corporeal body, but I will never be apart from Gesar. I am the guardian drala who resides upon his helmet, and I will be his chief protector."[18]

So saying, he remained in the space above like a shimmering, pure white rainbow. And then quickly recovering from the drala's appearance, Gogmo could hear from within her belly the first words spoken by her divine child, Topa Gawa.

> The song is Ala Ala Ala.
> Thala leads the melody.
> In case you do not know this place,
> In the body, chakras, and channels of you, my kind
>   mother,
> It is the heart chakra of truth.
> In case you do not know the likes of me,
> I am the boy, Topa Gawa.
> Listen, I have something to say.
> I have been dispatched on this mission
> To bring benefit to the people of this world.
> Though now just an infant,
> I have been selected to be a leader in this land of
>   humans.
> Along with this mandate, there must be a land where
>   I might rule,
> Reliable ministers,
> Peaceable citizens,
> Caring relatives,

18. Drala is a Tibetan term for a nonhuman spirit being, one that helps one in fighting one's enemies, whether material or psychological. They are all around us, and for some beings, such as Gesar, special ones accompany their birth and provide a degree of protection. In this birthing, we will meet the three drala who are born along with Gesar. According to tradition, whenever a human is born, there is the simultaneous birth of their drala protectors.

And a generous treasury.
Mother, tell me how this will come to be
So that I may be released from your womb.
Mother, tell me from which chakra shall I emerge?
First, the crown chakra of great bliss,
Second, the throat chakra of abundance,
Third, the heart chakra of dharma,
Fourth, the navel chakra of emanation,
Fifth, the secret chakra that holds bliss.
If you understand this song, it is sweet to your ears.
If not, then we are both out of luck.
Kind mother, keep this in your mind.

As she listened to this song issuing from within her, like the peahen that hears the sound of her peacock lover's thunderous caws, she was filled with ecstasy, and in that state, she offered this song to the being in her womb.

If a chieftain is up to the task,
Then leaders, warriors, and subjects will naturally sur-
    round him.
Have you understood this, Gogmo's baby?
According to the famous proverbs of the ancients,
When the geese fly north,
If the strength of their wings is not exhausted,
The boundless northern lakes will not turn them away.
When the golden-eyed fish are swimming happily,
If the strength of their bodies is not exhausted,
Endless is the ocean's depth in which they will play.
If you have indeed been sent by the gods to be our sover-
    eign chieftain,
Then you will not lack for ministers and subjects.
They will outnumber this world's blades of grass.

Concerning your family and relatives:
Your paternal uncle will be King Chipon,
Your older brother, Gyatsha Zhalkar,
Your worldly father, King Senglon,
And your maternal grandfather, Tsugna Rinchen.
For the treasury of prosperity:
First, there will be the tea treasure of China in the east,
Second, the silk treasure of Mi-nub in the south,
Third, the jeweled treasure of Persia in the west,
And fourth, the coral treasure in the wilderness of
    the north.
My throat, my heart, my navel, these three
Are the immovable chakras and channels.
Both the chakras of the crown and the secret place
Are the entranceways for coming and going.
Come through the crown down to the bliss-holding
    chakra,
And there will be the auspicious connection of good
    fortune.
May the people of the four borderlands become your
    subjects,
May your life reach its limit,
May you suppress with your splendor the three worlds,
And may whatever prayers you make be accomplished.
If this song has caused confusion, the fault is mine.
If it has been but idle talk, please forgive me.
Child of mine, keep this in your mind.

As soon as she finished the song, she painlessly delivered a child with the full bearing and carriage of a three-year-old. He was so bewitching that one could not look away. During his birth, his eyes were wide open, and neither he nor his mother made the slightest cry.

Immediately after the birth, the baby climbed onto Gog-mo's lap, and Padmasambhava arrived to give the infant an empowerment and long-life water. In celebration, his maternal grandfather, Naga Tsugna, then offered almond-flavored long-life amrita, and Magyal Pomra presented a ritual cake of one hundred tastes. Lord of Nyen Gedzo brought colorful silk and clothing. All the grand prophecies were thus fulfilled.

However, this miraculous birthing process was not over. Two more magical drala beings came forth. First, from Gog-mo's heart center arose an egg-shaped orb of blue light, from which appeared an infant with a human body and a snake's head.

Presently, he said these words, "I am the third-born son, des-tined for kindness. I too am without a corporeal body, but I will be the guardian of Gesar's weapons and armor. I am the younger brother, Ludrul Odchung [Naga Serpent Little Light]. My mark is the silken cape that drapes over the armor. I am the body protector who will never leave his side." Saying this, he remained in the space above as a radiant, multicolored light.

Lastly, from Gogmo's navel, a beautiful girl emerged, clothed only in an array of vulture feathers and rainbow light. Address-ing Gogmo, she said, "Dearest mother, I am your fourth child. As you can see, I too am without a body of flesh and blood. I shall be Gesar's sister, Thalé Odkar [Completely Luminous], the drala sister who accompanies Gesar's noble steed. I am the luminous beams of light that are able to illuminate any situation. I am the body protector who never parts from your young son."

At that moment, Padmasambhava spoke these words in song.

From now until the end of this eon,
May he be a leader for those who pursue virtue,

> May he become a jewel that fulfills whatever others
>   desire,
> May he be a great being who brings benefit to all,
> And may auspicious bliss prevail.

Countless deities had assembled, and they floated in the sky around the little tent. And as Padmasambhava finished his song, there came a symphony of music, a rainfall of flowers, and a dome of rainbow light blazing overhead. These celestial displays centered over Gogmo's modest tent where her four animals had also given birth.

As this drama was unfolding, Padmasambhava conferred upon the child the name Gesar Norbu Dradul [Jeweled Tamer of Enemies].

It was a fruitful, fertile, and phenomenal day—so much so that Gyaza soon became suspicious and went over to Gogmo's tent. Peeking in, she saw the enchanted boy-child who had just been born, sitting on his mother's lap. Gyaza was overcome with his beauty and calm. Soon Gogmo and Gyaza brought the child to see his half-brother Gyatsha, who took the boy in his arms, saying, "Now all my wishes are fulfilled. May all the buddha activity of this younger brother be perfectly accomplished."

Unable to resist, he added this somewhat arcane proverb. *"Two brothers together are the hammer of the enemy, two mares together are the seed of wealth, and two wives together are the ground and strength.* For the time being, I would think it good to call my younger brother *Joru* because he is so alert." And this name stuck until he matured into the name Gesar.

Gyatsha, contented, spoke to Gogmo. "Though you must be fully aware of this, as the older brother it is my responsibility to say it anyway. You must take especially good care of this child. Then again, I have great hopes for him as the signs and indications are clear. No one will be successful in creating obstacles for him. To be in accord with custom, a birth like this should be celebrated throughout Ling. I will go and discuss all this with my uncle, Chipon."

Gyatsha went before Chipon, and they conferred for many hours, after which Gyatsha offered a song recounting the events that had occurred. In the song, Gyatsha asked his uncle's advice about the child, particularly concerning his upbringing, and any insights he might have about the miraculous birth. And he asked whether Chipon, as the king, would host a grand celebration. Then King Chipon himself sang.

> This child has already had a miraculous birth,
> And if we, his close relatives, carry on about him,
> The villagers will think us arrogant and the boy Joru
>   a fake.
> Just as the lotus that grows out of the filthy mire,
> Unnoticed until it blooms,
> So radiant in its full flower,
> Has no need to be washed of its mud,
> Just so that lotus never forgets its earthly beginnings
> And is revered by all.
> In this same way, we do not have to revere Joru.
> If we just leave him alone,
> He will surpass even the mightiest.
> In his twelfth year, he will secure his karmic steed,
> And the throne will be secured with the same certainty
> As the sun rising over the peak of the eastern mountain.
> These are the words of the unmistaken prophecy—
> But do not let these words escape your lips.
> No one else knows this but I, Chipon.
> Until the boy reaches the age of twelve,
> We should go along with whatever he does
> Rather than counsel him with our advice.

Even if he calls forth the classes of enemies and demons,
Even if he reverses earth and sky, there will be no
    problem.
Of course you love him with all your heart, Gyatsha.
I, this old man, am now content.
Gyatsha, you and your brother will attain golden
    thrones,
And I, your uncle, will shepherd your intentions.
Denma will be the leader of the troops,
And the mighty warriors of Ling will line up before you
As precisely as rows of tigresses.
Karma such as this is the gift of the past.
Before long, the sun of happiness will dawn.
Were you listening, Gyatsha?
You, great warrior, hold this in your heart.

When Chipon had finished speaking, Gyatsha slowly and carefully considered the obvious and subtle meaning of this advice, and fully heartened, he gave up the idea of a grand celebration and rode back home to gaze again at his wondrous younger brother.

Meanwhile, in his own lavish tent, Trothung was beset with dark and nasty thoughts. His malevolent mood festered. Over and over in his mind he replayed how he had lost the beautiful naga princess, and now she had given birth to such an extraordinary son. Despite all of his scheming, his plans had backfired, and he had returned from Gog with nothing but a sore back, a headache, and a wasted week.

In his mind he had been tricked out of the spoils—Gogmo and her treasure. Worse, his unworthy brother Senglon had taken Gogmo into his own home, and now a most unusual son had been born. And if this were not enough to keep his rancor going, he fretted over the fact that there had been no strong leader to unify Tibet in quite some time. But now, with Gyat-sha's obvious strength and the birth of his charismatic half-brother, their clan was clearly in ascendancy. And that would mean that his brother Chipon, whom Trothung had always considered overrated, would now be in a position to unify and lead all of Ling.

Thinking of Joru's lineage, Trothung realized that Joru was the grandchild of a naga king, the son of King Senglon and the nagini princess, and the nephew of Manéné, who was famed as a powerful sorceress and great meditation master. Manéné was capable of great magic and always saw through Trothung's craftiness and intrigue. Moreover, Joru's mother, Gogmo, had the protection of the great guru Padmasambhava.

All bad for me. Worse than bad, played over and over in his mind, twisting his thoughts until the obvious popped up. *Death to the child, and the sooner the better. Now all I need to do is figure out how to get this deed done with no fingers pointing toward me.*

For three days, Trothung plotted, and at dawn on the fourth day, he mounted his horse and headed off to see Joru and his mother. He brought along balls of white butter, honey cakes, and many other sweet delicacies, all of which were filled with powerful, vile poisons.

Upon reaching their tent, he put on his sweetest voice and exclaimed, "Oh, what a joy! Gogmo has a boy. He is Akhu's[19] nephew. Only three days have passed, but already he seems to be three years old. Without a doubt, he is a son of the great Mukpo lineage. If his uncle gives him his first solid food, this will increase his life force and longevity. So now, on behalf of the Tag-rong clan, I offer to this wondrous child his first sweet food."

---

19. Akhu means "uncle." It often refers to Trothung, as it does here, although in Tibet it can refer to almost any older male relative.

Without any further ceremony, he gave Joru the butterballs and cakes, and Joru ate every morsel. Overjoyed, Trothung thought, *He surely will die now.*

But Joru just laughed, and all the poison flew out of his fingertips. Trothung turned away from Gogmo's tent and thought, *It is said that nagini bodies themselves are poisonous, so perhaps, because his mother is a nagini, he could never be harmed by poison. What now? At present, in the valley of the Upper Black Crag, there is a shaman and practitioner of black magic named Amnyé Gompa Raja [Grandfather Meditation Prince]. He has utterly debased views regarding life and is an evil and powerful sorcerer. He is the one for this job; I have worked with him before on various evil exploits.*

Thinking all of this in a flash, he turned back and said to Gogmo, "What this lovely baby needs now are some long-life protection offerings and ceremonies. As for the offerings, I can arrange those if you can just lay a clean cloth upon the ground upon which the ceremony can occur."

Gogmo nodded her assent, and Trothung took his leave. Directly Trothung went off to get Amnyé, who that very night had had bad dreams and was sitting in his darkened cave, attempting to cast spells and recite incantations to reverse the portents and ease the foreboding he was feeling. Upon arriving, Trothung made three quick prostrations to Amnyé and sang this rather perverse song about why it was necessary to liberate the boy Joru by slaying him.

> The song is Ala Ala Ala.
> Thala leads the melody.
> Wondrous protector, look upon me,
> Trothung of Tag-rong.
> In Ling, a land of the six grains,
> A land of the divine lineage,
> There resides a bastard demon child.

Through compassion, I gave him poison, but he did
    not die.
Now it is up to you to slay him with your evil magic.
Unless we can eliminate the enemy Joru,
His troublemaking will never cease.
Do you understand, honorable one?
From the very day this boy Joru was born,
He said that he would be the one to slay you,
Saying that it was your sorcery, thievery, and seduction
That had brought misery and suffering to Ling.
He said he would not abide your survival
But rather, when just a bit older, come here
To take your very head and arms.
Amnyé, you must act.
It is easy to extinguish a fire when it is small.
You don't even need water; it can be snuffed out with your
    thumb.
It is easy to subjugate an enemy when he is small.
You don't even need weapons; he could just be swaddled.
Through my cunning ruse, I have enlisted his mother's
    help.
You will be invited to bestow the long-life empowerment
    and bathe him.
You must place the black magic torma upon his crown
And the black magic substances into his mouth.
You must be the one to sever the stream of his life.
After this is done,
The prosperity bag called Petsé Nu-gu [Nine-Edged
    Little Sack],
A treasure source of all that is desirable,
Will be yours.
These words and this presentation

Must be kept secret, of course.
And on the day of Joru's demise,
You must come to the house of Trothung.
We will rejoice with song and dance,
And the prosperity treasure will be yours.
Amnyé, please keep this in your mind.

Pleased with his plan, Trothung had sung these words, beseeching Amnyé to kill baby Joru.

Mulling this over and recollecting his recent dreams, Amnyé responded, "I have been having bad dreams about being assassinated and have seen evil omens everywhere. The child you speak of may well be the source of these portents. As he is but three days old, how difficult can it be to kill him? As you well know, my power is very great, and I can, among many other things, break apart rocks and mountains. I can control the great turquoise dragon. Actually there is nothing I *can't* do." Given that Trothung's proposed payment sounded fine and reasonable, Amnyé agreed immediately.

Overjoyed, Trothung once again prostrated himself at Amnyé's feet, urging him on. "Of course your magic will work. Come today and kill baby Joru, and in exchange I will give you the Nine-Edged Prosperity Sack. Not only that, the province of Tag-rong will forever be your support."

The guru Amnyé replied, "Yes, this very night I will go, and tomorrow I will come to your tent so you can pay me for my trouble."

Thanking Amnyé, Trothung returned to Gogmo's place. So accustomed was he to his own disingenuousness that, as he related to Gogmo how he had thoughtfully arranged for the great guru Amnyé to give the long-life empowerment to baby Joru, he himself nearly believed that he had acted kindly. In the very next moment, however, he realized he had best not be around when Amnyé killed the infant. So he headed hastily back to his own encampment.

Baby Joru did not yet possess the armor, helmet, and weapons that were the usual dwelling place for those drala that had been co-born with him. Therefore, realizing that trouble was coming his way, he said to his mother, "Could you please bring me four little pebbles? Today the time has come for me to subjugate Amnyé Gompa Raja."

Gogmo had no idea why he would want pebbles, nor why Amnyé needed taming, but she did get the stones for him. Placing one in front, one in back, and one each to the right and the left, Joru visualized the pebbles as alembics, or chambers, for his personal drala. There was elder brother Dungkhyung Karpo, younger brother Ludrul Odtrung, and sister Thalé Odkar, and they were accompanied by a fourth, the great land spirit and protector, Lord Nyen Gedzo. These four beings rested above the pebbles and were further accompanied by nine hundred supporting, lesser drala. Because of the strength of Joru's visualization and meditation, all these drala beings then dissolved into the pebbles, therein quietly waiting.

By then, Amnyé Gompa Raja had left his cave and was lumbering toward Joru. When he was eight miles away, Amnyé shouted "*Phet!*" so suddenly and so loudly and with such force that the sky itself shook and rattled as though thunder and a great earthquake had collided. The force of his "*Phet!*" was such that hundreds of lesser protector beings that had arrayed themselves around Joru's tent were destroyed and disappeared like thin smoke on a windy day. But as Dungkhyung was there, along with the other personal protecting drala, Joru was unharmed.

Amnyé traveled closer, and when three miles away, he shouted another "*Phet!*" This time the seas roiled, and great waves appeared on previously still inland waters, causing lakes to overflow and rivers to escape their banks. Chaos descended upon all the nagas dwelling in waters for hundreds of miles around Joru and his nagini mother's little tent. They too disappeared swiftly and without a fish scale of residue into the seas of the great beyond. But the younger brother drala Ludrul remained firm, and Joru was unharmed, smiling and playing with his beads and other toys.

Still Amnyé trudged on, ever closer and closer to the tent itself until he was just outside, and shouted yet another "*Phet!*" this time attacking the land around Joru's tent. With great force, all the trees and bushes were stripped of their leaves and branches, and the smaller saplings were uprooted and flung from the area as large trees cracked at their bases. A great, thundering din resounded, and small animals fled from this scene of destruction.

However, Gedzo and his grand retinue stood their ground, and all within the tent was left undisturbed. Joru focused his mind and invoked the strength and power with which he had been born, directing it with a heart filled with tenderness and compassion. Terrible thunder and eerie lightening gave rise to a fearful scene of chaotic energy.

At that very moment, the heretic Amnyé stood at the door, and Joru quickly scooped up the four pebbles and flung them at Amnyé. From what the bards could put together from Amnyé's incoherent ramblings, he saw thousands upon thousands of terrifying beings of all colors coming after him—ghastly creatures adorned with frightful armor. All manner of spirits, dakas, and dakinis, a multitude too numerous to tally, appeared, out to destroy poor old Amnyé.

Never had he been so frightened. It looked as if those hordes of beings were about to cut his heart out of his chest and devour it on the spot. Turning and running away as quickly as he could, Amnyé did not stop running until he literally dove into the presumed safety of his own cave.

Meanwhile, Joru had sent one of his own emanations to Amnyé's meditation cave and, while there, had overturned his drinking water, dried up his neighboring spring, and carted off all of Amnyé's food. Amnyé returned to the cave, only to find this destruction. And as he turned, desperate to escape, he gasped in horror as he spied an enormous and well-equipped army approaching his tent.

Marching in lockstep, rocking Amnyé's cave, hundreds of boots all struck the ground in unison and approached relentlessly and with purpose. Fearfully Amnyé thought, *I must throw my most powerful torma at this frightening army to drive them away.* But just as the magician was readying his great weapon, Joru magically sealed the door of the cave with a huge boulder the size of a large yak. Finding himself trapped in his own cave but imagining himself still capable of victory, Amnyé sang.

> Joru, you demon cub, naughty boy,
> Listen with your ears and watch with your eyes.
> At a distance—magic; close up—needles.[20]
> We will see who is the best at knives and needles.
> Gods and protectors, dwelling above and below,
> Eight classes of the dark side, don't be idle.
> Appear now and protect your faithful servant from this
>   demon child.

So saying, with a great uproar, his Bon protectors gathered around Amnyé as he threw the great magic torma that he had been preparing as he sung. It struck the boulder, causing it

20. Here he is referring to sharp, needle-shaped knives that are used in combat.

to tremble. Then with the heave of a second, more powerful torma, and the utterance of cursing incantations, he was able to fracture the boulder, bringing down a torrent of meteorites, hail, and sparks.

But in its place, through Joru's power to emanate, stood Zilnon Padma Drakpo, one of Padmasambhava's wrathful manifestations—his skin dark red, his three eyes furious and bloodshot, a black vajra in his right hand and a nine-headed fierce black scorpion in his left, a garland of fresh human heads around his neck, and a tiger skin across his torso.

Amnyé thought, *Catastrophe is mine. All is lost.* In desperation, he hurled a massive explosive torma, his greatest weapon. To counter its force, Joru visualized Amnyé's cave as solid stone crafted entirely of black meteoric iron, and by the intensity of this powerful image, every last one of Amnyé's protectors was imprisoned in the cave, powerless to escape.

And so it came to pass that, when the great torma exploded against the side of the cave, the power of these protectors magnified the force of the detonation immeasurably. So much energy was released that Amnyé's body was atomized. His bones and flesh scattered like nuclear dust in a great gale wind. Not a single tooth or shard of bone was left ever to be found.

Through the power of Joru's meditation and his compassion, Joru separated Amnyé's consciousness from his murderous, protective death spirits and led him to the pure realm where his rebirth as a kind and wonderful teacher was assured. Finished with Amnyé, Joru entered the cave and obliterated all of the magician's ritual implements. He blessed two demons that had been protecting Amnyé, Bloody Single-Tress Demoness, and her brother, Life Essence Demon, so they would become great and powerful guardians of the glorious twin doctrines of Buddhism and Bon, installing them as protectors of these precious teachings.

All along, one emanation of Joru had remained back at the tent with Gogmo. Those who were there had seen Amnyé run off, and though they did not know what had happened next, in the end what mattered to them was that this three-day-old child had tamed the greatly feared, evil magician, Amnyé Gompa Raja, and caused him to flee.

The next day Joru awoke early. He said to his mother, "Today I have an important matter that must be settled. I must go to Amnyé's deserted residence and gather up what remains." Smiling a bit to himself, but not waiting for a response, he rose up, tucked in his little chuba, and left.

His mother thought to herself, *Padmasambhava reassured me that I do not have to guard this child too closely, even as an infant.*

Thus Joru went with his mother's blessing. As part of his plan, at midmorning, Joru first went to Trothung's encampment and recast himself to appear as a dead ringer for Amnyé. At the entrance to Trothung's tent, he sang this song.

> The song is Ala Ala Ala.
> Thala leads the melody.
> Most powerful protectors of the dark side,
> Help Amnyé today to sing this song.
> I am the butcher who killed the demon Joru.
> Last night during the middle watch,
> I was solicited for this cowardly act.
> Thus I went and flayed Joru's skin
> And threw his corpse into the rushing river.
> However, Joru, that ill-fated son of Gogmo,
> Although he possessed the power of a thousand
>   godly demons,
> First off, he had nothing but honorable intentions
>   toward me,
> Second, he had said nothing against you, Uncle Trothung,

And third, he intended to repay the kindness of the
fathers and uncles.

For these three reasons, when I cut his throat, he bled
milk.

I regret that I killed this one who so clearly was an
innocent.

Even though I regret it, it was at your command, King
Trothung.

You ought not to have said to kill this magical child,

But even so, you must hand over the prosperity sack.

That gift horse without incisors,

Seeing it is toothless, nevertheless you must accept it.

The same for you, chieftain of Tag-rong,

Now is the time to make good on your payment,

And I demand your magic staff as well.

If these are not presented at once,

I will throw a powerful torma at you

And disclose everything to Chieftain Gyatsha and your
brothers.

Be quick with your response. Bear this threat in mind.

After hearing this menacing song, Trothung saw that baby
Joru's flayed skin was draped over Amnyé. Not understanding
that Joru was posing as Amnyé, Trothung thought, *Joru has been
killed, but it is disturbing that Amnyé is so angry and filled with
regret. On the other hand, I really cannot blame him as I did weave
a false tale about Joru. But now he has gone too far in insisting that
I give him both the prosperity bag and my staff. As I have committed
to give the prosperity sack, I cannot renege on that piece, but I never
said I would give him my magical staff. I must find a way to put him
off. Still, I fear it is as the proverbs state, Power in another's hand is
no better than your own hair caught in a tree branch.*

Trothung continued thinking, *If Gyatsha and Chipon hear of this, not to mention my wife, Denza, my son, Nyatsha, and the rest, chaos will ensue. Yet Amnyé is growing old, and with any luck, it won't be long before he dies. For now I will go along with him since, having confronted the power of Joru and his naga ancestors, he is likely to be nearing his end. Not to mention the bad karma that I have burdened him with. When he dies, I will get my possessions back, but until then, as long as Amnyé is under the impression that I am upholding my end of our deal, he will keep our confidence.*

He turned to Amnyé and said, "Gracious sir, since you have accomplished what I asked of you, I can offer you the nine-edged sack and the staff. In addition, I will give you as much gold and silver as you desire."

Joru, still disguised as Amnyé, replied, "As you wish, but I do not want the sack or the staff after all. Gold and silver in good measure will do. Later on, remember that out of friendliness and mutual comity, I am now kindly letting you choose what treasure would be my payment. Moreover, since Joru was not only powerful, but it turned out, innocent, nothing can possibly suffice as the fee for committing the sin of such a murder. If I tell Gyatsha, Chipon, and the rest of your countrymen what has happened, they will do away with you forthwith. If you have something to give me, present it now. If you try to cheat me, you will suffer the full strength of my dark magic." He started to leave, mumbling his distrust for Trothung and recalling the proverbial warning, *The business is over, but the price is yet to be discussed.*

A frightened Trothung replied, "Please be calm. I will get you wealth beyond measure, provided this matter remains known only to us. Please take my staff and sack, and I will gather gold and offer that to you as well."

So saying, he pressed these items into Amnyé's hands. Then Trothung looked at Joru's skin hanging over Amnyé's shoulder and noticed that the eyes were winking and the lips were moving. Amnyé stood up, spun around once, and vanished into the air with a great clap. Trothung sat dazed, full of doubt and fear. He could feel his world slipping away as the ground upon which he stood became spongy, and panic overtook him.

A few days later, Joru was sitting with his mother and said to her, "This day is most lovely. Both the sky and my mind are sharp and clear. Perhaps something wondrous will happen."

At that very moment, Auntie Nammen Karmo,[21] the powerful meditator and sorceress, showed up in the form of a large turquoise bee the size of a small apple and sang these words of prophecy, buzzing so loudly in his ear that inattention was impossible.

> Your motherly aunt's prophecy is like this:
> Chieftain Trothung,
> It seems has evil intentions,
> But know well that his actions will transform into aid
>   for you, Joru.
> This is what you must do.
> Returning to the magician's cave, make it look as though
>   Amnyé has died.
> Place Trothung's prosperity bag and staff where your
>   uncle can see them,
> And then move the boulder that is the door to his retreat
> So that the entryway is just large enough for a rat to pass.
> Right now, Trothung is on his way to Amnyé's cave,
> Where through his own magical spell he will enter the
>   cave as a rat.

21. Auntie Nammen Karmo, also known by the affectionate term for auntie, Manéné, is a major influence on Gesar/Joru. She appears often with important advice. Considered by some to be similar to a muse or anima representing the inner life of Gesar or his feminine side or, from the Tibetan perspective, his wisdom aspect. Gesar draws strength and direction from her.

Once there, you must bless him so he cannot turn back.
Then you must force him to expel his demonic possession
And, until he swears, by drinking the oath water,
That he will not deploy his army,
You must not let him go.
His actions are two-faced and deceitful.
However, it is foretold that,
When you need to open the gates of the twelve fortresses,
He will be vital to your eventual success.
This then, my dear Joru, is what you must do.

Having heard her humming song in all its detail, Joru immediately went to Amnyé's cave. And placing the treasure bag and staff in plain sight, he saw the boulder that Manéné had mentioned and moved it into position so that only a small gap remained that was a friendly size for a rat, but not a man.

Meanwhile Trothung was mulling over his recent encounter with Amnyé. The powers that Amnyé displayed were greater than he thought possible. Moreover, he thought that, if Joru had indeed been successfully killed, word of the deed would certainly have reached him by now.

Trothung, deciding that he should confer with Amnyé, headed for Amnyé's cave. When he arrived, he saw blue smoke billowing above the meditation cave, leading him to believe that Amnyé was inside. A great boulder barricaded the entrance, but two small holes afforded a view of the cave's interior. He peered in and saw Amnyé, not breathing, and with his eyes wide open and staring straight ahead. He recognized his staff and prosperity bag leaning against the wall on the rock face behind Amnyé. Trothung rejoiced, thinking this was the best possible outcome. He had thought Amnyé would die but was relieved that it was so soon.

Immediately he transformed himself into a little rat, just

as Manéné had predicted. He went into the cave through the small hole, but now the staff and bag were no longer visible.

Trothung thought, *This must be some trickery. Perhaps I cannot see them now because of this little rat head with its tiny rat eyes.* So he removed his rat head, and his own human-sized head appeared atop the rat body.

Trothung looked all around the cave and saw the remains of a fire and a flood, but he could no longer see Amnyé's body, the staff, or the prosperity bag. They had all vanished because Joru had destroyed the illusion. Spooked, Trothung attempted to transform his human head back into a rat head, but his incantation failed since, at that very same moment, Joru had cast a spell preventing Trothung from reversing his own transformation.

Trothung desperately wanted to escape, but even though he tried mightily to push his human head through the hole, it would not pass. His terror increased, and he fervently supplicated his favored deity, Hayagriva, but alas, he could do nothing to free himself. Finally he slid his rat body out through the gap next to the boulder, but again his human head would not pass and was stuck inside the cave. At that very moment, he realized that Joru was standing at the entrance to the cave.

Joru rolled the boulder back just enough to allow himself passage into the cave but not enough to let Trothung's head out. He exclaimed, "What a sight! A bearded man's head is sticking into this cave. It can only be the head of a terrible devouring demon." Then Joru picked up the staff and whirled it around, preparing to smash the bearded head.

Petrified, Trothung screamed, "Dear sweet, precious Joru! You, the divine son of the gods, look. It is your sweet Uncle Trothung. Do not kill me. I know I have presumed and made a huge mistake, and through my magical powers, I transformed my own head, but now I cannot undo the spell. Please protect my life and save me! I promise to accept and do whatever you say."

Joru answered, "Uncle, you are possessed by a demon, and now the murderous death spirit has turned on you. You would have died had I not arrived. And that would have made me so very sad. It is as the proverb says, *Sons and nephews without fathers and uncles may be strong, but they are like tigresses wandering an empty plain. The people use such tigresses as a target for their stones.* Now come here."

Trothung tried to pull himself back into the cave, but now even the rat part of his body was stuck, and he despaired of ever getting free.

Joru went on, "All the murderous devouring demons must be around your waist because, if a rat's body were able to slip out through that gap, why could it not now get back in?"

Telling him that he should pray to his deity Hayagriva, Joru placed his right hand on Trothung's head and mentally invoked the deities as he entered into a penetrating meditation to remove the spell that possessed Trothung's body. Trothung promptly vomited a two-headed black serpent, and Joru killed the snake while leading the snake's consciousness to the pure realm. At that very instant, Trothung's rat body entered easily back into the cave.

"Although the demonic possession has been undone, Uncle, the problem remains that your swelled head is still attached to a rat's body. I am afraid that there is nothing further that I can do." Joru turned to leave and started down the road.

Trothung called after him several times. "Joru! Joru!"

Joru asked, "What?" and came back.

"Nephew Joru, please put an end to this magic, and I will obey your every command."

"I cannot reverse magic," Joru feigned. "However, as your

head is attached to a rat's corpse, I suggest that it be cut off and we cast away the corpse. Perhaps then your real head could be put back on your body."

Trothung said, "How can I dare do that? This rat body, though illusory, is my sole corporeal support. Please try to think of something else."

Joru pretended deep thought. Then he said, "Oh, Uncle, your intentions toward me and toward our country of Ling were particularly evil. Your inability to undo your own magic is your own karma. Though you take much pride in your armies, alone I could defeat them. On the other hand, if your sons Zigphen, Nyatsha, or Dongtsen were to meet an early death, I would feel as much sadness as if my own brother Gyatsha were struck down. You are a man who will stop at nothing, but your attempted treachery in Ling has been in vain. You must swear not to incite your armies to war nor to obstruct peace in Ling. If you promise from your heart, then it is possible that this magic could be reversed."

Having little in the way of choice, Trothung replied, "Yes, I am willing to both promise and swear."

He crouched beneath the staff and swore three times not to rouse his troops to combat with any of the lineages of Ling. At that very instant, Trothung's body was restored to its former state, and Joru ambled down the road, heading home and whistling a sweet tune.

As Trothung exited the cave, he found that he was able to easily dislodge the boulder (one that can still be seen in eastern Tibet) from its spot blocking the cave's door. Trothung remained confused as to whether all that had occurred was due to Joru's magic or rather had been caused by the same demon that had killed Amnyé.

The more he thought about it, the more perplexed he was.

Eventually he decided that it all had ended well for him. Even though he had lost a few precious possessions, at least Joru had not told Gyatsha, Chipon, and the others about it.

"Perhaps this Joru is not so bad after all," he mused.

From that time until Joru reached his fifth year, Trothung did as he had promised. Though, as this tale unspins, we will see this promise come to an end as change itself is our only unchanging inevitability.

CHAPTER 6

Wherein, following the dream commands of
  Padmasambhava,
Joru attires himself in the skins and hides of animals,
Behaves badly indeed, yet frees many demons,
And with Gogmo moves out of Ling.

FIVE YEARS had passed since Joru's encounter with Amnyé and his embarrassment of Trothung. On a full moon winter night, Joru was fast asleep in the tent he shared with his mother, Gogmo. Furs and hides of many animals were heaped upon them to stave off the frigid Tibetan winter air. Joru was having a vivid dream of Guru Padmasambhava, accompanied by a retinue of dakas and dakinis. Although he understood that he was dreaming, he felt their actual presence. And within the vividness of his dream, Padma and his retinue had begun chanting melodically to Joru this very song.

The song is Ala Ala Ala.
Thala leads the melody.
Now then, Joru,
Listen and we will tell you the way things are.
When those such as you arrive among human beings,
Your miraculous accomplishments unfold.
Yet, unless you can rule that land,
Those accomplishments are not worth yak dung.
Keep listening to our song.
The Ma Valley will be your homeland.

Its high mountain ranges connect with India,
Making Mother India's lineages of spiritual wealth close
    at hand.
The lower Ma Valley connects with China.
Hence the silken path of China's great tea commerce is
    close at hand.
To the west lies the path traveled by the bandits of Hor
And, joined with the Yak Mountain pass,
Makes a short path to Hor.
Finally, to the north, beyond the great marshlands
    of Ma,
Are the nomadic mara lands of Dud.
The great zodor, Magyal Pomra, whom we know well,
Is the principle land spirit of Ma.
You must take possession of these lands.
Be assured there will be nothing easy about your task.
There is famine, caused by plague-infested rodents
    called pika,[22]
Which lord over the grass and water,
And at every step along its trade routes,
A merchant's wealth is thieved by the Hor bandits.
A lone person walks this path in fear.
You, the great one, must conquer those lands,
But first, you must provoke the people of Ling to
    despise you
And cast you out.
Your behavior must be outrageous … beyond outrageous.
Make certain that they believe your mother, Gogmo, to be
    a demon rakshasi
And you then, her raksha child.
Moreover, you must break the humane laws of Ling,

---

22. A pika is a small burrowing mammal similar to a vole or a large mouse.

Defying the moral code of reasonable people.
You must cause the populace to have fearful dreams
And to believe you a monster.
It must come to pass that you are expelled from Ling
And hence come to dwell in the land of Ma.
And so it will be that, when the moon first waxes
In the year of the Wood Monkey,
You will take possession of the Black Earth Valley in
     Lower Ma,
Where your excellent karma will ripen.
The six tribes that dwell there will naturally come to
     your aid,
And once again your goodness will be celebrated.
Though these predictions might be met with disbelief,
All we say will come to pass.

As soon as Padma and his retinue finished their song, they disappeared like steam into warm air. Gogmo, being a dakini, could intuit Joru's dream, and she could already smell the beautiful valley of Ma and see in her mind's eye its fields and mountainsides strewn with multicolored wildflowers. When Joru awoke, he told his mother that he would need some new clothes. She listened as he spoke this proverb, *Once a boy is born, he will learn to provide for himself. According to karma, the necessary wealth will be within reach.*

Having said this and remembering the guru's instructions, Joru left, riding his magical staff. First he went to Seyu Mountain, and there on the ridge, he saw three antelope-demons. Quickly he slew them all, sending their consciousnesses to the pure realm, but he severed the head from the largest antelope buck, making it into a gruesome, three-pointed hat that he snugged beneath his chin with a tie fashioned from one of the antelope's leg tendons.

That very night he went down to Chipon's yak corral, stealing and killing seven yak calves that he knew to be afflicted by disease-demons. He took the untanned calf hides and wore them as clothing with the tails still attached, crusted with bits of blood, and muscle and tendon exposed. Then he went down to Trothung's horse corral, stealing and killing a demon-horse from which he made grotesque rawhide boots.

Rather proud of his new clothes, which he deemed worthy of the tasks ahead, he began to dig for pika demons, repeating to himself, *When I unearth the pikas, their burrows will collapse, ridding this land of demons.*

Just then the pikas' vast cavern did collapse, and instantly nine terrible pika demons were buried. Joru said to his mother, once again in proverbs, *"Being able to make your own decisions is more empowering than receiving the chieftain's pretty words. Having personal freedom to act brings greater happiness than assuming a thousand golden thrones."*

He continued, "Let us stay no longer under Chipon's rule. It is demeaning to both of us. We have no relatives, no family, and no worldly status. We do not need to flatter others with sweet talk. We should go where the weather is lovely and the land pleasant."

Remembering Joru's dream, Gogmo asked, "Are we going to the Ma Valley?"

Joru replied, "Someday, yes. But first, I have business in the lower valley of Drulgo [Snake Head Valley], where it is warm and the wild yams[23] are sweet to eat."

They packed their few possessions and began their journey.

Soon they came to a turbulent river crossing guarded by a demoness with the name of Sinmo Buzen [Cannibal Demoness

---

23. Very small and somewhat sweet, these wild yams are a favored Tibetan treat. They also have a place in Tibetan and Chinese medicine.

Child-Eater]. At this point in her already long life, Sinmo was comfortably set in her cannibal ways and unconcerned with the frightening appearance that she presented. The skin that had been hers for a lifetime fell in ceaseless wrinkles, blending almost imperceptibly into the creased and tattered yak-skin garment that had been hers for nearly as many decades.

Joru understood that her time had come to be tamed so he bid his mother to wait on the banks of the river while he led his unbroken colt into the Dza River[24] at its shallowest point. From there he could see the demoness in the process of devouring the corpses of four or five children, and in a loud and cheerful voice, Joru cried out to her, "Precious Sister! May your life last for one hundred years! Give me some fire, and I'll show you a trick that I know."

Seeing this harmless-looking little boy, she struck a flint, handed the flame to him, and asked, "What trick do you have to show me?"

He said, "If you stay here in the middle of the river, you will go hungry. But if you go to the far shore, over there you will find an abundance of young flesh. I have seen them, and they are yours for the taking."

But she protested, saying that she did not think she had the strength to ford the river. By now, she had waded close enough to Joru that he could wrap the tail of his little colt around her neck.

Urging her on, he said, "Now follow me. We can cross right here."

When they reached the middle of the river, jerking the lead rope, Joru turned the colt upstream and struck the horse's

24. The Dza River is continuous with the Mekong River. It is called the Dza Chu from its headwaters in northeastern Tibet until it reaches Tibet's border with China, eventually emptying out as the Mekong River into the South China Sea not far from Ho Chi Minh City in Vietnam.

hindquarters with his hand. The horse bolted, and the demoness' neck snapped. Joru guided her consciousness to an auspicious rebirth.

Mother and child continued down the road. They journeyed on to Drulgo Valley, and soon Joru met up with the fearsome demon, Khasé Rulu [Gray Beard]. He was daunting with an oversized and ugly mouth rimmed with sharp teeth. He was out on his rounds: gathering people up, bringing them to the river, and drowning them. His mouth was large enough to devour the drowned people whole, without chewing.

Tied to Joru's waist was a leather lasso eighty meters in length and tipped with a massive iron hook. He threw it so the hook lodged in the middle of the demon's heart, and when Joru pulled back on the lasso, the demon's heart instantly disgorged from his chest, killing him. He offered the flesh and blood of the heart to the drala and werma and transferred the demon's consciousness to the pure realm, thus setting him free as well.

They remained in Drulgo Valley, and Joru continued his horrific deeds. Slaying two bucks, he took only one rack as a trophy and left the bodies as carrion. Then he lassoed a mule and rounded up all the wild animals that were freely grazing on the slopes. Slaying them all, he built bloody walls with their flesh. He made corrals with their heads on fence posts and swirling lakes with their blood. Any traveler who passed through that desolate valley he took as a prisoner and freely ate their flesh. He quenched his thirst with human blood and spread out sheets of human skin as his seat. He stacked human corpses here and there across the landscape. Seeing this, godly and cannibal demons alike had their spirits broken. All who saw these gruesome sights were aghast.

For a year and a half, Joru's heinous activities continued. By that time, the Ling lamas, diviners, astrologers, fathers, uncles, and brothers had all been sent ominous dreams by the drala and werma. In addition, the rumors and stories of Joru's evil deeds were widespread. Everyone shared the same dreams and the same thoughts—that Joru was causing harm and spreading misery throughout the land and that despite all the previous good omens, Joru, the divine child, had turned out to be a wretched demon after all.

They began saying, "He is robbing all beings of their welfare and happiness, destroying the teachings of the Buddha, and eating whatever flesh he sees, and he has become nothing but another red-faced cannibal. Our hopes for him were so high, but now he is as disappointing as cold butter-tea."

Although they gossiped in this way, no one had the courage to stand up to him.

Shortly after the rumors, dreams, and omens had reached a fevered pitch, seven hunters from Trothung's clan of Tag-rong went on a deer hunt. Not finding any prey, they decided to stay overnight on a mountain crag. Instantly Joru commanded a demon horseman from that crag to detain the hunters, locking them in a guarded corral for three months.

During that time, Joru blessed their bodies so they had no need of food or water and appeared to be dead. After some time, a search party, which happened to include Drukmo, King Kyalo's beautiful daughter and Gesar's future wife, found only small bits and pieces of the corpses of their comrades as well as the remains of their horses. And so it came to pass that the entire country accused Joru of eating the horsemen, but still no one had the courage to confront him.

King Chipon, of course, had learned of Joru's terrible deeds from his advisers. He remembered the many glowing prophecies that attended Joru's birth, how he was born to overcome demons and maras through his incomparable warriorship, and he had believed them all. But now he thought that the only thing Joru seemed to want was the destruction of the peace, prosperity, and lawfulness of Ling. As king he could not allow this to continue.

On the other hand, Chipon realized that Joru *was* a child of divine lineage and they could not simply incarcerate or execute him. Thus he reasoned that a diviner, someone who could see into the truth of this troubling situation, should be hired. Weary of all this thinking, Chipon drifted off to a deep but restless sleep.

Toward dawn, he had a dream in which a beautiful dakini rode down from the mountains astride a pure white snow lion, holding a crystalline bow and a golden arrow and singing in a loud and clear voice this prophetic song.

> Leader, rightly seated atop a gilded throne,
> Lord of Mukpo Dong, King Chipon, listen.
> When the divine child manifests as a human,
> Although the land of his birth may be excellent,
> He must take possession of the Ma Valley,
> That place where the four maras are to be bound
> by oath.
> Just staying in Ling gets Joru nothing,
> And it gets Ling less.
> All the bad signs and inauspicious connections you see
> Are enlightened activities well beyond your
> understanding.
> Nevertheless, the punishment for his illusory killing
> of the hunters
> And the way to restore order to Ling
> Is to exile Joru to the valley of Ma.
> Within three years,
> Ling will be covered with sheets of white ice,
> Your animals starving, and your people poor.
> At that time the verdant Ma Valley

Will be adorned by the farmers' five-colored scarf,
And Joru will be your only refuge.
If you understand this, keep it in your heart.
If not, there is no concern as the words are self-secret.

The dream and the dakini dissolved, and Chipon awoke. The dream was fresh in his mind when a messenger from Trothung arrived. He recounted the growing catalogue of complaints against Joru and asked that a council be convened forthwith. Chipon agreed and sent the messenger back to Trothung to arrange just such a gathering. At this point, Chipon fervently wished the situation to be someone else's burden. It was as the proverbs say, *A man who would guzzle the ocean needs a stomach the size of the sky.* On the other hand, the proverbs also say, *Don't race with the tsen.*[25] *Don't throw dice with the maras.*[26] *Don't get too close with nagas.*

Eight days passed, and as the morning sun lit the mountain peaks, all the warriors gathered. Trothung feared that, as he had asked for the meeting, the most difficult task would fall to him, that of relaying the punishment to Joru. Chipon spoke first, requesting that all assembled contribute and speak freely.

Without a moment's hesitation, Trothung stammered a reply, "My brother Chipon, my dear nephew Gyatsha, and all who have gathered, I address you. I, Chief Trothung, have given great thought and pondered deeply on the political situation of Ling and in particular on the integrity of our clan and Joru's personal situation. Despite my brilliant mind, clear insight, and stellar awareness, I have not found a resolution to this problem. As you all know the dreams and predictions have been

25. Tsen refers to a class of powerful and negative nonhuman spirits that inhabit the earthly realm.
26. Maras are malevolent spirits whose main function is to perpetuate ignorance and confusion.

worrisome. Concerning Joru, it is as the proverb goes, *Even though there is no pain in the body, there is still pain in the mind.* Perhaps his is a case of demonic possession. If so, we must decide which ritual will relieve the demonic forces. Although I have heard talk of Joru's evil deeds, I myself have no wish to challenge him."

He spoke as if his words were entirely sincere. Chipon, Gyatsha, and the others agreed that the time had come to consult divinations and astrology. Various divinations were performed, using dice, divination arrows, and string. The astrological charts were cast. All agreed: Ling would never be at peace unless Joru was sent away. Gyatsha felt uncomfortable with this, but Chipon went on to add,

> The song is Ala Ala Ala.
> Thala leads the melody.
> The delicious foods are meat, butter, and molasses,
> But in poor health even these can cause life-threatening
>   illness.
> This magical child, the boy Joru, has come to harm Ling.
> It seems as though Ling's merit is exhausted.
> Boys and nephews, with the courage of tigers,
> Once they meet the wild beast enemy, they believe them-
>   selves heroic.
> Fathers and uncles who are like Meru, the king of
>   mountains,
> Once they encounter good and bad, are even more solid.
> The warriors of the lineage of Mukpo Dong,
> Once the enemy descends upon them, are fiercer than
>   before.
> As the child Joru brings harm to Ling,
> Let us send him away to a place where he may prosper
> And cast away this thorn in our side.

Those fourteen men and horses of Tag-rong
Have been slain by Joru,
And Drukmo's testimony is sufficient.
Joru's punishment is expulsion from Ling,
As our laws prevent any stricter punishment.
Let Joru's brother Gyatsha
Gather provisions for Joru's journey to the borderlands.
Who among our gathered warriors will be the courier?
Come forward now and proclaim yourself.

Choking up, Gyatsha said, "My little brother, when I think that he is to be banished, it breaks my heart. Nevertheless, the karma of his deeds must play out, and my king's command is wise and just. I have no choice but to carry out Chipon's wishes."

By that time, the powerful mountain spirit Magyal Pomra had been dispatched by Padmasambhava to welcome Joru to the Ma Valley. But Joru remained unmoving within his illusory disguise, surrounded by rotting human flesh, open skulls, and entrails. Being a nagini, his mother, Gogmo, was appalled by her son's consumption of human flesh. She struggled to keep the words of her father in mind. Although she often tried to think that Joru had created a magical illusion, at other times his cannibalism seemed all too real.

Just as Gyatsha was volunteering to bring the king's edict to Joru, Denma objected, stating that it was his responsibility as commander and that he had been a warrior well before Joru was born.

With limbs as sinewy and taut as his own bowstring, he was a skilled archer. Denma continued, "Gyatsha, great warrior and loyal brother, you stay. This is my duty. I will go at once." And with a sweeping motion, he hoisted himself upon his great steed and departed before anyone could challenge him.

Having ridden for six hours, Denma finally arrived in Drulgo Valley and, looking around, saw pitched tents of human skin held down by ropes of intestines. Hundreds of fresh and rotting human and animal corpses were stacked against a fence, creating a wall ten feet high.

At first Denma thought, *It is truly horrendous what Joru has done!* On second thought, it came to his mind that, if Joru had actually killed hundreds of people, there would have been a much bigger uproar and all of Ling would have heard a great deal more about it. As it was, as far as he knew, there were only the seven men and seven horses that Joru was alleged to have eaten. Suddenly Denma realized without a doubt that everything he was seeing was but an apparition. He was awed at its intensity.

Denma had dismounted and had been sitting on the hard ground for a short while when Joru walked toward him, gnawing on a human arm. Denma waved his helmet with white plumed silken pennants in greeting. Joru called out as he came,

If a great cause and a person with great expectations
Are brought together, there is good fortune.
To a superior person this seems natural,
To a mediocre person this requires effort,
And to an inferior person it is elusive.
This must be the case here.

Denma rose quickly to meet Joru, and as he did, the animal and human corpses all vanished like the mirage that they were. Denma no longer perceived any impure appearances but instead saw only the bright midday sun shining down on a profusion of wildflowers and a throng of peaceful animals milling about. Denma removed his armor and weapons, starting to place them outside the entrance of Joru's main tent, but Joru brought them inside, explaining that they were necessary as talisman supports for drala energy.

Denma followed, entering Joru's comfortable and cozy dwelling. Fragrant, sweet incense filled the air, and Denma was overcome with emotion. At that moment, a profound and lifelong connection was forged between Joru and Denma. Denma offered an imaginary celestial feast, and Joru gave a spontaneous discourse in which he described the history of the Mukpo Clan and gave prophecies for the future.

Denma vowed fealty to Gesar for lifetimes to come, even if they were to be as numerous as the sands of this realm's many oceans, and followed with a song praising Joru.[27] In return, Joru offered a song in the melody "Nine Swirls of a White Conch."

> The song is Ala Ala Ala.
> Thala leads the melody.
> I am the young yet powerful Joru.
> Padmasambhava is my protector.
> My spirit father is the nyen Gedzo.
> I am the grandson of Tsugna Rinchen, king of the
>   nagas,
> And the younger brother of dear Gyatsha of Bumpa.
> Now Denma, listen and I will tell you the way things
>   are.
> If I did not wish to depart,
> The six provinces of Ling would find it difficult to
>   expel me.
> However, to bring peace to these lands,
> I was sent here by the imperial gods,
> And I cannot accomplish this purpose living here
>   in comfort.

27. See Song Appendix, Song #3.

Banishment is the way Brahma shows me the path.
As the old proverbs state,
Only if you cross the treacherous crag
Will you arrive at the flat plain and fertile valley.
Only if you traverse the path of mind's misery
Will you encounter the wealth of mental joy.
The land spirit Magyal Pomra has come to receive me,
And I will go to the heartland of Ma,
But before long, you and I will meet again.
If you understood this discourse, it is sweet to your
   ears.
If not, there is no way to explain.

Denma's worries were completely put to rest, and as he was preparing to leave, Joru said, "When you return to Ling, say to the others, 'I didn't dare get close to Joru, but I yelled out to him to make clear our edict.' It is crucial that what happened here between us be kept secret. You must tell no one."

Denma arrived back at the Ling encampment and said to the anxious assembly, "Just as you thought, Joru is truly a cannibal. I did not dare get very close to him, but I called out our message, and he responded that he will come and present himself here tomorrow."

While they were glad to see Denma return safely, the prospect of Joru coming to their encampment filled many with dread. They had heard the stories, dreamed the dreams, and lived the omens, and most of them thought that, when Joru finally arrived, he was going to devour them all, swinging their intestines as lassos and sticking their heads on fence posts.

Trothung, more frightened than the rest, thought that, if Joru had reason to kill anybody in Ling, it was him. With sheer dread, he declared, "Everyone should put on armor, take up weapons, and assume a state of warlike readiness."

Testily, Gyatsha replied, "What is the reason for that? Joru's exile is punishment enough for his crimes against Ling. What more do you want?" Though everyone was on edge, they generally agreed with Gyatsha.

Suddenly Joru showed up wearing his hideous finery. On his head was his bloody antelope hat with its sinewy chinstrap and on his back the ugly dried calf-hide coat. Grotesque raw horse-hide boots adorned his feet. He came riding his white willow staff. On the other hand, and in striking contrast, his mother, Gogmo, was more resplendent than ever, riding her gray mare with a striking white blaze on its face.

Clearly the time had come to bewitch the minds of the inhabitants of Ling. And magically, just by seeing Gogmo and her son, their minds *were* transformed, and almost in unison, they intoned, "Oh, look how sweet Joru appears and how beautiful Gogmo is!"

But the tribe's King Chipon, privy to the secret and unequivocal prophecy that Joru was to be banished from Ling, took his responsibility to heart. He sang with the melody called "Long and Solemn Song."

> The song is Ala Ala Ala.
> Thala leads the melody.
> I am Uncle King Chipon
> And my song is a genuine account of how it is.
> The strong and solid four-sided castle of stone,
> Beautified by its juniper-timbered roof
> And adorned with its golden pinnacle,
> It may seem a mighty fortress that will protect us
> for a lifetime,
> But in an earthquake, it will be the hammer that
> smashes us.
> Whatever karma one collects is dirt piled upon them.

The boy Joru is the royal grandson of the naga king
    Tsugna,
The one we hoped would be the ornament of Ling.
Beyond that, he is the heart blood of the warrior Gyatsha,
And in an ideal world, he would have become an ally.
But something went awry, for he has killed the hunters
    of Tag-rong
And his thieving hands have stolen their horses.
These wrongdoings must be punished.
Massacring the wild animals roaming the mountains,
Imprisoning the travelers passing through the valleys,
Eating human flesh, and drinking human blood—
What he has done amounts to destroying the laws
    of Ling.
It became clear through our divinations and prophecies
That we must expel Joru.
Do you understand this, Joru?
The inevitability of karma unwinds.
Even as soft mushrooms can emerge from an unyielding
    meadow,
Likewise, Gogmo and Joru together
Must herewith depart from our land
With the aspiration prayer that we will meet again
During a time more pleasing.
Do not lose heart.
Whatever you need you will receive from Gyatsha,
Who will escort you on your way.
If you understand this song, it is sweet to your ears.
If not, there is no way to explain.

Thus he sang, and the song prompted a shared sadness, one familiar to any community grieving for a child gone terribly astray.

As he had promised, Gyatsha had obtained all the horses, yaks, and provisions necessary for their journey. Then Joru turned to his half-brother and said, "Do not despair. My exile shows that destiny is playing out in the unending cycle of karma. You do not need to be concerned, as, just yesterday, Magyal Pomra himself, the virtuous zodor[28] of the land of Ma came to welcome my mother and me to their land, and they too brought us provisions."

Joru leaned on his staff and spoke his piece to all of Ling, "Well then, great inhabitants of this divine land of Ling, although I have done nothing wrong, you wish to paint a picture of my supposed sins and faults. But here is the truth of the matter." And he sang.

> The song beings with Ala.
> Thala leads the melody.
> People of the six districts of Ling,
> Listen, for I have a few things to tell you.
> Appearances are not true but an illusion.
> It is difficult for the outer appearance and the inner
>   essence to match.
> Although the outer may seem good, it is false in three
>   ways:
> The sheen of a peacock's feathers may look good on
>   the outside,
> But the peacock is unclean on the inside, filled with
>   poison.
> A coward's armor and weapons may look good on
>   the outside,
> But inside he is gutless and crafty as a fox.

28. A zodor is a nature spirit generally associated with a particular location.

The face of a bedecked beauty may be lovely on the
    outside,
But on the inside, she is as phony as false treasure.
I, faultless Joru, banished from this place,
Do not deserve the reprimand of my uncle,
Yet I have no choice but to accept the burden of my
    karma.
I will accept the punishment of having broken the law,
But without the higher perceptions,
It is difficult to distinguish good and bad.
The uncles and fathers have been hard on me,
And now I must depart.
If you have understood this song, it is sweet to your ears.
If not, there is no way to explain.

He mounted his staff and prepared to depart for Upper
Chipu as his mother, Gogmo, sang this little song of beckoning.

Ho! Heed me!
All guardian deities who are the principal companions,
Be as a refuge for us, mother and son,
But also for the prosperity of these three—
The people, possessions, and livestock of Ling.
Just as tributaries flow into rivers and rivers, in turn, to
    the sea,
Foals follow mares and children their mothers,
So will everything follow after mother and son,
Rushing and overflowing until reality's truth dawns.

She called out *"Ho!"* three times. As she did so, the course of
the thirteen rivers of the Chipu Valley and the mountain peaks
above them turned in salute. The topography of this part of
Tibet remains marked by this greeting. Gogmo and Joru spent

some weeks in the Chipu Valley with Gogmo's old friend and benefactor, Ralo Tonpa, who had sheltered her when she first left her naga homeland.

Then at the time of the waxing December moon, they set out for the Ma Valley. Tonpa also tried to provision Gogmo and Joru for their journey, but they refused his kind offerings, taking only a broken, old hoe that he no longer needed.

After traveling some distance, they came to Lower Ma. Joru lit a fire and made strong and delicious tea that he offered to his mother. Gogmo, feeling energetic, picked up the hoe and dug a bit in each of the four directions. In each hole, she found sweet yams, said to be the size of a horse, yak, dri, and a sheep in the east, south, west, and north, respectively. This was a sign of great auspiciousness, although Lower Ma was a dark place controlled by pika demons that had gnawed the tall grasses, turning the land black as pitch. All the vegetation had withered and died, and first the livestock and then the people of that land had either starved or moved away. It was a bleak and barren land with little to recommend it.

Joru realized that the time had come to eliminate the pika demons, and he put three kidney-shaped god-demon life-stones into his trusty slingshot.[29] Preparing to empty their mountain hideouts, he sang this song.

> The song is Ala Ala Ala.
> Thala leads the melody.
> You who are embodied as pika demons
> Have decimated these great grassy plains,
> Devouring its flowers and leaves

---

29. In Tibet as well as many herding and nomadic lands, a slingshot, similar to the South American bolo, is a very powerful weapon. As the shepherd boy David slew Goliath, so a trained person could expect to cast a stone at speed for fifty to one hundred yards.

Until only the dust of the black earth remains.
As it is said in the proverbs of the ancient people of Tibet,
It is a pika that turns the earth to black
And a thief who destroys the district.
Your negative karma produced this rebirth.
Ruining the green meadows, you have banished all joy
    from this land.
This very day with my slingshot,
I will empty this realm of pika demons.
May their negative karma be severed,
May all beings know true happiness,
And may every species rest in ease and comfort.

Then with a mighty effort, he loosed his slingshot. The stone struck, instantly killing the three principal pika demons, and with the roaring sound of a thousand dragons that followed, the whole colony was annihilated. By the strength of Joru's meditative awareness and compassion, their little pika minds were placed in the state of liberation.

Meanwhile, there were merchants from Ladakh en route to China with some two thousand mules. The mules were carrying assorted loads of gold, silver, and precious silks. As they came into the valley, seven vicious Hor bandits overcame them, binding and beating even the oldest among them. Joru came to where they were being held and overheard the din of their collective sobbing.

Harshly, Joru told them, "If you must cry, then go home and cry! Forget about crying! You're not even supposed to laugh here. You must apologize to me as I am now the landowner here, and you must make offerings to the mountain zodor Magyal Pomra. Refuse, and my deadly slingshot will find your skull." Menacingly, he loaded a stone.

The three merchant leaders begged him, "Dear Joru, we

are just merchants from Ladakh far to the west of here." They told him in detail how robbers from Hor had overcome them, beaten them, and stolen their goods. "Please help us to recover our goods, and we will do whatever you command."

Joru replied, "What a pity! I rule over this land, and even the Lord of Death is not allowed to come and pillage here. Why would I fear a few butchers from Hor? In exchange for helping you to recoup your possessions and wealth, from now on, merchants traveling from Ladakh must bring me gifts and offer scarves as well as whatever I ask for safe passage."

Even though they quickly nodded their assent, they wondered how it could be that Joru, who still appeared as a small, oddly attired child, would be able to do as he had promised.

Meanwhile the seven robbers had already arrived at the Plain of Achen and were divvying up their booty of mules, jewels, and other goods.

Joru arrived, riding his trusty staff, and shouted at them in a haughty, booming voice, "Take heed, you seven thieves from Hor! I am Joru, and you cannot raid merchants on my land. I am the ruler here and cannot abide what you have done."

Overwhelmed by the sound of this mighty voice, the leader of the bandits said, "What a commanding voice is coming from such a small boy. He must have concealed power."

He urged the bandits away, and they fled, leaving all of their booty behind. The bandits could see their king, Togtog Relchen, up on the slope of the Nine-Pointed Vajra Mountain where he was hunting with ninety-nine of his men. They watched in alarm as Joru threw three stones with his slingshot, striking a crag above their king and his hunting party, letting loose a landslide that tumbled down and killed all one hundred men and their horses. Immediately, through the power of his realization, Joru led their consciousnesses to the pure realm.

Summoning the local drala and werma to help him, Joru

snatched the helmets, armor, swords, and other items that had belonged to King Togtog Ralchen and his men and gathered up every last one of the Ladakhis' stolen golden boxes and mules. Riding his staff, he made his way back to the merchants. Joru returned their possessions, which, merchants being merchants, made them as joyful as men could be.

And although they tried to give a large share back to Joru, he refused, not caring a bit about riches. He simply said to them, "I do not want any of your wealth, but someday I will count on you for a favor. For now, know that your passage is safe, and go in peace." Joru then departed for Lower Ma.

Nearly simultaneously with the Ladakhi merchants, three wealthy merchant chiefs from O-mé Mountain in the Sichuan Province of China were traveling with four hundred thousand bricks of tea and one thousand attendants, on their way to the high plateaus to their west. They had heard of the terrifying Hor bandits and were fearful of meeting up with them, even though they were traveling with quite the garrison.

They had arrived at the Turquoise Valley in Ma and set up their camps. Having transformed his little sorrel colt into a great and mighty steed named Noble Mount, Joru galloped with aplomb into the encampment and halted the horse right in front of the merchants.

He said, "I am King Joru with only this horse, the excellent steed, Noble Mount. I am worried that the bandits of Hor will make off with my horse before I find any buyers in this vacant land. As you possess fabulous wealth, I am willing to sell you this magnificent animal."

Some of the merchants thought, *This cannot be true. It must be some kind of ruse. Even the emperor of China does not have an animal like this.*

A skilled magician was asked to examine the steed. After checking the horse, he confirmed, "There are no traces of deception present here." And the chief merchant accepted Joru's offer, saying he would pay whatever Joru asked.

Joru replied, "This horse of mine is one of two brother flying horses, and frankly, he is going to cost you dearly. His head is so fine that it is worth a hundred boxes of gold, his ears are worth a hundred boxes of silver, the four hooves are each worth a hundred boxes of silk, the tips of the hairs on his coat are worth a hundred mules, and the roots of those hairs are so fine that they are worth a hundred ewes. Additionally there must be a tip for the mare, and I must insist upon a fee for myself for removing the halter and a contribution for the celebration we must have in my honor."

One of the merchants spoke aside to the others. "This horse is only a bit better than my most excellent horse, the one I sold to the Tag-rong Clan for a hundred, very small pouches of gold and a hundred ingots of silver half the size of a horse's hoof. Besides, even if each of us were to put in all of our own wealth, it would not total a hundred boxes of gold. This horse trader does not understand the value of horses, gold, or silver. Whatever the case, we cannot be sure that he is not a horse rustler from Hor whose bandits are capable of great thievery."

The merchants spoke amongst themselves and decided to kill Joru, steal the horse, and send it back to China with the magician.

The chief merchant returned to speak with Joru, saying, "The price you quoted is ridiculously high, an insult really to all of China. We will simply seize the beast."

Joru retorted that the horse and land they stood on belonged to him. Accusing them of trespass, he demanded that they leave with both haste and an apology.

If the merchants weren't angry before, they were furious now, and they began to stone Joru. But as soon as they killed one Joru, two emerged. When they killed two, four appeared.

They killed four, and then there were eight. And on and on. Finally the valley was filled with a Joru army.

Some of the Joru emanations began to pack up the Chinese merchants' encampment, others started leading the mules away, and still more tied up the merchants and beat them. Joru left, leaving the merchants there, hog-tied and without even a needle's worth of wealth or provisions. In terror of being left to die, they watched the great band of Jorus leave for Lower Ma. However, one miniature Joru remained there, and the merchants begged him to spare their lives.

He said, "We Jorus may have anger, but we do not hold a grudge. A grudge is a waste of time in the mind of the enlightened and compassionate. In exchange for promises of loyalty, we will not steal your possessions."

The merchants were relieved and said to each other, "This must be a magical emanation. We merchants must apologize for our ignorance and do whatever he says."

Then the miniature Joru untied them and restored their camp as it had been, with each merchant back in his own tent.

Then the real Joru appeared and said, "You have killed many of my emanations. If I took all of your possessions in revenge, it would not be enough. But I don't want your goods; rather you must vow that, from this day on, every Chinese merchant who travels through here will greet me with a silken scarf and a pick of the bricks of your best tea. Moreover, you must build me a palace in the place called Ma Drodro Lu-gu'i Khelkhung [Speckled Lamb's Kidney Cavity]. When it is completed, I will return every bit of your wealth, but until then, I will provide only what you need to survive. But my ultimate gift to you is that, from this day onward, wherever you go, I will protect you always from the Hor thieves."

Joru continued, "Yesterday some merchants from Ladakh were robbed by the seven Hor bandits of Achen. I pursued them, recovered the stolen goods, and returned them to the merchants. And later today they will arrive here, also to build a palace for me."

And just as Joru had said, the Ladakhi merchants and their mules arrived and made their encampment. Through his magic, Joru produced a feast with many varieties of food and much drink. The merchants offered three tan mules laden with boxes of gold, five white mules laden with boxes of silver, and seven sorrel mules laden with boxes of silk. The merchants from China offered a thousand bricks of tea with khatas and their oath to obey him.

The very next day, all the merchants from Ladakh and China went to Ma Drodro Lu-gu'i Khelkhung to build a four-storied palace with four pagoda-like fortresses in the four directions and to make the supports for a fifth story.

Joru told them, "If the provisions I have given you are exhausted before the building is completed, you can come back for more."

Each group of a hundred men was given a cache of tsampa and a load each of butter, tea, and meat. Then two Jorus arrived to be supervisors. The tea merchants from China were tasked with building the east, west, and north pagodas, which were thereafter collectively known as the Tea Castle. The merchants of Ladakh were only asked to build the southern pagoda.

During the construction, the food provided for the merchants not only was not exhausted but did not decrease in the slightest. Upon completion of the palace, Joru threw another magnificent celebration and presented all the merchants with bountiful gifts, after which he sent them happily back to their respective countries. It became well known that, through Joru's blessings, these merchants prospered as never before.

Later on, the fifth story of the palace was built jointly by the nyen Gedzo and the mountain spirit Magyal Pomra. Since the stones for its walls were carried by many snow lion cubs, the roof laid by the gods, Nyentag, and others; and the wood carried from Siblung Nag-gyal Chugmo [Shady Valley Rich Royal Forest] by tigresses, it thereafter became known as Sengdruk Tagtsé [Lion Dragon Tiger Peak].

Perfectly accomplished, without and within, for some time the palace was maintained by the gods, nagas, and nyen who resided there. This is how it became known that the upper (the highest) story, was built by the gods. The second (the middle) story was built by the nyen. And the third (the lower) story was built by the nagas.

CHAPTER 7

Wherein, blanketed by snow and wrapped in icy air,
The inhabitants of Ling become desperate
While the land of Ma blossoms in an eternal spring
And Joru distributes his land to the glad people of Ling.

NOW IT HAPPENED that, when Joru was all of eight years old, he knew that the time had come for Ling to be established in the land of Ma. So he sought out his grandfather, the naga king Tsugna Rinchen. And finding him in a nearby clear blue spring, he asked him to make it rain. With nagas having dominion over water, this was the work they loved best, and thus the king was happy to aid his grandson, the son of his beloved and self-sacrificing youngest daughter.

And so a great rain poured down from the heavens, and then, with the help of the land spirits he had befriended, Joru turned that tumultuous rain into a snowstorm that malevolently descended on the entirety of the land of Ling. From the first day of winter, the snowfall was such that, if an eight-foot spear were to be put into the ground, only the tip would be seen, and soon the tip would be covered as well.

Even by the harsh standards of the Tibetan winter, this was a storm like no other. Not even the shriveled grandmothers and grandfathers, huddled freezing in the corners of their cold tents, could remember either such a storm or so miserable a winter. Therefore, a council of elders and leaders was convened. Daily, animals were dying, food was rapidly becoming scarce, and people were beginning to starve.

The leaders knew that no one would survive if they simply stayed put. After considerable discussion, it was decided that four groups of able warriors would be dispatched in the four directions to search for a place where there would be food and shelter from the ravages of this great winter storm. Each group was to travel for one week in its designated cardinal direction and then return and report back. Three of the groups found only more snow and even greater desolation, but the warriors who had traveled to the Ma Valley came upon its fertile, grassy green hills and warm, inviting climate. Edible grasses such as barley and herbs and other vegetation were abundant, and well-fed livestock continually grazed the plateaus.

While they were exploring the land of Ma, the warriors encountered traveling merchants from China and Ladakh—the very same ones who had encountered Joru. And having labored to build his fortresses, they were no longer preyed on by robbers and thieves. The warriors questioned these merchants about the land and its leader, asked them who the owner of this land was, and inquired if they knew if some of it might be for rent or sale.

The merchants replied, "Previously this was an empty land, known only for the bandits who terrorized merchants. Then the one known as King Joru came here. He is the lord of the nonhuman godly demons. His great strength has overcome enemies too numerous to count. Because we all present him greeting scarves and portions of our tea and other goods, we are able to travel here in complete safety and no longer fear the ruthless robbers and bandits. If you want to rent or purchase some land, you must request it of him."

The warriors of Ling knew well Joru's reputation and were afraid to approach him themselves, and instead they returned home, as they had been instructed, to make their report. A fortnight had passed, and everyone convened to learn what had been found. Three of the search parties explained that they had come across no land without snow and desolation, but the group that had gone to the land of Ma told of a lush and verdant land.

On the downside, they had ascertained the ruler of the land to be Joru, and hanging their heads, they confessed that they had been too afraid to meet with him. A low and agitated murmuring spread through the crowd and was reaching a fevered pitch when Gyatsha thundered, "We have no choice. It is clear that Ma is the land for us to settle. Joru may be the ruler, but I am his older brother. I have no reason to fear him and will travel there to approach him. What else can we do? However, I should not go alone, but rather accompanied by a few armed warriors so as not to appear needy and weak."

Five brave warriors volunteered, and the band of six tacked their horses and departed for Ma.

Intuiting their arrival, without warning, Joru suddenly appeared in their line of sight. He had placed a black nyen stone the size of a man's fist in his slingshot and was standing about the distance of an arrow's flight away. Without a greeting, he sang this song.

> The song is Ala Ala Ala.
> Thala sets the melody.
> If you do not recognize me,
> My name is Little Chieftain King Joru.
> Now listen here, you six bandits.
> Some time after I arrived here,
> Three Ladakhi merchants' gold, silver, and mules
> Were stolen by seven bandit brothers from Hor.
> I pursued them,
> And though the seven mounted thieves escaped,
> I killed their king with my slingshot

And took his nine-pointed meteoric sword.
I returned to the merchants their wealth—
Their gold, silver, and silk as well as their mules—
Taking only a two-year-old colt as my first bounty.
But a thousand Chinese merchants with their porters
  came
And tried to steal my little colt, plotting to kill me.
They I imprisoned, threatening them with death,
And their tune changed to a lovely melody.
They offered a thousand bricks of tea and silk scarves,
But the only amends I required
Was that they build the palace tea fortresses,
And that was my second bounty.
Today you six bandits
Must have come here for some deviltry.
This slingshot that I hold in my hand,
Watch as I aim toward the cliff in front of you.
It will be split as if by a thunderbolt.
The stone that I next throw
Possesses the strength of the Nyentag drala
And will demolish the bodies of you six men.
Your six horses will be my third bounty.
This pleasing mandala of the divine valley of Ma
Is no place for you bandits to wander.
If you have understood this, it is sweet to your ears.
If not, there is no way to explain.

Having sung, he whirled the slingshot, and great waves of
sparks and flames shot forth. The stone launched, and the rock
face exploded into dust. The booming sound filled the entire
valley, causing several of the mighty warriors to faint.

It was then that Gyatsha took his white silken offering scarf from his inner coat and, waving it over his black-haired head, said, "Joru, have mercy on us. Don't you remember me? I am your brother Gyatsha Zhalkar, and I have come with these five wise men to meet with you."

Without wasting a breath, Gyatsha related to Joru why he had come, explaining in detail that the land of Ling was enduring a winter without end. The cattle had died, the milk of poor mothers had dried up, their infants were starving, and hunger gripped the entire country. Searchers had gone out in the four directions and found that it was only Ma that had somehow been spared this terrible winter.

Gyatsha went on to say that he had been sent with these five seasoned warriors to beseech Joru for his kindness, compassion, and generosity. He explained that he was there to plead that they might rent or purchase some of Joru's land where the citizens of Ling could resettle.

Gyatsha made it clear that he, Joru, was their last chance. The leaders of Ling had swallowed their pride. They would rescind all of their previous accusations and complaints against him. He finished by somewhat sheepishly saying, "We would like to apologize for casting you out."

Joru ran to receive them. Taking Gyatsha's horse by its bridle, he said, "Alas, Gyatsha, my brother, I failed to recognize you. Please do not be angry with me. Come. Let us talk."

He invited Gyatsha and the five warriors into his tent, which looked deceptively small from the outside but once inside was quite spacious. Through magic, the space had transformed. Inside, there were chests of tea, gold, silver, and more, which gave a feeling of prosperous charm and conviviality.

The Ling warriors were overwhelmed, not so much by the richness as by the warmth of the greeting. They feasted and spoke freely and intimately of the situation in Ling, and the

occasion concluded with Joru offering Gyatsha and each warrior a white silk scarf and singing a song of auspicious connection called "Long Haunting Melody that Invokes the Divine."

> The song is Ala Ala Ala.
> Thala leads the melody.
> It is as the ancient proverb says,
> *A starving beggar may dream of finding food,*
> *But when he awakens, his stomach is painfully empty.*
> The chieftains of Ling analyze and cogitate interminably,
> But blind to the pure nature of their own minds,
> Continue to mistake illusion for reality.
> Last year, they identified me as the demonic force;
> This year they accuse the snow.
> What is it with you people?
> In this great lion's belly, the land of Ma,
> The flowers and grasses are in bloom.
> You are welcome to stay in Ma for as long as you like,
> There is no need to pay for the use of the land and its
>   bounty.
> I offer this to the elder and younger brothers of Ling
> And especially to you, Gyatsha.
> It is not mine to possess.
> Entrust carefully in a leader
> Endowed with virtue and wisdom.
> Do not tarry in the barren land of Ling.
> Brothers, bear this in mind.

Gyatsha and the warriors were greatly relieved to hear
Joru's song. For the first time in many months, they smiled and
radiated good cheer. Joru accompanied the warriors as they
returned hastily to Ling to bring their families the good news.
The Ling citizenry gathered straightaway to discuss the possi-

bility of an exodus to the Ma Valley, with Chipon making the final decision that, yes, they would go.

But as with all firm decisions, nagging doubts arose insidiously as the people of Ling began to speculate about how Joru might divvy up the land. Those who felt that they were assuredly Joru's friends were buoyant; those who were not so sure were rather anxious. Most anxious, of course, was Trothung, who now knew Joru to be innocent of most of what he had been accused, while at the same time recognizing that his own voice had perhaps been the loudest in Joru's condemnation.

Although he was both rattled and ashamed, Trothung thought it best to get in a good word early. In his sweetest voice, he said, "Dearest nephew, may all your wishes be fulfilled, and please, may it be in your heart to give me a most excellent portion of land."

Joru replied with a smile, "There is no need to worry, wondrous uncle. Put your mind at ease. It is no problem to give you a piece of land that will truly be unlike any other."

Then in the midst of the assembly, Joru donned his trusty antelope hat and sang a song describing the division of the lands of Ma, called "Quelling the Great Gathering through Splendor."[30]

In this long and eloquent song, Joru divides up his kingdom and gives each of the thirty warriors a parcel singularly chosen for them. To Trothung he deeds a particularly challenging piece of land. Joru also distributes much of the wealth that he had acquired from the traders to the people of Ling that they might prosper in their new homes.

The great relief that had spread throughout the citizenry evaded Trothung, who felt that he had been snubbed, though his portion of land was actually fine and he had very little

30. See Song Appendix, Song #4.

about which to complain. This did not for a moment keep him from complaining. From that day onward, the local land spirits of Ma protected the people of Ling, and prosperity was shared by all.

A few weeks later, Joru announced the opening of the gates to the treasure fortress. The people of the six districts gathered as flowers rained down, and the sky became a dome of rainbow clouds. Joru's accumulated wealth was revealed, including statues of Shakyamuni Buddha, Avalokiteshvara, and Tara, as well as musical instruments, a white conch, magical drum, thundering hand cymbals, and so forth. These gifts were entrusted to the six tribes. Beyond that, offered into their general wealth were Gogmo's naga treasures, including the maroon urn, the blue tent with nine partitions, and the gold-lettered *Twelve Volume Prajnaparamita Sutra*.

At this time, Joru's father, Senglon, and Kyalo Tonpa Gyaltsen were named as the two principal leaders of Ling, while Chipon stepped down to be an elder advisor. This set up a strong connection for the future, when their lineages would together lead Ling toward a joined destiny.

CHAPTER 8

With some prompting, Joru creates a false prophecy,
Which, delivered to the gullible Trothung, spawns the
    idea of a race—
A great horse race for the warriors of Ling
And, as its prize, great wealth, the throne of Ling,
    and Drukmo.

A NUMBER OF YEARS had passed, and Joru had grown in stature and strength, becoming a young man. But despite all that he had done for the people of Ling, soon enough their regard for him had faded, much as a combatant's ardor wanes when the challenge is lost. Left to their own designs and now more confident of forging their own destiny, their memory of the harsh winter had dimmed, and Joru's role in delivering them to this land of fertile valleys, bountiful barley, and thriving livestock had begun to seem less significant. In fact they had started to doubt that he had had any part in it. To make matters worse, Joru's behavior continued to be quite eccentric. Although he had given up the corralling of human bodies and the eating of flesh, he persisted in defying the general ways and customs of the people. When he spoke, no one could fathom his meaning as he talked in riddles that stopped the minds of all who would listen, twisting logic until no end could be found and sending them away staggering and holding their heads.

After a while Joru and his mother had tired of the endless innuendo and the growing contempt displayed by the leaders, warriors, and citizens of Ling, and in a conciliatory act, they had moved to Lower Ma, some distance from the Ma Valley proper. The people of Ling breathed a deep and collective sigh of relief, and in turn, Gogmo and Joru had respite from the churlishness of the Ling populace.

Lower Ma was not as pastoral as the Ma Valley. In fact, it was a frightful land populated by fierce female spirits called *menmos* who danced chilling dances and ate raw animal meat. Joru felt more in his element, as did Gogmo, who, having been borne of naga stock, also tended toward the dicey. In these lands lived the tsen, a class of lower gods who favored gambling and misadventure. They were long-lived beings, without much of a sense of humor outside of a great appreciation of irony and mishap.

It is said that they still roam the earth and that occasionally they can be seen out of the corner of one's eye. As it happened, Joru got along fine with both of these spirit groups and lived contentedly with his mother in Lower Ma. He continued his meditation practice and spent many hours dwelling in luminous equanimity. During the day he joked with humans, mostly the traders, with whom he remained friendly. In the evenings he played dice with the tsen, and at night he challenged the demons to games of chance. The tsen loved foot races, and as a spirited teenager, Joru joined in, racing and gambling on the outcome. Much to the delight of all, he generally won.

All in all, Joru and his mother had settled into quite a comfortable routine, enjoying their life together. Also Gogmo was relieved that Joru had given up the flesh-eating and skin-flaying activities that were so upsetting.

Some months later, a bright spring day dawned with an endless sky so deeply blue and cloudless that one's heart ached from its sheer intensity and brilliance. Joru and Gogmo were sitting outside, drinking their morning tea.

It was into this charming domestic scene that Auntie Nammen Karmo appeared to Joru and, this time, not as a turquoise bee. As usual, Manéné was something to behold. She was in the guise of a beautiful female goddess, with long black tresses flowing down over the curves of her flawless skin and a radiant smile on her lovely face. She was naked except for bone ornaments encircling her arms, waist, and ankles. She was riding a proud white lioness that held its head high and appeared to gaze in all directions. Arrayed in space behind her, each on a lotus throne, were a hundred thousand dakinis equally as beautiful as the glorious Manéné herself. As Joru composed himself, she sang this short song of prophecy and instruction. He hung on her every word.

> The song is Ala Ala Ala.
> Thala leads the melody.
> Listen to your sweet auntie's song.
> *In this vast plain of patterned fields,*
> *Blue-green stalks of grain have shot up.*
> *But unless they yield a good harvest,*
> *The shoots are nothing but forage,*
> *Their growth expended without fruition.*
> Joru, you have been born in the land of Ling.
> It makes little difference that once you bested your fool
>   Uncle Trothung,
> Your life will still have been for naught.
> Unless you take your place as a chief of Ling,
> Your name is just another word for dishonor and
>   disgrace.
> Your great steed roams the northern wilderness.
> It too is twelve years old.
> If you do not take possession of it this year,
> The horse will forfeit its life to your sloth and stupidity.

Your wife, ordained by the grand prophecy,
Is to be Kyalo's daughter, Drukmo.
Unless she becomes your bride this year,
Her life too will be wasted and her powers squandered.
This is what you must do:
Tomorrow in the predawn light,
Bring to Chieftain Trothung
A false prophecy from Hayagriva
That says to him that he must host a festive warrior
    gathering
At which he will announce that the rider of the fastest
    steed
Will become the leader of Ling and win Drukmo as his
    wife
And moreover will be heir to the treasure of Drukmo's
    father, Kyalo.
Trothung knows that his son's horse, Turquoise Bird,
    is the fastest,
And in his pride, he will see himself the master of
    the bride, Drukmo.
You must capture your steed with the lasso of great
    emptiness
And work diligently in order to merit the fairest
    of maidens.
If you understand your grand aunt's words, fine.
If not, there is no way to explain.

Thus she sang, and the wisdom of her words pierced Joru's complacency as an arrow through soft flesh. He thought, *Auntie is right. Since I was born, I have never really shown my true form. Other than at the moment of my birth, I have been concealed, like a lotus still encased in mud, by this unsightly little body and strange clothing. For years I have been wallowing in my own filth and have accomplished nothing of value. Probably the time has come for me to prove myself worthy. I must succeed in all that Auntie commands of me.*

At just this time, Trothung was in solitary retreat, at that very moment meditating on his visualization of his *yidam*,[31] Red Hayagriva. Hayagriva is a wrathful form of Avalokiteshvara, the bodhisattva of compassion. He is pictured in a fierce pose, with three eyes and the head of a horse, snakes in one hand and a scepter in the other, and adorned with a tiger skin around his waist and bone ornaments around his neck, arms, and ankles.

It was this image upon which Trothung was concentrating his mind. He had completed a full day of contemplation when, at the stroke of midnight, Joru, disguised as a raven, flew into Trothung's meditation cave. After circling thrice around Trothung's shrine, the raven perched gently on Trothung's right shoulder and intoned the false prophecy into his ear. From his state of alternating dreaming, meditation, and wakefulness, this is what Trothung heard.

> The song is Ala Ala Ala.
> Thala leads the melody.
> I am Red Hayagriva and have this to offer
> To you, one who pursues my blessings,
> You, Trothung of Tag-rong.
> The time has come for Ling to find a true leader,
> And to this end, you must proclaim
> That your family will host a great festival.
> Gather all the kinsmen of Ling
> To undertake a magnificent horse race.

31. Yidam practice is a form of individual visualization practice wherein the yogi or yogini visualizes himself or herself as the yidam and connects with its particular aspect of enlightened activity. The visualization could be that of a buddha, a bodhisattva, a protector, a guru, or an historical figure.

Three great prizes awarded to the winner—
The Kyalo daughter, Drukmo,
The Kyalo wealth treasury,
And the throne of colorful Ling.
All three will go to the rider of the fastest steed,
And that will be none other than you, Trothung.
Among the great horses of Ling,
The fastest steed will be victorious
And Turquoise Bird will be that steed.
If you understood these words, hold them in mind.
If not, this prediction and command will remain
    an enigma.

The raven sang into Trothung's right ear, repeating the song over and over, and not long after, Trothung began mindlessly nodding his head in dulled agreement. He had never before had such a clear communication from Hayagriva despite how intently he had meditated, recited mantra, supplicated, or made offerings.

Yet he was rather skeptical until his gaze shifted to the loquacious raven. He watched in wonder as the raven dissolved right into the heart of the Hayagriva statue that was the focal point of his rather elaborate shrine. And so it was that, with this final flourish from the raven, Trothung rather impulsively fell for the prophecy. He bolted up and went to his wife, Denza, who was with him in retreat, roughly shaking her awake, already relating in an excited and grandiloquent manner what he had just experienced.

Denza sat up and bent her head into her palms, with her still long and luxurious silken black hair falling over her face. She had been married to Trothung for many years and had borne him three sons. Despite the difficulties of being Trothung's

wife and the hardships of the Tibetan climate, she had a youthful verve and playfulness.

While not particularly happy about being awoken, Denza
was a thoughtful, considerate person, and she mulled over what
she had heard before she spoke. She knew Trothung very well,
sometimes too well from his point of view. She well knew his
lust for another, younger wife, as he was often blinded by a bit
of smooth skin or a lively manner. But she was also cognizant
that, according to the oft-repeated prophecy, it was Joru who
was ordained by the gods to be the bridegroom of Drukmo
and the master of Kyalo's wealth, as well as the destined king of
Ling. Essentially she thought Trothung a fool living in a fog of
pride, seduced by Drukmo's beauty, and covetous of both Kyalo's wealth and the throne of Ling. Having weighed the risks
and benefits of speaking the truth, she sang.

I am the daughter of the king of Den
And your wife, Trothung.
I may not know one foolish prophecy from another,
But I suspect I can ferret out the truth.
Here in the Ancient Black Fortress
That hoarse cawing of the midnight raven
Seems to be either a magical illusion crafted by the maras
Or a neurotic delusion formed in your fool brain.
What it is not is a true prophetic vision.
You are a tired, old, clouded meditator
Lacking insight and compassion.
To one such as you, no true vision *could* appear.
This seems not to be the truth,
But a false prophecy set up by Joru.
When the Chieftain Trothung's
Butt is burning with desire,

He cannot wait for the darkness of nightfall to enter
   his bed.
When he is led around by his genitals,
He cannot even wait for sunrise to get up.
Don't be this way tonight; just rest.
And when the sun rises early tomorrow morning,
We can discuss matters and decide what must be done.
What we should do is fetch our three sons
To lead a discussion with the ministers of Ling
To contemplate and consider your vision.
If the minds of these men and your so-called prophecy
   concur,
We will go forward to plan for the horse race.
Since you were the recipient of this prophecy
And believe it true [though so many others were false],
You had best be certain to understand it with painstaking
   accuracy.
Think hard on what karma may ensue.

Denza sat, motionless. Although her words rang with the
clear, cold steel of truth, Trothung was blinded by his desire
for Drukmo and deaf to what Denza had said. He could think
of nothing but Drukmo's countenance, which so beguiled him
that his eyes saw only her face and his thoughts went only to
her body.

Not only that, Hayagriva's prophecy seemed to promise him
great power and wealth. Additionally local spirits conjured by
Joru had brought down wave after wave of desire for Drukmo
in the minds of not only Trothung but all the other men of Ling.

The more he thought about it, the more certain Trothung
became that his son Dongtsen's horse, Turquoise Bird, would
win the race. Painting his future with the thick brush of arrogant fancy, he imagined that, once Drukmo was brought into

their home, Dongtsen would relinquish her to him, making it uncomfortable to stay with Denza. Thus he decided to break ties with his wife without delay by blaming her for trying to ruin his connection with the prophecy.

Besides, he thought, *if I cast Denza out only after Drukmo has already arrived in my home and my bed, people will accuse me of having no conscience and Drukmo of being a careless and thoughtless girl. An enormous scandal would ensue. Better to rid myself of Denza now.*

Imperiously, Trothung spoke to Denza. "You meddlesome woman, you have attempted to destroy this golden prophecy with your evil words. You have tossed your own false omens, like ashes, into the face of my connection with this sacred prophecy. I care for you no longer."

Denza was not surprised by her husband's words and thought, *A proverb tells us, Just as karma from past lifetimes cannot be sidestepped, wrinkles on one's forehead cannot be erased. Likewise, I cannot separate from my karma with Trothung. Day or night, I have always spoken to him with an open heart, yet not only does he not listen, he becomes angry. I should know better by now that it is useless to try to explain myself.* She resigned herself to begin making preparations for the festival.

In the morning, Trothung's messenger rushed to sound the great army gong that calls all of Ling to council. And two weeks later, when the sun rose over the azure eastern skies and illuminated the highest mountains in its golden hues, the Thirty Mighty Warriors, the Seven Super Warriors, and the Three Ultimate Warriors—Falcon, Eagle, and Wolf—all came together.

They came with drala flags and pennants fluttering on their helmets, longevity knots billowing behind their bejeweled cloaks, and their swift-gaited horses dazzling in formation. Once they had all arrived, the messenger began to relate the details of the planned festival in Tag-rong and recounted exactly how Trothung had received the prophecy. He sang this song in the melody of "Gently Flowing River."

> I am the personal minister of Chieftain Trothung
> Sent here on an important mission
> That will determine the future prosperity of Ling.
> A fortnight ago in the predawn hour,
> Trothung received this prophecy from Hayagriva:
> In the field of wealth of Kyalo
> Grows the sprout of well-born Drukmo,
> And now her youth has reached full maturity.
> If one of our kinsman does not claim and cherish her,
> She will be seduced by the majesty of a foreign throne.
> But a seat on our golden throne, along with Drukmo
> And Kyalo's precious wealth,
> Will be awarded to the rider of the fastest steed,
> The one with the destiny to be our king.
> In this way, Tibet will see its fruition in this world
>   realm.
> This is the vision seen by our Chieftain Trothung.
> Let us gather to celebrate and discuss the details,
> And then on the fifteenth day, the steeds will line up,
> And the kingship, the wealth, and Drukmo's hand
> Shall await he who wins.
> Therefore, you warriors should agree that,
> No matter who is victorious,
> You will abide the decision without regret
> And align with the glorious prophecy.
> If you can hear this song, it is an ornament to your
>   mind.
> If not, there is no way to explain.

Thus he sang, and although Gyatsha, Darphen, Sengtak, and most of the warriors saw no problem with the wager itself, they also knew that Trothung's son, Dongtsen, owned the kingdom's fastest horse, Turquoise Bird. They could not avoid thinking that Trothung's plan was self-serving, but they held their tongues, waiting to hear what their elder, Uncle Chipon, would say.

Chipon contemplated all that he had been told. He knew Joru truly to be the predicted winner but also that Joru's wild, magical horse was far away and had yet to be captured. Thus he thought it would be better if the race could be delayed several months. Chipon's brown wrinkles and sparkly eyes hinted of a keen mind that was wise enough to know that even prophecies of the gods often need just a bit of human coaxing.

Chipon smiled as he said, "All that you have said sounds true. Drukmo is renowned, Kyalo is rich, and Ling must have a single chieftain to be unified against its many enemies. I see no problem with wagering these great prizes on the horse race, but if the race is held now, the mountain passes will be slick with ice and the plains inundated with dust storms. It would be safe neither for rider nor our beloved horses. We should put the race off until early spring. I suggest that, on the day of the next full moon, five days from now, we gather all the people for a festival and then work out the details for the contest."

Feeling that this was a sensible and straightforward plan, the warriors nodded in agreement and promised to return on the appointed day.

The messenger went back to Trothung and relayed the outcome of the meeting and Chipon's suggestion. Trothung was overjoyed and felt that the warriors' agreement had confirmed his prophecy, driving out any lingering doubt. Now he believed in the raven all the more and was thrilled with the plans. At the same time, each warrior of Ling, from the ancients to the adolescent boys, yearned to win the lovely Drukmo. The local spirits commanded by Joru had intoxicated their minds until every male ached for her, and since only King Chipon and Denma knew that Joru would win the race, each warrior believed that the throne was well within his reach.

While Joru's brother, Gyatsha Zhalkar, did not doubt Joru's power, nonetheless, he worried that Joru could lose. Gyatsha had known Joru since his birth and had witnessed some of his unconventionality. Moreover, he was not sure that Joru even wanted to win the race, and he was rather anxious about the whole plan.

Then as the full moon day arrived in that twelfth and darkest month, all of Ling arrived for the festival. With great dignity, the elder fathers, uncles, and gurus gathered with flowing cloaks, long, gray beards, and many a tale of previous daring exploits. Led by their elders, the women of Ling came, elegant in their mutual respect and self-confidence.

Like full muscled tigers and freshly blossoming flowers, the young warriors and youthful maidens assembled in a state of joy and wonderment. Then the great mediator Werma Lhadar sang a song to arrange the seating. The song went on as the warriors and leaders of the land assembled according to rank and ended with this refrain.

> In our great tent on the highest seats of all,
> Each man, please sing of your pleasure,
> And each fair maiden, step out a lovely dance.
> Kinsman, cheerfully meet and discuss your plans.
> Today, on the occasion of this festival,
> May the blue sky show that there are no spirits aligned
>   against us,
> May the dense earth show no enviousness among us,
> May all disaster be gone from greater Tibet.

The feasting began, and there were meats, cheeses, and other fare to eat. Tea, liquor, and other beverages flowed like a springtime's gushing river. The adults sang with good cheer, and the fair maidens and young men danced and exchanged coy glances with each other. As the celebration peaked, Trothung raised his voice in song.

> On the face of the mirror of my luminous empty mind
> Blazed the splendor of supreme direct knowledge.
> Like a garland of thunderbolts, the prophecy arose,
> Unbidden, with a meaning spontaneously clear.
> Concerning Drukmo,
> The prophecy warns that she soon may be lost to us,
> Lest we not wager her as a prize for the horse race.
> Not only her, but the golden throne itself,
> The seat of the one to be the sovereign king
> Must be laid on the wager,
> All to avert further turmoil in Tibet.
> Whoever wins, whoever loses, there will be no regret.
> I will make the arrangements,
> But all the fathers and uncles must meet and concur
> As to the distance and route of the horse race
> And the date on which it will take place.
> Warriors, keep this in your minds.

Though Trothung was not well loved by many of them, on that day, the mighty warriors began the discussions in good spirit.

The clan leader, the imperial King Chipon, rose and said, "I have decided that the race should go on. However, we must make certain that all who belong to the lineage of Mukpo Dong, irrespective of their station in life, have been told about the race and the prizes. Then no citizen can afterwards claim ignorance and political deception, and we can avoid any disputes. Furthermore, if we do not postpone the horse race for another five or six months, then, as is well known, *A foolish girl churning frozen milk in winter will not get butter, but only freeze her hands. A foolish boy racing his horse on winter's frozen soil will lose his mount, an embarrassed ass on hard ground.* We will postpone the race until spring and now let the council make the best decision about the route."

On cue, Gyatsha Zhalkar proclaimed, "So be it, this horse race shall now go forward, but let us not forget that my younger brother, Gogmo's son Joru, is of the lineage of Mukpo Dong. As the proverb says, *It may be only a small piece of flesh, but it is a shank of a very tender lamb.* Although Joru is small, he is Trothung's nephew, and his horse, equally small, is of noble lineage. Both mother and son were exiled, although it appears now that they were innocent. Unless he is called to the starting line of the horse race, then my clan will not compete in the race. Nor will we vie for the valuable prize. Although I do not expect that Joru could win, if we do not invite him, the race will be tainted beyond redemption."

Then Gyatsha shook his great frame, flexed his biceps, and, grimacing outwardly but smiling inwardly, took his seat. Trothung, with a dark mood brewing, thought, *That Joru, with his contemptible mother Gogza, is like the proverbs. Ignoble, having never seen what is higher, bringing ruin to the ranks, having never seen nobility. Dung does not become gold, although cats think their litter precious. Joru is of no use to this land of Ling, but my fool brother Chipon has brought him up, and Gyatsha followed his lead in saying that he must join in the race. To my mind, Joru is naïve enough that, were he to win, he would give the prize away, not knowing its value. And should he decide to rule, he would make such a muddle of it that he would soon be overthrown.*

Trothung's mind quieted enough for him to feign agreement

and say, "Gyatsha, you are right. I cannot help but regret that Joru, a worthy son of Senglon and the divine child of Gogmo, has yet to join in the contest. Indeed he should be invited, but first let us turn our minds to determining the length of the race, its course, and when it will take place."

Trothung's son, Dongtsen Apel, proud of his swift horse, Turquoise Bird, joined in and suggested a race of thousands of miles, starting in China and ending in India. Everyone knew that he had said this because of the legendary speed and endurance of his horse.

Sengtak, one of the great warriors, realizing that Dongtsen's words were being poorly received, thought, *If there is going to be a discussion, there is no point in bringing up things we cannot agree upon. There must be a way to work this out.*

After an uncomfortable silence, he blurted out, "If there is to be a horse race that will be renowned throughout the world, take the azure firmament as the finish line and look to the dense earth for the start."

Then the brawny but wise and reasonable Gyatsha said, "Let us make the finish line Crag Mountain of Gu-ra and the starting line the Downs of Ayu. We will prepare a great smoke offering, and the spectacle can be easily viewed from the grand hill of Naga Downs."

As this proposal seemed fair, a consensus was reached. With joy and gratitude, the warriors once again returned to their homes.

However, there were two men who were still anxious about the result. Gyatsha was thinking, *Dongtsen winning would be disastrous for all of Ling. Underneath his steadfast exterior, he is a hothead and completely devoted to his evil father, Trothung.*

And Trothung, fearing that something unpredictable and uncontrollable could happen if Joru were in the race, was mulling over what could be done to keep him from participating.

And as Ling was plagued by the same inequity that seems universal to human society, a group of impoverished men worried that shame would be brought down upon their clans because they lacked the wherewithal to equip themselves for such a race.

CHAPTER 9

Wherein Joru's invitation comes from Drukmo's hand,
Their meeting, long in coming and long foretold, is won-
  drous indeed.
Obstacles are cleared, and connections are forged.
A magical steed is captured, and equine lore elucidated.

K ING CHIPON had a problem and was alone at the edge
of the great encampment, worrying. The wind was
rustling, and the air was cool. The sky was clear, but
his mind was unsettled. He looked at the throng of warriors
and pondered the predicament. He knew that, according to the
prophecy, Drukmo must be the one to invite Joru to the horse
race, but he was uncertain of how to ensure this. He knew that,
in all things strategic, good timing was essential. He strode
over to speak to Gyatsha and Denma.

He told them, "Of course it would be fine for me or anyone else to invite Joru, but there is karma to consider. It was
Drukmo who wronged Joru in her accounting of the deaths of
the seven hunters, and to some degree she is responsible for his
banishment. In order to resolve and heal this rift, she should be
the one to invite him. She is young and inexperienced, and she
may be reluctant or even afraid to go, given his wildness and
his reputation, but you must convince her to do so."

Gyatsha and Denma first approached Drukmo's father,
Kyalo. He was by far the wealthiest man in all of Tibet, and his
encampment reflected that as sharply as the moon is reflected
in a clear, calm lake. There was a great central fortress-tent, and

149

many wooden outbuildings surrounded on their four sides by masses of smaller but still impressive tents.

It was within this veritable city of tents that most of the inhabitants lived. Each tent was draped with elegant woolen tapestries spun from the fur of yaks. These were decorative but also utilitarian as they served to keep the tents warm against the cold of the Tibetan winter. Tradesmen and craftsmen as well as warriors milled around the fortress. There was a grand temple in the largest tent with an assembly hall richly appointed with thangkas and statues. Butter lamps burned continually, and offerings were made in abundance. It was a grand sight, an inspiration for all who lived there and for those who visited.

After discussing the matter briefly with Kyalo, they sought out Drukmo and learned that it was just as Chipon had thought: Drukmo was reluctant to make the trip and especially fearful of traveling alone and unprotected. But Gyatsha launched into the reasons that this task was falling to her, in particular recounting her testimony, which had ultimately proven to be false.

He made a strong case that it was her patriotic as well as her filial duty to be the one to invite Joru and thereby resolve the karmic debt that she had incurred. Going on in the melodious tones favored by great warriors and impressive orators, he was able to convince her, and she finally agreed to seek out Joru and formally invite him to the horse race. Denma and Gyatsha, who were used to parlaying with fellow warriors rather than maidens, were both slightly surprised and quite relieved by her quick assent. They mounted their horses before she could change her mind and cheerfully galloped off to report this good news to Chipon.

Drukmo was apprehensive in the face of this task and wondered how fate had brought her to this point. Indeed she was a privileged soul, daughter of the wealthy chieftain Kyalo.

Throughout her charmed life, she had been able to avoid misfortune as money avoids an unlucky gambler. She was purported to be a living representation of White Tara, whose beauty and compassion, keen mind, and clear insight she embodied.

She was a trustworthy friend on whom anyone could rely with confidence. She was both enthusiastic in her passions and exceptional in her morality. She stood with the bearing of limber bamboo, and her shiny black hair swayed like delicate branches. Her face shone in the conch-white of the rising moon, her cheeks glowed a rosy-red, and her dark almond eyes were as fathomless as a mountain lake. Her lips had the beautiful lines of a lotus, and upon her tongue rested the white syllable AH representing unfettered pristine awareness:

She was well spoken, and her songlike voice rested comfortably on the ear. She was said to be skilled in the arts of love, and from every angle she was faultless. Her hair was perfectly parted in the middle with the right and left plaits resembling the spread wings of a garuda, the magnificent mythic bird of Tibet. The hair falling down her back was tied so it would not fly in the wind. It was studded with precious amber and other stones. So that the fine hair at her temples would not flutter, it was held down by thin loops of turquoise and coral.

She wore a long colorful necklace of dzi beads interspersed with red coral, and as she contemplated her coming journey, she held blue turquoise prayer beads and a ruby amulet. She had a sapphire bracelet and a golden ring shining like the rising sun. Her chuba was lined with a beaver pelt and spotted with nine layers of pigment arrayed in the traditional astrological trigrams, and her silken boots were banded with the colors of the rainbow. Her clothes were of silk brocade encrusted with jeweled ornaments. Even the sun and moon would lose their luster in comparison with her. Even a divine, celibate rishi would feel desire for her. Even the radiance of the dazzling lotus would be stolen away by her, and even an enemy as murderous as Yama the Lord of Death would do whatever she asked. In a word, she was wondrous beyond imagination, and no one who met her was ever quite the same.

So this precious being, Drukmo, sighed, packed provisions, tacked her horse, mounted, and set out for Lower Ma.

Joru knew that she would be coming, and soon he could sense that she was on her way. He knew this to be confirmation of the grand fate and prophecy that his Aunt Manéné had brought to him in his dream. He felt that things were falling into place, and with the optimism of youth, his aspiration to bring benefit to others was rekindled. When he told his mother that he was leaving to meet Drukmo, Gogmo said that she very much looked forward to their return as she was tiring of hearing only the shrieking of the pikas and the cawing of the crows.

After four hours of traversing difficult terrain, Drukmo had come to a neighboring valley, a dreary and deserted place in the foothills. Looking anxiously in all directions, she saw only a massive, empty plain surrounded by great mountains, with no landmarks in sight. Since she was traveling alone and wearing precious jewels, she became even more fearful. Joru had intentionally disguised himself and now appeared in front of her as an imposing and formidable warrior. He was dressed in traditional armor and sat atop a great black horse with a braided mane studded with silver clasps. He had a deep scar running from his right ear to the edge of his long Manchu-style mustache, and he was thick necked and broad shouldered. Those who could see deeply would spy a bit of a twinkle in his dark, piercing eyes and a grin behind his facial hair. Brandishing a black-bannered spear, he sang this song to Drukmo.

The song is Ala Ala Ala.
Thala leads the melody.
I am known as Nyima Gyaltsen of Weri,
A man who delights in the raw flesh of his enemy
And washes it down with the brute's heart blood,
Taking his possessions without a qualm.
Never letting anyone get the better of me,
I know no pity for the weak and powerless.
Now then, you flashy, fleshy young girl,
I have a few questions for you.
A person carrying valuables on their back
Must have some plan in mind.
For if not, why carry all that baggage?
I watch merchants from Ladakh and Tibet
With mules laden with boxes of gold,
Aiming to buy silk from the Chinese looms
And bring it back to central Tibet.
Their desire for wealth is clear to anyone burdened
    with eyes.
Nothing could be more obvious.
Merchants from China have yaks loaded with boxes
    of tea.
Their aim is to trade for white silver
And bring the precious metal back to China.
This too is clear as our azure sky.
So now we get to you,
A lovely girl whose gold is her body and beauty.
Perhaps her aim is to attract a rich man.
But to rely on what your mind desires is a fool's errand.
The proof of this is that your wealth will be mine.
Perhaps you have come looking for a good match,
But it seems you will only find yourself naked.
Let us see if this is true, flashy young girl.

Your jeweled ornaments gleam like those of the nagas
    below,
And your body shines as though you are a daughter
    of the gods,
But having no refuge or protector, misfortune is your
    fate today.
Now I will tell it like it is:
Your bracelet of pure gold,
Your dzi stone ornament,
Your earrings of excellent white turquoise—
These three jewels alone, worth the fortune of a lifetime,
Are displayed here on your lovely body.
Tell me honestly how these came to be yours.
Tell me of your parents and what you truly seek.
Be candid in your reply.
It is said that all meeting is the result of previous karma
And that karmic debts follow a body like its shadow.
The best choice is for you and I to be together for a
    lifetime,
You leading the life of a robber's wife.
If not that, then perhaps we have sex this once
And me taking only your horse and jewels.
If not even that, you return to your homeland with noth-
    ing at all
While this robber absconds with all your riches.
Think about it; what is your fancy?

It was with a grand swagger that the disguised Joru spoke
these words, and Drukmo, frightened but still with her wits
about her, replied,

I am more than a bit disheartened,
But listen now to my story,

Bearing in mind
That to strike a tiny flea with an ax,
To shoot a poison arrow at a honeybee,
Or to be a warrior who overcomes a defenseless girl
Will mark you as an unworthy lout.
No courage in that, my good warrior.
The worst choice is for me to be your wife.
Beyond that, sex between us will never happen.
I have no warmth toward you,
And you will be just an outlaw who violated me.
People will deride you, and both of us will suffer.
As for the jeweled ornaments fastened on my head,
The garland of dzi stones adorning my neck,
And the gold jewelry on my body,
These treasures you can take.
But the small turquoise knob adorning my hairline,
The clothing that protects my modesty,
And my chestnut mare, my ride back to Ling,
Leave these to me as my rightful portion.
How has this trouble arisen?
Trothung instigated this foolish calamity,
And then Gyatsha cajoled, prevailing upon me to make
    this journey.
Lastly, I owe a karmic debt to one known as Joru.
All this has conspired against me,
And now my fate is in your hands.

Thus she sang, and she stood there bravely, expecting the worst, but surprisingly the warrior responded, "What you say has the ring of truth, and I am not such a bad fellow. I won't rob or ravish you. In return, you must come back in one week's time, ready to hand over the riches you have promised. As a token of your good word and to seal our agreement, leave me your gold ring as a keepsake. And who is this Joru fellow? Is he a yak, a pika, or some nasty wild beast? Tell me about him."

Relieved at the robber's sudden turn, Drukmo laughingly replied, "He is a human—not a wild animal. Though some think him rather beastly. The people of Ling have called him a pika-killing, sniveling, demon-necked, notch-nosed laughingstock, not to be taken seriously, yet there are many tales of the depth of his meditation as well as of his skills in magic. In any case, he certainly is a strange one. He delights in stirring up mischief among humans, gods, and demons, and nothing cheers him as much watching the wealthy have a taste of hunger and the poor make good. He is happier in the body of a beggar than in the robes of a chieftain. He has turned his back on the affairs of his own state and lives among the pikas, squabbling with them over land and water. Other than wild Himalayan yams, it seems he needs no food. In actual fact, however, he is of the royal lineage of Mukpo, the rightful son of Senglon and the half-brother of the great warrior Gyatsha. But you would never know it as he dresses like a vagrant who wanders the ends of the dusty earth, followed only by an animal stench. Alas, I am on my way now to summon him."

Suddenly thinking that she might have been too long-winded in her answer, Drukmo made a quick promise to the robber to meet up again in seven days' time, and then she pressed her vajra-ornamented gold ring into his hand, watching it appear to shrink in size as it dropped into the hollow of his large and calloused palm. Much relieved at her seemingly good luck, Drukmo mounted her horse and headed on her way to look for Joru.

She came to a beautiful trio of snow-covered peaks that were the gateway to the Lower Ma Valley. Beyond the mountain pass of the Seven Dunes, which ran between the peaks, there was Joru who now appeared as a charming young man, relaxing and chatting with a group of seven well-armed, young horsemen.

Drukmo cautiously approached them and was first taken in by Joru's appearance. His complexion was as creamy as a conch shell, but his cheeks had weathered to a coppery bronze. He was not tall, but his lean shoulders were squared, and he stood with a bearing that suggested humility and kindness. He radiated an inner peacefulness, and she felt herself irresistibly drawn to him. Though she had never been more awake, her mind was blank, and she stood motionless as Joru sang this song to her.

> Young woman, as you might have suspected,
> I am not from around here.
> I have come from the golden land of India
> And am the Indian minister Berkar.
> Lovely and honorable maiden,
> Are you traveling from Ling?
> I have a few questions for you.
> Within that country of colorful Ling,
> Who is the sovereign chieftain?
> The legendary woman Drukmo,
> Does she live there?
> And if I were to beg her hand,
> Would I have a chance to be hers?
> Is she as lovely as they say?
> Don't hide anything; speak frankly
> As my heart stirs within my chest.
> An exceptional maiden turns back from the sublime,
> Reflecting the transcendent into the earthly world.
> Her mind and thoughts are like a crystal vase.
> Her speech so sincere and her beauty so deep
> That men's lives are forfeit to her clarity.

If you are such a maiden, you will find truth in these
   words.
This minister has come here
And traveled this twisting road
Like a wind through unfamiliar lands.
From disparate ends of this world, our fate has brought
   us together.
There are more maidens than grass on the mountains,
But an eligible and worthy partner is seldom found.
If you are searching for yellow gold,
Only in the mountains will you find it.
Though long have I wandered these lands,
Until now my search has been without reward.
If you have understood these words, they are sweet to
   your ears.
If not, there is no way to explain.

He sang most beautifully, and Drukmo was overcome with
desire. Though she feigned indifference, it was as the proverbs
spell out, *Although her words maintain that she feels no affection, her
smile betrays her lust. Although her heart wants to deny her desire,
sweet words escape her mouth. Although she tries to conceal her modesty, her inner feelings are transparent. Although her outer body of
flesh is clothed, her inner mind is nakedly revealed.*

Drukmo was nothing if not genuine and honest by nature,
and she dropped all pretense, prefacing her song with, "Though
you do not seem to recognize me, I am the one called Drukmo."

To the east, in the colorful land of Ling,
A great horse race has been set
With the golden throne as the victor's prize,
And myself, Drukmo of Kyalo,
To be given in marriage to the rider of the fastest horse.

Suppose you were thinking to purchase me,
You could not find enough gold dust to bear my price.
I did not expect to meet a minister from a distant land,
But here, on my way to bid Joru to the race,
You appeared, as though to escort me.
It seems to be a fateful bit of karma,
This happy union of rainbow colors.
You, Berkar, a minister from India,
And I, Drukmo of Kyalo,
Whether we connect depends on previous karma.
If you understand this, it is sweet to your ears.
If not, there is no way to explain it.
Keep this in your heart.

But from the start to the finish of her song, Drukmo had been struck by the single idea that, in her naïve honesty, she was acting the fool. She realized now that she was actually speaking to Joru and not to some handsome Indian minister, and she felt wobbly and on the verge of fainting.

Joru feigned misgivings of his own and said, "It is hard to trust the words of someone you have just met. Are you really Drukmo?"

"I am indeed," she swore. And her mind raced as she thought, *Joru is clearly a master of illusion and great meditator. Perhaps I should be making some sort of offering.*

But Joru and Drukmo's hearts opened to each other, and their young bodies entwined. It is said that their ecstatic bliss resounded throughout the heavens, and the inner emptiness of the phenomenal world and the luminosity of space merged in their union. They pledged their vows to one another, swearing an oath.

To seal their decision, Drukmo gave the so-called minister from India a lovely white offering scarf with nine knots, and in turn, he gave Drukmo a crystal bracelet. Scarcely able to part, they planned to be reunited and then went their separate ways. Never once did Joru admit to being Joru, and after they parted, it seemed so dreamlike to Drukmo that she began to doubt what had just occurred.

She was continuing on over the mountain pass alone, unsure if she should still be searching for Joru or turning around to go home. She scanned the landscape for clues, and wherever she saw a pika hole, she saw a Joru. Frightened by this magical display, she dared go no farther, and she stopped her horse short and watched.

After a while, Joru dissolved his many emanations into one, and that single Joru killed a large pika and then just sat and waited. Drukmo stood up in her stirrups and called out to him. Joru turned to her and, mistaking her for a demoness, pulled out his slingshot, and he loaded it with the pika's innards and sang.

> Hail to you, horsewoman—
> Disguising a devious demoness!
> Your gratuitous splendor
> Threatens this skilled exorcist.
> But when I target a demon,
> That demon will be led to bliss.
> This colorful, short slingshot has great precision,
> And this waste and intestines are the earth's power
>   substance.
> If you are a demon, your spirit will be liberated.
> If you are a human, you will be released from all
>   obstacles.
> If you understand this, it is sweet to your ears.
> If not, it cannot be explained.

Thus he sang and, whipping the slingshot three times around his head, loosed its contents, spraying Drukmo's hair and teeth with the pika's entrails. Instantly she became as hairless as a copper ladle and as wrinkled and toothless as an old crone. Realizing what he had done, Joru sought out his mother and poured out his story.

"Today Drukmo came, just as I had hoped, but somehow I just saw her as a demoness among a mass of demons, and I tried my best to tame them all. And only after it was all over did I realize that it was Drukmo who had been struck straight on, and now she is a fright to behold."

Gogmo ran immediately to Drukmo's side and reassured her that they would find a way for Joru to undo what he had done. Less heartening was her comment that "Joru is very powerful, but sometimes his magic goes awry."

She led the still shaking and rather mistrustful Drukmo back up to the tent, where a troubled Joru paced. He didn't hesitate to say, "I see now that you are Drukmo. I mistook you for a wicked demoness, and it was in my desire to liberate her that I cast this spell. Please allow me to make it right."

Then Drukmo sang[32] of her suffering and began the invitation to Joru that had brought her there in the first place. Her song ended with a pleading refrain,

> Well then, good sir Joru,
> When you came to the land of humans,
> It fell to me, Drukmo, to unite with you.
> You are a lord of magical illusion.
> You must transform me into a vessel of splendor,
> Ageless, youthfully radiant,

---

32. See Song Appendix, Song #5 for the beginning of Drukmo's lament.

Free from illness, and gloriously endowed with
  well-being.
Among the eighteen kingdoms,
The eighteen fair maidens are equally sublime.
Yet may I be transcendent,
And together may we accomplish all that is good.
If you understand my song, it is an ornament to your
  ears.
If you do not, there is no way to explain.

Joru, still feeling contrite, spoke quietly. "There is just one thing that I must mention, one request I must make of you before the spell is reversed and your transformation complete. There is an errand that you must embark on very soon. There lives one wondrous horse in the midst of the great roaming herds of wild kyang.[33] It is karmically destined to be mine, just as it has been throughout the succession of my previous lives.

"Truly, it is neither a horse nor a kyang. Rather it is the all-knowing steed that not only understands and speaks human language, but is clairvoyant. The sacred prophecy avows that only you, Drukmo, and my mother, Gogmo, are capable both of recognizing and capturing this magnificent creature. Once you are in sight of it, if it seems that you might be unable to catch it or that once you do that it will be lost, then and only then, at that desperate time, you may call out with intense yearning to my drala siblings.[34] They will come with their magical lasso.

"If you do catch him but lose him, that would be Gogmo's fault, and if you cannot recognize the horse, it is your own fault, Drukmo. And if you fail to coax and place a harness on his broad neck, then the blame falls to you both. Finally, if your

33. Kyang are the largest of the wild asses common to the Tibetan Plateau.
34. The drala siblings are the beings who were co-born with Joru.

CHAPTER 9 | 163

call to the drala siblings goes unheeded, then they are to blame. Promise that you will catch the steed, and with that promise, you will become so splendid that the sun will turn away with envy."

With no small measure of trepidation, Drukmo swallowed hard and pledged to try.

Joru closed his eyes and stood, his body motionless as a mountain, his mind still as a great lake without wave or wind. His breathing slowed and then stopped. Drukmo and Gogmo sat transfixed as Joru, in a very low hum, began to chant in a voice as though from some other land.

> Deities from above and below, meet with the earth
> spirits.
> Gather the splendor, beauty, and blessings
> Of the goddesses of the three times and manifold
> worlds
> And confer them here upon Drukmo.
> Likewise may her speech and mind be blessed
> By nagas and nyen alike.
> The carriage and kindly presence of sacred Tara—
> Confer upon Sengcham Drukmo's body.
> The sweet sound of the celestial musician's lute—
> Confer this upon Sengcham Drukmo's speech.
> Concentrating the wisdom of the three worlds—
> Confer all this upon Sengcham Drukmo's mind.
> May she be the ornament of all the maidens of the
> world.
> May this song come true.

Joru opened his eyes and gazed deeply into Drukmo's eyes as he touched her wrist lightly with the fourth finger of his right hand. At that moment, there was a sudden shake to the land, flowers rained down, and a sweet smell pervaded the air. Time slowed, and the trio was momentarily suspended in its slackening, but when the moments resurged, Drukmo's beauty was resplendent and her equanimity unbounded.

Despite this turn of events, Drukmo was reluctant to enter Joru's tent when she saw that it was filthy. However, Joru gazed into the sky, summoning down lightning, thunder, hail— a furious storm. And hence Drukmo had no choice but to enter. He served her a meal of pika flesh and sweet potatoes. The food had been infused with the hundred flavors of the gods, and soon Drukmo realized that she had not eaten in some days. She was ravenous and ate and drank, and she generally over-indulged until she had made herself quite ill.

A great nausea overcame her, and she vomited over her lovely dress, Joru, and Gogmo. This cleared her mind, and she remembered why she had come there in the first place. Wiping herself off and apologizing to Gogmo and Joru, she returned to her song of invitation.

> I, a young woman, Drukmo of Kyalo,
> Have come to Lower Ma to invite you, Joru.
> At times, the sun of happiness dawns,
> And at other times, the dark tempest of fear storms.
> My thoughts, like a flag on the highest peak,
> Were so blown by the wind of fleeting experience
> That I had forgotten the very point of my mission,
> But it is here that it truly rests.
> Thinking now on what I have been sent to say,
> The very fabric of this story unravels.
> On the merits of Trothung's Hayagriva dream—
> Or prophecy, or imagination, or whatever it was—
> There will be a great horse race,
> And the winner will take me as his bride.

That hero, big brave Gyatsha,
Enjoined me to seek out his brother Joru
And invite him to compete.
Guilt-ridden about our previous karma,
And not daring to defy Gyatsha, I came here.
My plea is that you, Joru, join the race
And that you as well, Gogmo, come to Ling.
I will be able to capture the noble kyang,
And, Joru, with this magical steed,
You will take your seat on the golden throne.
The people of Ling, happy as fish in water,
Will be all the happier as you show your astonishing
    power.
If you understand this discourse, it is sweet to your
    ears.
If not, there is no way to explain it, and all is lost.

Then Joru said, "Drukmo, you and my mother, Gogmo, must first capture this karmic steed, and only then can we go to Ling. Once there, it will fall to me to display the power of which you speak, winning the race and becoming the king as well as your husband. But that is not the sole purpose of my birth, as only together can we bring peace and prosperity to this troubled land and defeat the enemies of Ling. I will face the mara demons and am fated to put an arrow through the forehead of the terrible demon Lutsen.[35] Bards will sing of it, and volumes will be written. But know this: without the horse, none of this will come to pass, and Ling will only decline further into despair and turmoil. So, my queen-to-be and my precious mother, do not fail."

---

35. Lutsen is the terrible demon king of Dud and the subject of one of the best known of the Gesar tales.

When Joru had finished, Gogmo and Drukmo sat in silence, contemplating the importance of the tasks ahead. They shared a little more chang and retired as the fire in the center of the tent turned to embers.

After a troubled sleep, Drukmo awoke with the thought that she had no idea how she would recognize the horse, and lurking in the back of her mind was the nagging thought that, with Joru being a master of illusion, perhaps this was all a trick of some kind. She went over to Joru, who was rekindling the fire. She pointed out that, if he were such a master, why could he not summon the animal himself? And if that were not possible, then at the very least he could tell her how to identify the great steed.

"You are quite right to ask," Joru replied. "To answer your first question, if I act alone, benefit will not come to Ling. As for your second question, here too you are right to ask. Unless the characteristics and markings of this special horse are elucidated, you will not know him."

Accordingly Joru sang the song that describes this steed and also conveys much of the horse lore so central to the livelihood and culture of the people of the Tibetan high plateau.

My dear mother, who was the abode of my body,
And kind Drukmo,
Please listen with gentle ears.
Discursive thoughts are convoluted, like a sheep's second
stomach,
Sometimes cheerful and sometimes grim.
Conversations can be like an artist's drawing,
Looking good from the front but nothing there from behind.
Drukmo's determination to catch the horse
Comes from her mouth but not from her heart.
Mother's capture of the horse in the mountains

Is easy to imagine, but difficult to bring about.
You both must crank up your devotion
And give me your ear.
As for the horse, his father was White Sky Horse.
Even so, he is not called White Sky Horse.
His mother was Sorrel Earth Horse.
Even so, he is not called Sorrel Earth Horse.
He is not an ordinary horse, but a wild animal,
And free of any trace of the mundane.
There can be no mistaking him.
The markings of his coat will clearly distinguish him.
The horse's hair is not pale, but sorrel,
The color of ruby-reddish brown.
His four hooves are ornamented with wheels of wind.
The poll of his head is pyramidal, like a small mountain.
His muzzle is balanced as though secured on either
    side,
His throat, in the shape of a beautiful bell,
Is supported by the aquiline muscles of his neck.
His belly looks like a budding waterborne lotus
And is supported by four legs,
Firm and straight as the trunk of a tree,
Rooted in four graceful hooves.
Furthermore, this great steed has nine distinguishing
    features.
His forehead resembles a bird-demon falcon.
His neck is like that of a pika demon.
His face has the dreamy countenance of a goat,
With hairs as soft as those of a newborn rabbit.
His eye sockets resemble those of an older toad,
While his pupils look like those of an angry snake.
On his musk doe-like muzzle,
His nostrils flare and collapse like empty silken sacks.

The tips of his spy-demon ears
Have delicate hairs like the finest vulture feathers.
He is unmistakable
And has other unique traits beyond these nine.
His head and ears resemble those of seven animals.
He has eighteen special muscles,
As well as twenty heroic bones
And thirty-two hidden marks.
Such are the great qualities of a stallion
Complete in this supreme steed.
What is more, when he flies, he holds to the pathway
    of the birds,
And he understands and speaks the human language.
These are the characteristics by which you cannot
    mistake the horse.
As if that were not enough,
In the flowering meadows of the mountaintops,
He can be found frolicking with a hundred stallions
And sporting with a hundred mares.
His forelock calls forth the gods and his tail, the nagas.
His forelegs seem to summon him,
And his back legs are made to run.
This stallion of karmic connection
And Joru who gathers authentic presence—
We two are helpless but to join together.
Whether I go to Ling or not depends upon this steed.
Spirits and protectors, rouse yourselves.
Come today to support my mother.
May she and Drukmo know success.

Gogmo and Drukmo were encouraged by his words and
started into the hills to catch the horse, aided by spirits, nagas,
and nyen. They rode north and east, from valley to valley until

at last, looking down from a high mountain pass, they saw the face of Penne Ritra[36] and herds of kyang grazing the foothills.

At times, thousands of these stately animals could be seen grazing along a plain or hillside, and such it was that day when Gogmo and Drukmo came over the pass. Above the herd, a flock of vibrant falcons swooped and cawed in the noonday sun, their haunting calls harmonizing with the echoing thrum of horse hooves hammering the ground. And finally, within the herd, they saw a magnificent creature, a horse unlike the rest.

It was Wild Kyang, unmistakable with his turquoise mane and tail and his ruby coat. The tips of his hairs glimmered with swirling rainbows, and he pranced on his four hooves. From the front, he looked like burnished metal. From behind, he looked like a white vulture swooping for prey. His body was low to the ground, like that of a vixen stalking, and he undulated and twisted with the elegant ease of a fish. He moved with great beauty and symmetry. His hocks were full-fleshed, like those of a doe's thigh, and he had the delicate breast of a female crane.

Drukmo recognized him immediately as the all-knowing horse that Joru had described, and she turned to Gogmo, jubilant. Gogmo was thinking, *If it is my karma to catch him, so be it. Joru has said that this horse understands and speaks human language, so I will explain our purpose.* She sang out across the valley to the horse.

> Well then, Supreme Steed,
> I have a few things to tell you.
> The sharp arrow notched with gold,
> If left inside the quiver,

---

36. A great mountain lying in northeastern Tibet near the headwaters of the Mekong and Yellow Rivers.

Merely embellishes the warrior's costume.
Unless it serves to tame the enemy,
Its razor sharpness matters not.
The Supreme Steed honored by his title
May be the regal ornament of the mountains,
But if he does not stride beneath a golden saddle,
His elegant Mongolian gait matters not.
Joru, Wild Kyang, Gogmo, we three
Are karmically connected.
Therefore, Wild Kyang, Joru's horse,
Come here and stand by Gogmo.
First this cake made of five types of grain,
Second this drink, the finest of teas,
And third, this square woolen horse blanket
Are our gifts for the Lord of Steeds.
Ling's golden throne, a treasure trove,
And the bridegroom of Drukmo,
All will be wagered on you.
Joru has assured me that you are fluent in the human
    tongue.
Therefore Wild Kyang, hear my words.
Merely to stay and graze the open grasslands
Is well beneath your dignity and station.
Instead come and accomplish the benefit of others.
Help magnetize and lead Ling.
Wild Kyang, hold this in your heart.

She approached the herd, and the other kyang ran off. The divine steed quietly neighed and nuzzled Gogmo with affection. Raising his head toward the sky, he intoned this song in reply.

If you do not recognize me,
I am the messenger of the gods above.
I am the karmically destined god of the horses.
My full name is Lord of Steeds Ever-Increasing Wild
    Kyang.
Now then, Gogmo, listen.
It is hard to domesticate an animal that you have neglected.
It is hard to achieve without effort
And hard to have prosperity without merit.
It is hard to have children without karmic fruition.
I am the Supreme Steed, Lord of Horses, Wild Kyang.
I stayed in Red Wetland Pastures for three years,
Then on the Crag Mountain of Gu-ra for three years,
On the slopes of Yutsé three years more,
And now I have been in Penne Ritra for the last three
    years.
In the three months of summer, I roamed and grazed
With no shelter from the rains.
In the three months of winter, I endured the icy winds
With no blanket to cover my flanks.
In the three months of spring, I wandered, hungry,
Waiting for even three blades of grass to sprout.
I am a stallion twelve years old,
Too late to be saddle-broken.
Moreover, I have never heard of anyone called Joru,
Nor ever before seen the one called Gogmo.
And now that I have grown older,
I cannot imagine accepting a bridle
Or acceding to the mandate of the gods.
That sharp bit will never fit this square mouth.
That saddle blanket will never cover this broad back.
And Drukmo is meaningless in my eyes.
You must sow seeds in the three months of spring

If you wish a harvest of grains in the three months of fall.
You must feed cows in the three months of winter
If you wish milk in the three months of spring.
You must faithfully care for a steed
If you wish a mount that does not grow too wild for capture.
I care nothing for the beings of the human realm,
And since Joru has not looked after me,
Why would I continue as a horse, a mere animal,
When I can wander the ranks of the gods above?
If you understand this song, it is sweet to your ears.
If not, there is no way to explain.

The steed sang and then began to fan out his great wings as if to fly. Drukmo and Gogmo, fearing that he would bolt and be lost to them, supplicated the gods, invoking the names of Joru's drala siblings over and over. Although the minds of both mother and maiden had despaired, their hearts had persevered, and from the western sky appeared three beings of light, the sibling drala.

There came elder brother Dungkhyung Karpo, younger brother Ludrul Odtrung, and sister Thalé Odkar in a glorious spectacle, surrounded by a dazzling array of earth spirits, nagas, and nyen, all of whom sparkled with their own light, starry as diamonds against the bright blue sky. These spirits took many forms, both corporeal and spiritlike. They appeared as raptors and birds, snake and insects, various animal forms, and formless creatures—all giving out translucent beams of multicolored light. In the midst of all this beauty, confusion, and chaos, the drala siblings threw the ring of the lasso around the divine horse's neck. Bowing to Gogmo, they gently placed the other end of the rope into her right hand.

Turning to Drukmo, with the affection that comes from the sharing of intense experience, Gogmo spoke softly, "Drukmo of Kyalo, among the many herds of Ling, there is not one horse that equals this steed. No animal in any place or in any time can rival this creature."

At that very moment, Wild Kyang bolted and soared into the sky. As he flew, Gogmo, who was still holding onto the lasso, was pulled along behind. As they flew higher up into the space above, they could clearly see the countries of China, India, Persia, Mongolia, and the land of the maras. It was then that the wondrous horse broke into a song relating to Gogmo all that he could see.

> Look down, a spectacular sight can be seen.
> Far below is Vulture Peak Mountain[37] in India
> And, over there, Posing Elephant Mountain in China.
> Then that great mountain with five peaks
> Is Wutaishan[38] in China,
> And the mountain that resembles a pure crystal vase,
> The supreme site for meditation, is Mount Kailash.
> These are the four sacred mountains of our world.
> Look down! There is more to see.
> The earth is covered with clouds and mist.
> This is the land to be tamed by the boy Joru,
> And it is where this horse will accomplish the benefit
>   of beings.
> Gogmo, remember and keep this in mind.
> Far beyond is the land of Hor,

---

37. Vulture Peak Mountain is in the state of Bihar in northeast India. It is a sacred site where the Buddha taught.
38. Wutaishan is a great, snow-topped mountain in China that sits above the headwaters of the river Qingshui, a secondary tributary of the Yangtze River. It is sacred to Tibetan Buddhism as the abode of Manjushri, the bodhisattva of wisdom.

> Where you see that mountain resembling a white torma
>   offering
> And the castle that looks like a crimson Chinese knot.
> It is there that Joru and I must go
> And there that Joru and Drukmo's marriage will first
>   go awry.
> Gogmo, remember and keep this in mind.
> Since Drukmo alone knows my qualities,
> Gogmo, you must leave and return to Ling,
> And I will not stay here but go to the spirit land.
> If you have understood this song, it is sweet to your
>   ears.
> If not, there is no way to explain.

Thus Wild Kyang sang, and within an instant, he, with Gogmo in tow, had landed at Wutaishan. Joru was already there, waiting. He approached and had only enough time to stroke the horse's broad neck three times and whisper a few fleeting words into its ear. Then the great horse gave a lilting neigh, slapped its wings, and again flew up and across the sky like a meteor, landing back where Drukmo was still standing, hoping for the return of Gogmo and the horse.

Gogmo, panting and still clutching the horse's neck, was delighted to be back on solid ground. She led the horse over to Drukmo, who was saying that they had accomplished what they had set out to do and that it was time to give the captured horse to Joru and return to their respective homes. With the steed following and its lead rope firmly in Gogmo's hands, they headed on horseback to the encampment.

But as they approached Joru's tent, Wild Kyang tried to break away from them. When Gogmo could not hold him any longer, she called out to Joru that she was losing the horse.

Unperturbed, Joru replied, "Just release him. The horse and

I have already met, and I believe our connection to be strong. He will come to me."

Taking Joru at his word, Gogmo let go of the lead. The horse bounded playfully over to Joru, who affectionately stroked his muzzle.

"Ah, Drukmo," Joru said, "I have finally acquired Wild Kyang. Now it is time to return to Ling. You, a wealthy and experienced horsewoman from Kyalo, are familiar with the land's strongest and swiftest horses. Please expound on their qualities. Tell me. Is my horse superior, inferior, or equal, and how does he rank among the horses of my kinsmen?"

Joru had spoken accurately as Drukmo was indeed a skilled equestrian. She sang of the lineage and qualities of horses and explained at great length the attributes of the horse that she and Gogmo had brought to Joru.[39]

> That was a general explanation about horses,
> And now as to this divine horse—
> He is elegant and shimmers with rainbow colors,
> Eager to run and dazzling as he goes.
> He is an emanation of Hayagriva.
> His coat is not the usual piebald sorrel
> But the unabashed red of a ruby,
> Indicating that he magnetizes the assembly of Hayagriva
>   deities.
> He tosses his dark mane and tail,
> Indicating that he magnetizes an assembly of wrathful,
>   annihilating deities.

39. See Song Appendix, Song #6 for the beginning of Drukmo's Equine Soliliquy. This song embodies the importance of horse culture for the Tibetan people. It is full of detail, and worth the reader's time.

His teeth and muzzle are an unflinching white, radiant as
　　the moon's rays,
Indicating that he magnetizes an assembly of deities
Who pacify illness and demonic forces.
His underbelly is an opulent golden color,
Indicating that he magnetizes an assembly of enriching
　　deities
Who increase longevity and merit.
The downy vulture feathers on the tips of his ears
Indicate that he magnetizes protectors who illuminate
　　like a torch.
His shoulders are wheels of wind,
Indicating that he magnetizes the drala who have mas-
　　tery of long life.
The iron petals of his four hooves
Indicate that he magnetizes the drala who tame the four
　　maras.
This Ever-Increasing Steed, Lord of Horses,
Has all the marks of a sovereign of samsara and nirvana.
The height and majesty of his head
Is a sign that he venerates the Three Jewels.
That the size of his body is comparable to that of all other
　　horses
Signifies his mastery of bodhicitta.
That his tail and mane are thick and long
Signifies that his emanations are unceasing.
That his eyes are clear and sparkling
Signifies that he has the direct realization of the nature
　　of phenomena.
That he has a pair of eyes
Signifies that his understanding encompasses both
　　samsara and nirvana,
And that they see congruently

Signifies the ultimate inseparability of samsara and
   nirvana.
The elegance of his ears
Signifies that he is in harmony with the path of the two
   truths.
That these sense organs are complete on a single head
Signifies that everything is subsumed as one nature.
That he is adorned with the six sense faculties
Signifies that he maintains the conduct of the six
   perfections.
That he is agile on his four hooves
Signifies that he nourishes beings through the four
   gatherings.
The white of his pale underbelly
Signifies that he is unstained by the faults of existence.
That he can speak human language
Signifies that words themselves are without inherent
   meaning.
That he has wings to fly
Signifies that all appearances are illusory.
His bond of affection toward humans
Signifies that he looks upon beings with wisdom and
   compassion.
That he was caught with a lasso
Signifies that his buddha activity is ever increasing.
That he can shoulder you, a noble warrior,
Signifies that he can lead all beings on the path of
   liberation.
That his gait is smooth and swift
Signifies that he will accomplish the benefit of beings
   through skillful means.
To portray any ordinary stallion in these terms would
   be specious,

But it is in keeping with the true nature of this glorious
    steed.
That is not all.
Among the thirty winged horses of Ling,
Dongtsen's colt Turquoise Bird
Can claim the strength of a garuda in flight.
But where is the wonder in that,
As any creature that can fly has that quality?
Denma's Silver Colt and Trothung's Jagged Raven
Are said to be horses with the gift of speech.
But where is the wonder in that,
As other creatures have that skill?
Sengtak, Gyatsha, and Chipon
All have outstanding horses,
Yet these steeds' outer bodies and inner thoughts
Are none other than those of animals.
Although Wild Kyang outwardly appears as a beast of
    burden, a horse,
Inwardly he possesses the wisdom mind of a buddha.
To meet him is enough to close the door to the lower
    realms,
To ride him is to be carried to the citadel of peace.
To have encountered such a supreme horse is our good
    fortune.
And as if that were not enough,
It took a magical lasso
And the help of spirits, nagas, and nyen
To capture him.
He has wings to soar the sky,
Unrivaled even by a garuda,
And hooves to gallop the earth,
Without peer among the horses of Ling.
Joru, the finish line is in the palm of your hand.

If you have heard my song, let it be a melodious offering
    to your ears.
If not, there is no way to explain it.
Joru, take this into your heart.

Drukmo came to the end of her song extoling Wild Kyang
and comparing him favorably to other celebrated horses of
Ling. But as she was singing, Drukmo's previous karma was
awakened, and she realized in herself the very qualities of the
horse as she enumerated them. The splendor of the horse had
kindled in her an understanding of the illusory nature of per-
ception, and she was able to see both Joru and the steed for
the magnificent, majestic beings that they were. Her mind, her
heart, and her body knew great joy and profound peace.

CHAPTER 10

Joru and Drukmo travel together in strange lands,
But first, the horse's tack and gear is collected.
The magical steed is the object of heated negotiations.
A feast is held, and minds are becalmed.

ALTHOUGH HE WAS now in possession of the horse, Joru still did not feel prepared. Turning to Gogmo and Drukmo, he explained, "I could go to Ling, but this horse is not yet broken or trained, and I am without a saddle, a saddle blanket, or even a bridle. If I were to ride bareback, I would likely be thrown and the blame fall to Drukmo. Perhaps you, Gogmo, could lead the horse to Ling, and Drukmo and I follow. Of course, Drukmo, since you would have your own horse and I would have only a walking stick, I might fall behind."

Gogmo tacked her horse and rode off toward Ling, with Wild Kyang following on his lead.

Drukmo, wanting to show Joru that she was able to compete on foot with anyone, said, "Joru, I am quite swift. You should just ride my mare Dromuk [Roan] and I can walk. I will have no trouble keeping up with you."

Seeing that she had her mind made up, Joru agreed and mounted her horse, and they set off. After a short while, he saw a musk deer on the far side of the mountain and said to Drukmo, "See over there? That small black deer veiled in the shade of that mountain? It is a demon, and in order for it to have a good rebirth, now is the time to tame it, and moreover, unless it is immediately bound by oath, trouble will come to the entire valley. Please sing him a sweet song, and while he is distracted, I will rope him with the lasso."

Joru started off toward the mountain, and Drukmo, her pride swelling with this important task, melodiously sang.

> The song is Ala Ala Ala.
> Thala leads the melody.
> Through a verdant mountain pass,
> Joru and Drukmo are returning to Ling,
> But Joru is sidetracked by a deer that he has spotted.
> He claims it to be a demon that must be tamed,
> Perhaps to conceal his desire for its prized musk and
>   sweet meat.
> Phenomena are not truly existent.
> Joru himself is not real, but magical,
> You, the musk deer, are not real, but an illusion.
> And I, Drukmo, am not real; my song has no words.
> Whatever turns out to be true,
> Keep in mind that Joru intends to kill you,
> And I mean to deceive you with this little song.
> Musk deer are distracted by eating grass,
> And similarly, confusion befalls our own minds.
> Either the musk deer's life is over
> And Joru and I are acting in concert,
> Or Drukmo has been deceived
> And Joru and the deer are conspiring.
> I cannot tell the difference.

As she sang, Joru threw the lasso, and the loop caught the musk deer by the neck. The deer was unusually muscular and fierce, and when Joru pulled it in front of Drukmo, the deer attacked her as Joru simply looked on. Picking up a great stone,

Drukmo bludgeoned the deer. She smashed its skull, and its blood spattered. The deer's eyes glassed over, and its spirit departed.

Joru affected disbelief and said, "Drukmo, it was I who was to be the one to tame the deer and lead its consciousness to the pure land, but you have killed him. Now the opportunity to tame him is lost, and the deer's death was for naught as its good rebirth is not assured. Not only that, you have dishonored your father's entire tribe."

Aggrieved, he continued, "When it comes to the horse race, have you forgotten that you are the prize? Now you are covered with the brains and blood of the poor creature. How can I not tell your father and the warriors of what you have done? You pretend to care about evil versus virtue, but you lifted that stone and took his life. Bloodthirsty one, from whence did this come? Was it pride, was it hatred, or did lust push you forward? Maybe I was wrong about who the demon is." And he sang.

> The song is Ala Ala Ala.
> Thala leads the melody.
> Listen, I will tell you how it is.
> *Meditation that is without learning*
> *Is like an arrow without a bow,*
> *And learning without practice*
> *Is like a bow without an arrow.*
> *It is hard to unite these two,*
> *But if done, makes for an authentic teacher.*
> *Mistakes that are made through lack of understanding*
> *Are like the suicide of a madman.*
> *Having understanding but applying it mistakenly*
> *Is no different than being an animal that licks its own ass.*
> *Words without deeds*
> *Are like birds without wings.*

Saying that Joru does not exist but is an illusion,
This means nothing.
Saying that the musk deer is an illusion,
Why kill an illusion with a stone?
Now I am hard-pressed not to take action.
But if you think my decision unfair,
Then bring me from your father's treasure
The golden bridle called Wishing Gem
And the golden crupper called Wish-Fulfilling.
Do not place them among the prizes, but give them to me.
If you do, then Joru will shut his mouth.
Drukmo, keep this in mind.

Thus he sang, and Drukmo looked down at her bloody hands in disbelief. She felt queasy and faint. It was as though her mind had lost all bearings and she was in another world altogether. Prepared to accept that she had no choice but to give the golden bridle and the saddle ornament to Joru, she promised them to him.

All of a sudden, Joru leapt onto Drukmo's horse, spurred it into a gallop with his white willow staff, and took off on the mountain pass, swift as an arrow. Left in the dust was Drukmo who, although she indeed could run as fast as anyone in Ling, could not keep up. The pass climbed the steep face of the mountain, and the way was studded with strewn rocks and fissured with crevices. As she scrambled upward, Drukmo became winded and exhausted and was now covered in sweat as well as in blood and brains.

When at last she reached the top of the mountain pass, she gasped and pulled up short, as just before her on the path was Joru's neatly severed head. Midway down the neck it was dismembered, and thick, red blood oozed onto the ground. Immediately Drukmo assumed that this was entirely her fault and was karmic retribution for the vicious way in which she had killed the deer.

She turned and instinctively started slowly down the mountain, trying to collect herself. Fifty yards down the dusty mountain path, she saw Joru's severed right arm with the sleeve still partially stuck to it. Shards of bone lay on the ground, and the arm, which had been sundered above the elbow, almost imperceptibly seemed to be moving. A little farther down was his right leg with the shoe still on, and now, looking around, she could see organs and guts strewn everywhere. Her mare Dromuk stood sweating, with Joru's other severed foot and leg still in the stirrup.

Drukmo looked back at the head where Joru's two eyes were wide open and bulging from his head. According to Tibetan burial ritual, this was the worst way to die, and even seeing one in this state would result in generations of suffering.

In accord with custom, she threw ashes on his eyes and shouted, "Turn back those cursed dead eyes of yours!"

Then this beautiful maiden gathered all the pieces of his scattered body and buried the bloody body parts under some white stones. She thought, *Now at least no one will walk on Joru's pitiful body. What a gory end he had, and my own end now awaits me. I cannot return to my homeland now. Perhaps only my death could bring peace to my parents and to Ling.*

The poisonous Lake Weri was nearby, and Drukmo mounted her horse and left this terrible scene. As she headed toward the lake, she reflected on the vanity of taking her own life, but reaching the shore, she supplicated her personal deity and opened her mind, thinking, *I will transfer my consciousness and that of Joru to the pure realm and my illusory material body to this poisonous lake.* With this thought, she covered her head with her cape and called on all the deities for help.

The song is Ala Ala Ala.
Thala leads the melody.
Hoping to attain happiness and well-being,
But merely succeeding in producing a harvest of
    suffering,
It is hard to accomplish the purpose of one's goals.
Though it is said that the essence of this life is suffering,
Happiness and suffering are just ripples on a vast ocean.
Since Joru has died, should I regret my own death?
Delighting in the objects of desire
Brings pleasure to the five sense faculties.
May the unobstructed luminous emptiness of my mind
Mingle inseparably with the mind of Joru.
Unsullied by the confusion of hope and fear,
May we mingle as one in the space of awareness.
This karmic illusory material body
Produced through the three poisons[40]
Is well suited for this poisonous lake.
May all the buddhas and bodhisattvas
Come to lead us to the pure land.
May I accomplish these words of truth,
May my sweet mare Dromuk return to Ling,
And may my kind parents be free from suffering.

Thus she sang. She was standing at Dromuk's side gently slapping his flank, urging him to turn and gallop to Ling, when she thought that it seemed as though the horse was being held back. She turned, and there was Joru, pulling on her horse's tail. She was overwhelmed and burst simultaneously into tears and laughter.

---

40. The three poisons are the conflicting emotions of passion, aggression, and ignorance.

Sheepishly, Joru said to her, "Drukmo, never have you looked so lovely! As the worldly proverb says, *Cloyed by happiness like a buck howling in the wilderness. Cloyed by suffering like an owl laughing in the darkness. Cloyed by a full stomach like a wolf still crying for meat.* You are too beautiful. Even blood-spattered, you outshine the sun. Your father, Kyalo, is too rich, such that nobles bow at the mention of his name, and the young men, smitten with your melodious voice and besotted with your beauty, cherish you too dearly. Wherefore is the suffering that causes you to want to throw yourself in the lake? As I am not dead, I have no need of consciousness transference. But until now I did not appreciate the depth of your sadness."

Drukmo protested, saying, "Oh, my dear Joru, I thought you dead, and I was heartbroken. I had no idea you were using your magical powers. Torment me no further with such tricks. Just come along with me to Ling. I do not mind if you tell others of all this, for it is as the proverb says, *A person with a busy mind who leaves home will return with many kinds of stories.*"

Joru responded with a playful song.

The song is Ala Ala Ala.
Thala leads the melody
Drukmo, it seems that you are brimming with wisdom.
The way you take even my playfulness as real
Shows clearly just how far your view goes.
Intending to end your life in the lake
Indicates that your meditation has reached the unchanging state.
Your prayer for Dromuk to return to Ling
Indicates that indeed you have severed all attachment.
There exists a golden saddle with nine circular designs,
A karmic treasure that can be found in the middle lands
of the nyen,

And a saddle blanket marked at the corners
With the nine astrological divination numbers
That is the karmic wealth of the nagas of Lake
    Manasarovar.
Wild Kyang and I have not yet obtained this tack,
But we cannot race without them.
If you give both of them to me,
I will stop doing magic
And speak nothing of what has occurred here.
Drukmo, keep this in mind.

Drukmo thought, *Despite his apparent death, Joru appears very much alive and none the worse for it. Everything he does must be simply a magical display. Mental conceptions and perceptions cannot be trusted, but still it would be best if no one heard of my foolish mistakes. I have my family's good name to consider. Even if I must steal these things, it is up to me to get them.* With that thought, she calmed down enough to go with Joru.

From there, the mountain pass opened onto an expansive plateau thickly carpeted with wildflowers. Drukmo became tense as she remembered that this was where she had met the Indian minister Berkar, who might or might not have been Joru. As their tryst replayed in her mind, she felt her neck stiffen and her breathing become clumsy.

Nervous that Joru would notice, she turned her face away and pretended to embark on a detailed study of the surrounding wildflower field. But Joru appeared preoccupied with thoughts of his own, and she relaxed as they continued on to a spot where they could stop for a brief rest. Their solitude was interrupted when a large, white pika emerged from his burrow along with a number of smaller brown pikas and a rather finicky Tibetan snow finch, all of which shared the dusty underground abode. Drukmo was aghast to see that the white pika was wearing the very scarf that she had given to the Indian minister. The pika offered this song to Joru while the snow finch pecked at the appropriate times for emphasis.

> The song is Ala Ala Ala.
> Thala leads the melody.
> I am the youthful, clear-eyed pika Gapa Limig,
> The Grand Poobah of the pikas,
> Here to greet Joru.
> This white scarf with nine knots
> Was in possession of that maiden from Kyalo
> A mere few days back.
> With nary a thought, she rather crudely lay
> With the Indian minister Berkar,
> And so this previously pure scarf is now known
> As the Secret Tryst of Shacking-up Scarf.
> Since they promised to be true to each other, it is also
>   their Pledge Scarf,
> And as they took an oath three times, it is their Oath Scarf.
> Caring neither for the spoiled maiden
> Nor his own sworn vows,
> The minister gave this scarf to me,
> And now I pass it on to you, Joru.
> What I have to say is with pure intention.
> Without regard for her body, she hooked up with him,
> And not minding her mouth, she pledged an oath.
> Seeing that, this pika meditator had some thoughts.
> I thought this maiden girl was like butter,
> Easily melted away by the sun of happiness.
> I thought this maiden girl was like a flea,
> Biting the warm bodies of those who have shown
>   great kindness.

I thought this maiden girl was like the springtime
   weather,
Cold and warm, up and down with each passing day.
When I see that, this meditating pika is saddened.
I think the brethren of Ling have made a mistake,
The prize being already defiled.
Joru, I think a wrong path awaits you.
Joru, keep this in your mind.

Drukmo now experienced remorse beyond any she could
have imagined, thinking now that it was only in her mind
that the minister Berkar was Joru. *When would she pass beyond
illusion?*

She stood helpless as Joru said, "Drukmo, I had no idea you
would do something as crude and disappointing as this. I who
have tasted the heart blood of men and animals am shocked if
what the pika just said is true. This I must certainly tell to the
people of Ling. This is the very place where you had lain down
and shared your body and promises with the Indian minister.
How can I let your father offer you as a prize along with his
wealth and the throne of Ling?"

Drukmo, with her tears now flowing freely and full of shame,
bowed down to him and said, "Sweet Joru, listen to me." And
she sang.

The song is Ala Ala Ala.
Thala leads the melody.
Listen, for I have something to tell you.
Those who are confused by ignorance are called
   sentient beings.
Without confusion is to be the Buddha.
In the intrinsic nature of things as they are,
Liberation and confusion are mere words.

Not understanding that until now, I was confused.
Confronted by your unimpeded magical powers,
I believed every manifestation to be your illusion,
And solidifying them, I became confused.
First, in that narrow valley passage,
The frightening bandit on a black horse,
And then, beyond the mountain pass of the Seven
  Dunes,
The man in white sporting a topknot.
Thinking that these were your magical emanations,
Through aversion and attachment, I was confused.
This consciousness is like a drunken elephant.
Lead it where you will with your hook of compassion.
First of all, I confess all my past evil deeds
And pledge from this day onward not to commit them
  yet again.
With this vow come three prayers:
First, may your omniscient mind be free from
  obscuration,
Second, may your loving-kindness not abandon me,
Third, through your power may you seize the golden
  throne.
It is difficult to be the bridegroom of the maiden
  Drukmo,
But if mandated by the heavens, it is made easier.
It is difficult to be the leader of the citizens of Ling,
But if skill and accomplishment unite, it is easier.
If you understand this, it is a supreme ornament to
  the ears.
If not, there is no way to explain.

Thus she sang, and Joru sat on the ground frowning, occasionally pushing a few sticks in the dirt. Finally he looked up

and said, "It is difficult to untangle confusion and apparent reality, but listen to my little song."

The song is Ala Ala Ala.
Thala leads the melody.
Joru's mind is empty of magical emanation,
And Drukmo's mind is empty of confusion.
Within this magical display of the appearance of
    empty reality,
Confusion and emanation are merely empty words.
When you see the mind's nature as without self,
Confusion vanishes like a rainbow in the sky.
If there is any obstruction, there cannot be omniscience.
If there is any partiality, there cannot be love.
If there is any interruption, there cannot be power.
If we do not take the swift path,
Then proclaiming the benefit of others is just empty
    speech.
If you have understood this, it is sweet to your ears.
If not, there is no way to explain.

When he said this, Drukmo was overcome with emotion, and her attachment to the things of this world dissolved. Because of her previous karma, her mind could pierce Joru's words and grasp the essential nature of the reality that surrounds us all. All the doubt she had toward Joru disappeared. She understood that Joru was not only her life's companion but also that he must win the race and become king. This she shared with Joru, and then they traveled arm in arm to Ling. Thus it was that Drukmo did in fact fulfill her mission.

She said to Joru, "When it is time for the horse race, come to the tents of Kyalo. There will be a saddle for the horse, a rider's horsewhip, and my good wishes."

They then returned to her father's home, and after speaking with her parents, Drukmo and Joru went to find Gogmo and to fetch Wild Kyang. Gogmo and Joru, mother and son, were reunited and welcomed back into Ling, though some trepidation remained.

For instance, when any of the warriors asked Joru how he came to own Wild Kyang, he told various stories, never telling the same story twice. Not surprisingly, some of the warriors felt that once again Joru was sowing confusion wherever he went. Nonetheless, in the end, it still seemed best that Joru had been invited to the horse race.

One day, riding Wild Kyang, Joru, with his nine-edged prosperity bag hidden inside the breast pocket of his chuba, arrived at Trothung's door, announcing himself and calling for a celebration. Trothung was immediately dumbstruck by Wild Kyang. He had never before seen such a perfect creature.

"Well, nephew of mine, I am delighted that you have come here today. We had the banquet yesterday to precede the great horse race, but I will certainly arrange another."

Although Trothung had been talking to Joru, he had been staring at Wild Kyang and now asked, "Where did you get this horse?"

Joru replied, "Oh, this little colt of mine? It was born to a mare that belongs to my mother and me. Unfortunately, since he has never been broken, he is unable to be mounted. For eight years he has been running free in the cold mountains to the northwest. Now I am supposed to run him in the horse race of Ling. Uncle, what should be done to make him ready to race?"

Trothung said, "Joru, this horse is of no use to you. You need a horse that you can ride easily so you do not get hurt. To be capable of competing with the fastest steeds, a horse needs to have the best constitution, and the rider must be in complete control. Though certainly this horse is graceful and a beauty, his shortcomings are too great, and he will not win. I will trade you my most experienced and powerful steed for Wild Kyang and throw into the bargain his tacking and anything else you might need."

Joru replied, "I did not realize that my mother and I missed the banquet, but if you have another, I will be able to properly meet the warriors and leaders of Ling. Afterward, you and I can talk about trading horses. This particular horse is very precious to me, but you are right. If I do not trade it, I will not have a trained horse to ride. On the other hand though, it will sadden me to trade it. I must think of my dear mother as we will need to provision ourselves for the next few seasons. When one lives among civilized people, there is so much to consider. Perhaps if, along with thirteen scarves and thirteen silver ingots stamped in the shape of a horse hoof, you also give us thirteen pouches of gold, my mother and I could seriously consider such a horse trade."

Nearly drooling at Joru's words, Trothung said, "Your terms seem reasonable indeed. I just might be able to accommodate such a bargain. I would rather give my hard-earned wealth to my dear nephew than to some stranger. Let us agree on this, and I will host a banquet."

Joru agreed with his uncle's proposal.

Trothung darkly thought, *Now it is crystal clear that the prophecy of Hayagriva has always been true. I have heard tell of a magical horse like this, but I had never seen one. It is this unrivaled beast that will assure my victory. After I host the banquet and offer the gold and silver, the horse will be mine.*

The very next day, the celebration began with fresh dri milk, fragrant Chinese tea, plates of delicacies, sweets, and fruits, portions of marbled meat, and nine rounds of beer. Thirteen scarves with perfect fringes, thirteen silver ingots, and thirteen pouches of gold were all placed before Joru.

Trothung toasted, "Dear nephew, may your wishes be fulfilled. In any one lifetime there is much happiness and sorrow." He sang a song that ended with these words,

> *Without merit, wealth will not come your way*
> *Whether you work hard or not.*
> *Without wisdom, a daughter will never know happiness*
> *Whether she is good-looking or not.*
> Without strength, you cannot rule the people
> Whether you win the golden throne or not.
> And moreover, this untamed, wild horse will put your
>   life in peril.
> Therefore, let uncle and nephew trade horses.
> If you understand this, it is sweet to your ears.
> If not, there is no way to explain.

Thus he sang. For many hours, Joru ate and drank. He took on the appearance of total drunkenness even though his mind was sharp and his being was suffused with loving-kindness. He gazed up at his uncle and over at Wild Kyang, laughing, and deftly slurred his words into this song.

> The song is Ala Ala Ala.
> Thala leads the melody.
> Listen here, for I have something to say.
> First, the innocence of a child,
> Second, the willfulness of a youth,
> And third, the impropriety of the elderly—
> It is difficult for there to be happiness from beginning
>   to end.

A chieftain's mind and sights are set on wealth.
The ministers turn the law on its head.
Together they bring punishment to the innocent.
It is impossible to call them kind-hearted.
Uncles with deception and mountains of conflict,
Relatives with hearts more rotten than a corpse,
A helpless nephew was exiled to the borderlands.
Conquering the enemy and caring for relatives are both
    difficult.
In business, Uncle, you are spiteful to the core,
And I am naturally clever.
While Wild Kyang can easily fetch a high price,
In the end there is no deal to be had.
Ultimately, relatives are burdened by animosity.
In the end, friends take sides in disputes.
Bosom buddies wind up divided by slander.
It is difficult to say that one values another.
Uncle Trothung, while you have many schemes
And I am quick to act,
To find common ground is difficult.
Shepherds tend sheep and yak,
But when the time is right, the owners take their fleece.
Some work the fields and acreage,
But the ripened harvest goes to the owners.
Fathers and uncles stockpile food and wealth,
And in a pretense of generosity, they fill our gullets.
But the fuller my stomach, the more I value my horse.
The more I drink, the more I miss Drukmo.
I have decided against trading my horse;
Being a wealthy king means nothing to me.
If you understand this, it is sweet to your ears.
If not, there is no way to explain it.
Uncle, keep this in your mind,

And I will keep my horse.

Thus he sang, and putting the thirteen scarves and the gold and silver into the nine-edged prosperity bag that had once belonged to Trothung, he prepared to leave.

Unhappy and nearly beside himself, Trothung snapped, "If we are not going to trade horses, you cannot make off with my silver and gold."

But Joru retorted that he had promised only to consider the horse trade and reminded Trothung of his previous treachery, saying, "The wealth of which you speak is but the cost of our continued good relations. You must remember how you solicited the help of the assassin Amnyé and how that all ended. And how clean your reputation remains since I never made public your part in that whole situation."

And though Trothung could never quite resolve what had happened, he decided it was best to leave things as they were. Still, as Joru led Wild Kyang away, Trothung was left feeling that somehow he had been swindled.

A few days later, Joru and his horse arrived at Drukmo's tent, and Joru called out, "Drukmo, you promised the saddle for the horse, the whip for the man, and your good prayers for my mission. Now, the time has come when I need these things."

Indicating a seat that was strewn with blue silken brocade cushions, Drukmo's father, Kyalo Tonpa, offered Joru an auspicious greeting scarf and told him the story of how he had come to possess the saddle, the halter, the saddle blanket, and the golden whip.

Many years ago, Kyalo Tonpa had been out hunting in the foothills of a nearby mountain with his two brothers when a mendicant teacher approached them. He was old and withered, with a stringy beard and musical eyes. Tonpa went on to explain that the old man had given them these four equestrian implements, which he had said represented the wealth of the naga protectors and that he, Tonpa, in particular had been entrusted to keep them until a suitable sublime being, one possessed of magical powers, appeared.

Tonpa ended by saying, "At the time of your birth, Joru, I had such magnificent dreams of Ling's future and the power of your presence that I knew that you must be that being spoken of by the teacher. It brings me great joy that my daughter Drukmo can present these to you now."

Drukmo offered the tack for the horse and the whip for the man and sang this sacred song that opens the great secret, dwelling within the steed's heart.

The song is Ala Ala Ala.
Thala leads the melody.
In the sky, excellent is the alignment of the
    constellations,
In the space between the heavens and the earth,
Excellent are the indications of good fortune,
And on the earth, auspicious is the time for humankind.
Within this divine horse Wild Kyang
Dwells the great secret of the five senses.
Sight, sound, taste, smell, and feeling
Abide within his eyes, ears, tongue, nose, and bodily
    form.
By thrice waving the golden whip that fulfills all wishes
This great outer secret will be revealed.
This supreme horse possesses an enlightened mind,
Yet the flourishing of unimpeded awareness is obstructed
    by emotionality.
Freedom from accepting and rejecting is the inner secret.
In turn, this secret will be revealed by waving the golden
    whip.

The secret wisdoms of omniscience, loving-kindness,
  and power
Grace this horse but are obscured by the veil of dualistic
  mind.
Freeing the mind that dwells on concepts is the method
  of the great secret.
Today my waving of the golden whip will clear the veil,
And the horse will be imbued with the wisdom of naked
  awareness.
For this divine horse today
May the three secrets be opened
Through the wish-fulfilling whip.
Moreover, the wool saddle blanket marked with the nine
  astrological signs,
The golden saddle patterned with nine circles,
And the golden bridle and girth that accomplish all
  desires
Are the karmic treasure of the nagas, nyens, and gods,
And in them the life force abides.
Today, may Wild Kyang be so adorned.
May you, Joru, the son of Gogmo,
Keep those beings suffering from confusion
Away from the path of the lower realms,
And may you be able to turn their minds to the dharma.
This is my prayer.
May you, Joru, the son of Gogmo,
Fully perfect the four buddha activities
Of pacifying, enriching, magnetizing, and vanquishing,
And accomplish the uninterrupted benefit of beings.
This is my prayer.
May you, Joru, the son of Gogmo,
Be the refuge and protector of humankind
And the chieftain of the land of Ling.

This is my prayer.
This great steed Wild Kyang,
Commended by the imperial gods
And born at Mount Meru, the king of mountains,
Was captured by your mother and I.
Today I offer to you this horse, adorned with jewels.
May you inherit the wealth of Kyalo Tonpa
And become my husband.
That is my prayer.
May this great steed with magical wheels of wind
Let no swift ones go before,
And may he not fall behind.
May these well-intentioned prayers be realized.
Joru, keep this in your mind.

Thus she prayed. The tack for the horse, the whip for the man, and all good aspirations were received, and Joru took his place among the ranks of competitors. Chipon, Gyatsha, and a crowd of warriors greeted him warmly as he rode onto the parade grounds. The warriors had been telling stories of their own glory and that of their comrades, and now they offered advice to Joru and adorned his neck with colorful scarves. The horse race was about to begin.

CHAPTER 11

All the great warriors gather, and the citizens congregate.
Drukmo and the other maidens are dressed in their finery.
Long awaited, the unrivaled spectacle of the horse race
   begins.
Despite, or perhaps because of all this, tricks are still afoot.

T HE SNOW had melted and pulled the dust with it into the
fecund earth. Spring had arrived with its annual promise, and the prophesied horse race was about to begin.
The young warriors and young women of Ling blossomed with
youth, every bit as hopeful as the spring. The householders,
men and women alike, had abandoned their usual routines,
with an ease allowed by the constancy of their daily effort. The
elders, matriarchs, and patriarchs, seasoned by the joys and
sorrows of this life, savored their age with its attendant familial
and societal respect. Each spectator was dressed in his or her
finest apparel, and together they were every bit as colorful as
the wild-flowering plains.

They milled around their usual gathering place known as
Tagthang Tramo [Colorful Tiger Plain]. Here could be heard
the roar of the dragon as well as the melody of the cuckoo and
the mind-captivating trilling of the lark and, mingled with the
sweet sounds of the crowd's anticipation, the harmony rever-
berated across the plain as the warriors readied for the race.

First in majesty and importance were the eight brothers
of the Serpa of Upper Ling and the nine tigerlike sons of the
Elder Lineage. They were garbed in clothes of a golden color

that shimmered brightly as the sun. They were surrounded by family, both close and far-flung.

The six tribes of Ombu were headed by eight heroes of the Middle Lineage accompanied by their kin. Clad in white, with their familiar white yak-wool chubas, they were both as radiant and as tranquil as a blanketing snowfall. On each chuba was a single semiprecious stone: lapis lazuli that looked like a bead made of the evening sky, coral like cooled fire, or opal like the milky moon at the horizon.

Next came the four tribes of Lower Ling, headed by the seven brothers of the Lesser Lineage, again with their families. These impressive warriors wore outfits of intense azure blue, deep as a cloudless sky on a winter morning.

To the right were the tribes of the Ga Clan; to the left were the tribes of Dru. The eighteen tribes of Tag-rong, the ruddy people of Ta'u, the clan of Denma, and so on were arrayed on both banks of the river. All of the mighty warriors of Ling were gathered in their full regalia, their hearts full of joy and expectation.

But there was one among them whose hunger for the race had nearly reached a boiling point. Believing he had received a true prophecy from Hayagriva, Trothung was overcome by greed and lust, barely able to feign composure. Along with him came his sons Dongtsen, Zigphen, and Nyatsha, followed by the rest of his kin. In their pride, they were certain that no horse but Dongtsen's Turquoise Bird could win the race.

In the same way, parading majestically, came warriors from the Greater, Middle, and Lesser Lineages. It is said that the Greater Lineage warriors were confident as lions, the warriors of the Middle Lineage flamboyant as dragons, and the Lesser Lineage warriors, brave as a mongoose confronting a cobra. Drukmo's father, Kyalo Tonpa, the arbiter Werma Lhadar, the judge Wangpo Darphen, and the four gurus of Ling were all on hand as spectators. These elder men represented the pinnacle of Tibetan culture, wisdom, and learning. Their renown reached from Persia to China and from China to the south of India. The air itself exuded confidence, pride, and desire.

Meanwhile, Joru had dug deep into his old chest and retrieved his unsightly antelope-buck hat and his blood-encrusted calf-skin coat. Nor had he forsaken his horrible horsehide boots. He looked as out of place as a filthy beggar at a king's banquet. With a bit of illusion, the great steed's appearance was transformed as well, and now Wild Kyang looked rather ordinary and quite beneath his silver saddle and elegant tack.

Set to compete, the warriors lined up and headed toward Ayu Downs where the race was to begin. By that time, the Seven Fair Maidens, Drukmo, Ne'uchung, Pekar, Chipon's daughter Yudron, Denma's daughter Dzédron, Yatha's daughter Sertso, and Trothung's daughter Tromo-tso had arrived and were ready for the race to begin. They wore silken garments of every color, their hair was woven with jewels, and they wore anklets and bracelets of dzi beads and precious stones. They made a juniper smoke offering and then joined the other spectators to watch the race from the top of Naga Downs.

After the burning of more juniper incense and the chanting of propitious verses by the elders, the riders left the starting line, and the speculation, not to mention the betting, as to who would win reached a crescendo. Many opined that there could be no winner other than Dongtsen, while just as many others clamored in disagreement.

At the finish line of Crag Mountain, the ritual masters of Ling had gathered to fill the sky with lhasang smoke from thirteen smoke-offering vessels. Fragrant columns of sacred juniper and cedar smoke poured from the many chambers. Diviners and astrologers haggled over who might emerge victorious, and all manner of foretelling was invoked as they circumambulated the many stupas and hoisted banners. The sounding of the white conch invoked the protection of all the guardian deities.

From the outset, the Seven Fair Maidens of Ling were like goddesses moving through pleasure gardens, swaying gracefully as they offered juniper smoke and prayers. Then as they watched the spectacle from Naga Downs, Ne'uchung, Drukmo's close friend and cousin, was reminded of several recent and prophetic dreams that she had had. She gave them voice in a song. Her dreams had portrayed Joru not only as the destined winner of the race, but as a leader and a husband to Drukmo, his queen, and foresaw that good fortune would come to Ling. Drukmo, though she remained uneasy, took heart from the dream.

On the other hand, Tromo-tso, Trothung's daughter, was rather upset by Ne'uchung's song. Sneering, her head rocked back and forth like a hand drum while she swung her hair in annoyance. Bolts of displeasure shot from her eyes, and her nose wrinkled in irritation.

Her face simmered with anger, and when she could no longer contain herself, she spoke up. "Ne'uchung, listen to me. You, a mere mendicant's daughter, are both ignorant and arrogant. This dream-prophecy of yours is of no value. My father, Trothung, received golden, prophetic words directly from Hayagriva, the deity himself."

And with a song of her own Tromo-tso reiterated the prophecy that Trothung had relayed to the entire country, along with the conviction that her brother Dongtsen would triumph and the throne would pass to her family. She dismissed any thought that Joru was more than a short, poor beggar dressed in rags and oblivious to the proper manners of citizens. Summing up she added,

If there is a scarf for the one who comes in last,
That is all that that fool Joru could possibly win.
Dongtsen alone will wear the victory scarf.
If you have understood this, it is sweet to your ears.
If not, there is no way to explain.

Tromo-tso waited for a response, but Ne'uchung realized that further incendiary words would serve no purpose, as the race was underway and the victor would soon enough be known. Wisely she pretended temporary deafness. Drukmo saw the wisdom in Ne'uchung's silence, and though she realized that it would be pointless to argue, she couldn't help but speak.

She called out, "Long life to all of you, sisters! The outcome of the race will settle our differences. Please hear my song."[41]

Drukmo went on to remind them of the importance of the race and the difficulty of predicting the future. Then she named each warrior who was competing and described their particular virtues and attributes as well as those of their horses. She turned her singing to the progress of the race, becoming increasingly dismayed as Tromo-tso's words seemed to be coming true. Her brother Dongtsen was in fact well out in front on the lead horse, Turquoise Bird.

Gyatsha and a trail of warriors lagged behind and after them came straggling clusters of ordinary citizens on horseback, all still imagining a reserve of energy that would propel them ahead. Last of all was Joru who, Drukmo now saw, was accompanied by a lowly beggar named Khyishi Buyi Gu-ru [Gu-ru son of Khyishi], generally known sarcastically as Gu-ru.

Joru seemed either oblivious or unconcerned by their last-place position. As she finished her song, Drukmo took notice of Chipon's concerned expression and wondered anew how her

41. See Song Appendix, Song #7.

fate might unfold. She was so disheartened that now all she could bear to watch was the ground at her feet.

The horse race was now well underway, and the cadre of racer-warriors was heading out of view, rounding the foothills of a mountain to the east. A continuous and thunderous clamor filled the air, ricocheting from the hundreds of hooves battering the ground. The earth vibrated, and the heavens seemed to quiver. It created such havoc and chaos that the resting spirits of the land were stirred from the semi-conscious mental state in which they lived.

Three sister spirits in particular were roused, directly into a state of fury. Bent on protecting their homes, Tiger Head, Leopard Head, and Black Bear Head emerged from their caves and in spirit-thought communed, *We three sisters can see nothing but destruction and defilement of our land by these many horses and their arrogant riders. The zodor are distracted by the race itself and do not seem to care about or even notice the consequences. But we see what is happening, and in retaliation we will bring disease to the warriors and death to the horses. Today all of Tibet has offended us, and we will shower them with our wrath.*

At that moment, the riders and spectators saw a small black cloud in the northern sky that, with frightening speed, grew so large that the earth joined the sky in deepest darkness. And in tandem, a frigid wind howled across the land. As the sisters prepared to add walnut-sized hail and devastating thunderbolts, Joru realized that, even if it cost him the race, he had to stop these three sisters and their wrathful actions.

Without hesitating, Joru left the course of the race just as the last of the riders passed from the view of the spectators. He confronted the sister spirits as they sat together, positioned before a blazing fire, and performed their aeolian magic. He revealed to them the power of compassion to heal the wounds of the earth, and the sisters saw that, if Joru were to win and rule over

Ling, the sacredness of the environment would be preserved. They developed devotion for Joru and a deeper understanding of the interconnectedness of all beings. They withdrew their magic and retreated to their respective caves to contemplate what they had just been shown.

The darkness drained away, leaving the expanse of blue sky over the race area. Joru finally realized that he had fallen far behind and galloped toward the course. He soon caught up with the beggar Gu-ru, who was also lagging, and decided to offer him a deal. First he reminded Gu-ru that he, Joru, was Gogmo's son and destined to win the race.

Just that morning, Joru went on, he had overheard Drukmo saying that, if there were a pair of contestants who raced together on the same horse and won, they would share the prizes and that she could accept this result if it brought peace and prosperity to Ling.

Joru pointed out the obvious: they were both almost hopelessly far behind. But then he intimated that, although his own horse might appear to be an ordinary horse, he was in fact the fastest steed running. And despite Gu-ru's added weight, they would be assured victory, even riding double. After they won, they could easily share the kingdom, all the money, and Drukmo herself. Joru suggested that the beggar's only chance of winning was for them to join forces.

Suspicious, Gu-ru thought, *This Joru has evil intentions toward everyone, and he was cast out of Ling. Now, woefully behind, he has latched onto me, feigning camaraderie. Like so many others, he is probably planning to rob or kill me.*

He said to Joru, "You are full of lies and treachery, and I have a lifetime of experience in the risks of gullibility. As the proverbs say, *On top of not having enough to eat, a debt is incurred.* I may be a beggar, but I am not a fool. The throne of Ling, the wealth of Kyalo, and the hand of Drukmo, this is not a prize that could be split, and even if one of us were somehow to win, either way I would not want to share it."

Insulted by the whole exchange, Gu-ru cracked his whip and raced ahead, leaving Joru and his horse in a cloud of dust. Joru lowered the golden whip, barely grazing Wild Kyang, and the horse took off. Wild Kyang pulled up alongside Gu-ru's horse, and without breaking stride, kicked its flank. With that, the horse was flung a mile away into the mountain foothills, while at the same time Gu-ru was swallowed whole by Wild Kyang.

With considerable alarm Gu-ru found himself inside the steed's stomach, but just a moment later he had been expelled in a great pile of steaming horse manure. Man and horse thus defeated, Gu-ru was left with no hope of continuing, and he returned home.

By now Joru had caught up with Sheep-a-peep Ngo-luk. This great and handsomely muscled warrior was called Sheep-a-peep because he was so beautiful that even sheep craned their necks when he passed. Joru sang a song to put him to the test.

> The song is Ala Ala Ala.
> Thala leads the melody.
> If you do not recognize me,
> I am Joru, Gogmo's cherished son.
> I am of the Mukpo Clan
> And heir to the lineage of King Senglon.
> I alone have received the name Joru.
> I was unjustly expelled from Ling
> With no choice but to stand up for my own dignity.
> Well, Ngo-luk,
> Among handsome men, you are the most handsome.
> While I, Joru,
> Among ugly men, am the ugliest.
> Among sons who come from the same paternal lineage,

How is it that some are handsome and others ugly?
Among the ancient arrows of a single quiver,
How is it that some are short and others long?
We should apportion appearances fairly,
With bodies neither handsome nor ugly,
Height neither tall nor short,
And wealth neither great nor small.
Over my many previous lifetimes,
I have been virtuous
And without evil thoughts.
Why is it that I am cursed with this ugly body?
Therefore, you and I
Must balance our outward appearances and our inward
    qualities
And share beauty as though we were one.
If you have understood this, it is sweet to your ears.
If not, there is no way to explain.

After Joru sang, Ngo-luk thought deeply about what he
had heard. He had often wondered about his own physical
beauty and why others, much more virtuous than he, were
unattractive. Joru certainly was ugly. Yet what he said pointed
toward a deep understanding. Acknowledging this, devotion
and faith for Joru arose in this beautiful man's heart. He suddenly understood that we live in a world of illusion, filled with
arbitrary appearances and karma too complex for an ordinary
person to grasp.

His respect for Joru deepened, and he felt very lucky to have
had an intimate meeting with him. He sensed that likely Joru
was testing him or at least playing some kind of joke.

Reflecting on this, he said, "I have no possessions worthy
of you, Joru. But please grant me your blessings and protection. Furthermore, everything that you find contemptible about

your appearance, give to me, and if I have anything you deem worthy, please take it for yourself." He offered this song.

> The song is Ala Ala Ala.
> Thala leads the melody.
> If you do not recognize me,
> I am called Ngo-luk of Agé,
> One famed for his good looks.
> But appearance is mere flesh and skin.
> *Handsome* and *ugly* are simply two of mind's endless
>   labels.
> Either way the body is fare for vultures and dogs.
> A guru may look good in robes,
> But without experience and realization, is only one more
>   stuffed shirt.
> Beauty is a matter of clothes and adornments,
> But without virtue it is a sham.
> Being handsome does not keep you warm.
> Being attractive does not fill your stomach.
> Beauty and ugliness are mere aspects of mind's
>   confusion.
> You who are the wondrous being, Joru,
> May your buddha activity be limitless.
> If you have heard this, it is an ornament for your ears.
> If not, there is no way to explain.

Along with the song, Sheep-a-peep offered his colorful hat. Joru replaced his own antelope hat with it and in appreciation gave Ngo-luk a crystal vase filled with ambrosia as well as a multicolored scarf. Then he rode on, with Wild Kyang gathering speed and raising his own cloud of dust as he overtook many of the warriors. Glancing back, Joru saw the learned diviner Kunshé Thigpo, now a few paces back.

Joru pulled up gently on the reins and held up his horse until the diviner was alongside and respectfully begged for a divination, emphasizing that, in spite of previous assurances of his victory, he was now quite far behind. Feeling like one lone yak amid a massive herd, Joru was ready to give up, but as was customary, he gave a golden coin to the diviner who saw the sincerity and desperation in Joru's request for a prophecy. Although they were in the midst of a race with so much at stake, Joru waited patiently for a response.

Knowing that his customary divination would be too lengthy, Kunshé Thigpo took out his divination cord. The divination cord has six strands into which the soothsayer concentrates his mind and, placing four knots, reads the relationships between the knots and the colored strands, revealing the prophecy. Compared to the usual *mo* divination done with a nine by nine or eighteen by eighteen board, the cord divination had the great advantage of the rapidity with which an answer could be given. So it was that the diviner placed the knots and let the threads fall. Reading the divination, he sang.

> The song is Ala Ala Ala.
> Thala leads the melody.
> May this telling be true and clear.
> As for Joru, the child of Gogmo,
> If he races will the victory scarf be his,
> And with this victory, will he become a good leader
> And Drukmo's worthy bridegroom?
> With the six strands of the divination cord,
> May this prediction be swift and unerring.
> First, the sky knot of the life force is cast
> And confirms the vastness of your skillful means.
> Second, the earth knot of the life force is cast
> And foresees the immutable quality of your compassion.

The throne will be yours
And all beings will find happiness in your reign,
Drukmo will become your wife
And, though your marriage will see separation,
You will ultimately return to each other.
Joru, good fortune will follow you.
No divination could be better than this.
If you have understood, it is sweet to your ears.
If not, there is no way to explain further.

Joru took these tidings to heart. The erudition and wisdom of the diviner were evident. Joru placed a stainless white scarf around Kunshé Thigpo's neck, with a sincere request that, if he, Joru, were to win the race, the diviner would become his trusted advisor.

Then after a moment, Joru sped off on his horse. Eventually he caught up with the doctor Kunga Nyima. Knowing the doctor to be quite proud, Joru thought it would be amusing to tease him. He took off Sheep-a-peep's fine hat, replaced it with his own hideous antelope-head hat, and pretended to be extremely ill. He complained of nearly every symptom that he could imagine: that his body was always cold, that he was unrelentingly fatigued and depressed and that he had insufferable insomnia, racking pain in his upper abdomen, and icy winds in his lower abdomen. In fact, he said, he had such pain in all his limbs that he could barely move and his sweet mother had given up all hope. He rolled off of his horse in a miserable heap in front of the doctor and moaned.

Kunga Nyima thought, *I do not have all my healing potions with me, but I can check his pulses, and I do have a few remedies. Maybe if this is a short-lived illness, I can cure it.*

He carefully checked Joru's pulses, examined his tongue and his skin, and looked into his eyes. Nowhere could he see signs of disease. It occurred to him that this known trickster might be testing him. Adopting an optimistic manner, he explained to Joru that he was just fine, and that he should show courage and continue the race.

Much impressed, Joru thought, *This doctor is no imposter.* Placing a white scarf around Kunga Nyima's neck, Joru said that he envisioned that the doctor would one day be the court physician. Once again he rode off.

On he went, faster and faster, and soon he heard Chipon shouting to him, "Joru, what have you been doing? You fool, you had best hurry! Can you not see that Dongtsen is about to seize the throne?"

Joru replied, "Uncle Chipon, fast or slow, it does not matter how I race. It is not about speed. I am neither the tortoise nor the hare. Do you understand me?" So saying, off he rode, in a direction away from the throne and away from the finish line.

Needless to say, Trothung's greatest fear was that Joru would beat Dongtsen, so that when he saw Joru riding off in the wrong direction, he was beside himself with joy.

More certain than ever that Hayagriva's prophecy would turn out to be true, he shouted to anyone who could hear, "Now Dongtsen will win for sure!" And then he called after Joru, "Joru, what are you doing racing back and forth like a madman? Do you not see that my son Dongtsen is winning this race?"

Playfully, Joru answered, "I have reached the golden throne twice already, but I did not want to sit on a brocade cushion. However, although no one is ahead of Dongtsen, recall the words of the proverbs, *Although a man should not sweat, his forehead is sweating. A horse should not quiver, but his calves are quivering. When good fortune comes to the mouth, the tongue accidentally pushes it out.* No matter how high your position in Ling, it will not help you win the wager today. No horse is faster than my

Kyang, and he has not yet broken a sweat." Dissembling, he said, "Actually, I am not sure I am meant for the throne or it for me. And though I reached the throne earlier, unseen, I did not claim it. Perhaps I will drop out, and in that case, maybe Dongtsen *will* win."

Rattled, Trothung thought, *If I do not stymie Joru, who knows what will happen?*

Then he said, "Nephew, you are right. The winnings of this contest will be a curse, and the race itself is a farce, luring reckless youth and leading them astray. I completely agree with you: the throne is no great prize. To be sovereign over these unruly hordes will offer nothing but heartache. The wealth of Kyalo would only be a noose around your neck; you would be envied and despised and then betrayed by your dearest friends and closest relatives. And marriage to a highborn woman like Drukmo is bound to bring suffering. It's clear that your only prize will be misery and sorrow, my sweet nephew."

Joru replied, "Yes, Precious Uncle, perhaps your words could be true, but I have some thoughts."

> The song is Ala Ala Ala.
> Thala leads the melody.
> Uncle, I have no need for your advice —
> My repugnant antelope-head hat that vexes the fathers
>   and uncles
> Urges on the day that I wear a chieftain's white helmet.
> My calfskin chuba that houses the lice that bite
>   my skin
> Drives my desire to wear a long-sleeved cloak.
> The insults and spittle that rain down on me
> Guide my intention to be a just and able leader.
> Enduring the loneliness of being without a companion
> Fuels my longing that Drukmo and I bond.

In fact, the time grows short and my intention stronger.
Now, Uncle, keep this in your mind.

Abruptly Joru rode off into the wind, back toward the thick of the race. This upset Trothung, but now he saw that there was nothing more that he could do.

Soon Joru saw his elder brother Gyatsha a few paces ahead and thought to himself, *Now there is a man who wouldn't hesitate to raise his sword toward an enemy. There is still time for one more prank.* He disguised himself as a great shadowy warrior atop a strikingly black horse and bore down on Gyatsha, brandishing an iron spear and shouting *"Ki! So! Ho!"*

Gyatsha saw him barreling down and thought, *That has to be a mara or a rakshasa trying to disrupt this country's great day. What an insult to Ling and all the warriors. Even at the cost of my life, I will fight this assailant. Whatever the outcome, I will have no regret.* Gyatsha grabbed the handle of his sword, drawing it from its scabbard, and then swung it over his head and pointed it threateningly at Joru's neck. The disguised Joru drew his own sword and sang.

> The song is Ala Ala Ala.
> Thala leads the melody.
> Well then, man in white riding a pale white horse,
> Listen, for I have some stories to tell you.
> Last wintertime, Drukmo of Kyalo
> Was traveling alone across the valley when I met her.
> She promised me
> All the wealth and possessions of Kyalo,
> Saying they were hers to give.
> The time has come for me to claim my prize,
> But first I will fill the hills with corpses
> And the valleys with blood.

Either I will conquer all of Ling
Or I am not the great warrior of Dud and Hor.
If you have understood this, it is sweet to your ears.
If not, there is no way to explain.

Gyatsha, proud and loyal warrior that he was, replied, "All this, the wealth of Kyalo, is no one's for the taking, least of all yours, a demon of Hor. If I allowed this, I would be shamed, and I will know no shame. I possess a great sword, melded by mystical blacksmiths and forged of limitless power and hardest steel. That sword and my determination make the outcome certain."

Joru, still impersonating a demon warrior, accepted the challenge, and Gyatsha raised his sword and struck with lightning speed, putting his full strength into a single blow. He expected to encounter dense armor, but his sword struck only empty air. Spinning in a full circle, he saw Joru in front of him, smiling at his scowling face.

Joru, having confirmed Gyatsha's selflessness and thinking that he might have gone a bit too far in what he had thought a test, said softly, "Gyatsha, if you, big-hearted and kind, are not interested in the throne or its status and you take time off from trying to win the race to protect Ling, then being the beggar that I am, I certainly am not entitled to the victor's prize. Do you understand?" As he was speaking, he had dismounted and, dressed in his coarse calfskin chuba, which crawled with lice and maggots, now stood looking respectfully up at Gyatsha.

"Joru," Gyatsha said, "there is no point in my being put to the test since the divine prophecies of the gods and gurus repeatedly say that it is you who will quell the four maras and win this race. You are the one who will be victorious over the enemy. I was only thinking to protect Ling; that is the reason I was going to fight the warrior. I have neither hope nor desire for the golden throne or Drukmo, and were I to win, I would step aside for you. As they say, 'A buddha never tires of working for sentient beings.' Joru, now is the time for your magical powers, for if you delay any longer, you will lose, Ling will decay inexorably, and only war and misery will be left."

Thinking that Gyatsha was probably right, Joru mounted his horse and rode off to meet his karma.

CHAPTER 12

Aunt Manéné makes her last appearance, cajoling
   her charge.
Joru finally rouses himself and wins the race,
And feasts and celebrations are held as he takes his
   rightful place as Gesar.
Trothung and Denza have a final go at what it all
   might mean.

L EAVING GYATSHA BEHIND, Joru had continued onward in
       the general direction of the golden throne and the finish
       line. A crashing sound interrupted the rhythmic throb-
bing of the galloping horses. The entire sky shook, but the
ground quaked only below the hooves of Wild Kyang, and
Joru, startled to his core, was nearly tossed off of the saddle.

He looked up, and in the space in front in the midst of shimmering rainbow light, five white clouds had appeared. Atop
the clouds were the five nearly all-powerful Tsering [Long Life]
Dakinis. They held longevity arrows and trays filled with jewels, precious objects, burning incense, and candles, and each
held her unique personal object of power. Most impressive of
the five was Manéné, seated on top of the middle cloud and
holding an arrow in the crook of her arm, a mirror in her left
hand, and a treasure vase in her right. They radiated outer
strength and inner wisdom. Surrounding this grand assem-
blage danced a retinue of countless other dakinis. Horizon to
horizon, the sky shook.

At that moment, Manéné turned the sky an icy black and

roused a bitter wind that froze Joru to the spot. She twisted up her face and yelled, "Joru, yours is a most exalted rebirth, and yet you squander it. Auspicious signs marked your birth, flowers rained, and celestial beings blessed your baby body. Padmasambhava himself arranged the Buddhas to impart power to you. The country of Ling needs you. Compete like there is no tomorrow because, if you lose, I can assure you that you will wish tomorrow never to come. Dongtsen has moved ahead of you and is within grasp of the throne. Your faults of overconfidence, sloth, and distraction will prevent you benefiting anyone but yourself. Your drala siblings might be able to catch the horse Turquoise Bird, but not its rider, Dongtsen. The time for your foolishness is well past. I assume you understand my words?"

With that, unimaginably the sky grew even darker and the air still colder, and with another loud clap, Manéné and her entire retinue disappeared, leaving Joru shaken.

Meanwhile, downhill from where they were, was the golden throne, deep in a ravine to the side of a prominent rocky outcropping. Dongtsen was perilously close to winning when Joru's brother Gyatsha and the drala Nyentag caused Dongtsen's horse to go lame. Turquoise Bird struggled heroically to go on, but he collapsed.

Dongtsen tugged on his bridle and put the whip to his horse's side, but the poor beast could not right himself. Realizing that he was nearly upon the throne, Dongtsen abruptly ran toward it, abandoning his horse. But the land spirits and Joru's sibling drala magically kept moving the throne farther and farther away. Dongtsen ran faster and faster, but the more Dongtsen ran, the farther out of reach the throne moved. Just as Gogmo could never catch up with her dri, so Dongtsen could not gain the throne.

At that moment, Joru and Wild Kyang tore into the ravine.

However, it appeared to Dongtsen as though there were many Jorus, all chattering to each other, like crows, about eating the flesh of the fallen horse and speculating that, if they ate Turquoise Bird, his flesh would be fat and delicious. Some of them began to remove Turquoise Bird's tack. They pulled out their knives as if they were about to start butchering the poor animal.

Dongtsen turned back from the throne, at full tilt sprinting to his horse. He beseeched the many Jorus, calling out, "Please do not hurt my beloved horse! I will do whatever you say."

These words had barely left Dongtsen's mouth when the many Jorus vanished. The real Joru replied that he had no wish to harm Turquoise Bird but extracted a promise from Dongtsen that, if in the future he had need for the horse, it would be his to use. Then with his mouth at Turquoise Bird's ear, Joru screamed the sound of "*Ki!*" three times. In an instant, the horse revived and began cavorting about. Dongtsen was overcome with emotion but nonetheless elated.

Joru crossed the finish line. Some riders were still streaming through the ravine, but others, seeing their defeat, had slowed their mounts to a trot or had already alighted and were milling about. To the cheers of both spectators and contestants, Joru ascended the golden throne. As he did, he was transformed from his ugly, brutish boyhood to the full magnificence of an adult warrior.

The major and minor marks of his body blazed forth, and his true nature blossomed. No one could remember such a day in their lives or in the lives of their ancestors or their ancestors' ancestors. History itself was silenced as this congruity of an entire country's karma was entered into the great book that records all. It had been through the culmination of both earthly and cosmic forces that Joru had attained the throne. Joru had hidden the majesty of his true form, just as the clouds obscure the sun or the beauty of the lotus is hidden in the mud from which it arises.

From the rainbow tent of the sky, the many deities and guardians sang songs of auspiciousness. A fortnight of astonishing celebration and feasting ensued, culminating in a day and night when the midday sun, the full moon, and the stars of the night were simultaneously visible. This marvel was witnessed by beings below, upon, and above the earth.

As the commotion set off by the end of the race was winding down, the supreme deity Hayagriva, Lord of Horses Wild Kyang, neighed three times, causing the door of the treasury of Crystal Crag to open. Magyal Pomra, the local spirit of the mountain; the nyen Gedzo, the local spirit of the earthen plains; and Gogmo's father, the naga king Tsugna Rinchen, came forth to welcome Joru who had now taken his rightful and prophesied name: Gesar Norbu Dradul. He revealed the many treasures found in Crystal Crag. Among them were magical helmets, shields and armor, a life essence amulet, a tiger-skin quiver, and leopard-skin bow case, as well as armor, a belt, and boots. As he donned these items, he became the great warrior that he was destined to be.

Brahma offered prayers and ninety-nine divine arrows. The sky god Rahu offered a great bow, Magyal Pomra an elegant woven steel sword, Gedzo a lance, the naga king Tsugna a lasso, Vajrasadhu a slingshot, the drala Nyentag Marpo a thunderbolt, and King Lijin Harleg a great ax. Warriors and chieftains alike offered scarves, treasure vases, animal skins, a precious rightward-coiling conch, silk brocades, jewels and gems, turquoise, and coral. Each bowed to Gesar in turn and made his or her offering.

Every citizen of Ling gave what they could, great or small, and heaps of ceremonial scarves were piled high before Gesar. Many of the drala brothers and sisters of Gesar, as well as

Manéné and her dakini compatriots, manifested as young children, beating drums, blowing conches, sounding cymbals, dancing wildly, and offering scarves. They produced a raucous and delightful din.

Just as the extraordinary was beginning to seem ordinary, the people of Ling were beginning to doubt what they were witnessing, wondering if it were real, or rather a dream or an illusion. Gesar sang this doha called Unceasing Natural Vajra Sound.

> Ala is the way the song is sung.
> Thala sets the melody.
> If you do not recognize me,
> I am of the ancestral lineage of the nyen
> And a descendant of the water-bound nagas.
> I was given the name Joru among the earth-bound
>   humans
> By my brother Gyatsha
> And my spiritual name Gesar Norbu Dradul
> By Guru Padmasambhava.
> I came to this world realm
> Not to wander in impure samsara
> Nor to dwell in the pure state of nirvana,
> But to work for the welfare of all sentient beings.
> Please attend to my words.
> I am the dharma sovereign who teaches the ten virtues.[42]
> All the mighty warriors of Ling
> Are pure in this way,
> Though from the womb they are thick with obscurations.
> Some have total recall in their dreams,
> And others only a glimpse of meditative experience,

42. See glossary.

But ultimately all are pure and their courage unrivaled.
I, Gesar Norbu Dradul, have come to the golden kingdom
    of Ling
To promote the happiness and well-being of all people,
To establish the Buddha's teachings,
And to uphold the dharma of the ten virtues.
In the regions of the demons of the dark side,
The sacred dharma is not understood.
Nor are the teachings of cause and fruition respected.
They have not been liberated through forceful means,
And they lack the fortune to be tamed with peaceful
    compassion.
In order to directly pacify all of them,
I will lead the wrathful army.
Other than the general enemies of the Buddha's
    teachings,
I, Gesar, have no personal enemies.
Other than the general welfare of all beings,
I, Gesar, have no personal aims.
It has fallen to me to accomplish the general welfare,
As has been prophesied.
If we spread the teachings of the Buddha
And place all sentient beings in bliss,
The welfare of Ling will be accomplished as a matter
    of course.
From this day onward,
Be brave in knowing that it is virtue
That is the swift path for perfecting the two
    accumulations.[43]
If your mind overcomes dualistic fixation,

---

43. The two accumulations are merit and wisdom.

Your body and speech will not be mired in samsara
and nirvana.
All beings born into evil, even if slain,
Unless they cross the threshold to ultimate bliss,
Nothing will have been accomplished.
Now, people of Ling, will you accept me?
Do you have confidence in me?
Until now, my name and my form were hidden
As the time to tame the maras had not yet arrived.
Today I show myself directly.
May all sentient beings be liberated,
And may their minds turn to the pure and sacred
dharma.
If you have understood this, it is sweet to your ears.
If not, there is no way to explain.

Thus he sang, and everyone took his teaching to heart. No one spoke a contrary word. All beings, gods and humans alike, threw flowers of celebration, while Chipon brought out the *Mother Chronicles*, the original, ancient chronicles of the Mukpo Clan, and offered them to Gesar along with many more ceremonial scarves, singing,

The song begins Ala Ala Ala.
Thala leads the melody.
The sky is filled with everlasting victory banners.
In the middle, the virtuous mark of the humans
Is the sound of the victorious gods as *Ki! Ki! So! So!*
Below, among the offerings of the nagas,
Is the wish-fulfilling rain.
The gods celebrating with delight,
The humans joyfully dancing,
The merriment of the nagas,

Together set the clouds in motion.
Demons wail at their loss.
I offer this single white scarf to you, Gesar,
So that all the drala and werma above
May be like the sun and its rays,
Inseparably accompanying you.
Given that you possess stainless wisdom,
It is not appropriate to offer you this prophetic book.
Nevertheless, I will place these ancient chronicles in
    your hands.
May I, the sovereign of the clan of Rong, Chipon Gyalpo,
Be inseparable with you as my lord and I as your
    minister.
By offering you this single white scarf,
Together may our buddha activity transform all to
    dharma.
Never separating from you,
May the purpose of beings be perfectly realized.
From this day onward,
The wishes of Ling will be fulfilled.
Prepare to sing the songs of delight,
Prepare to dance the dance of happiness.
Keep all of this in your heart.

The entire populace developed deep, irreversible faith and
devotion. From the earth itself, music resounded, while white
flowers descended like snow from the heavens. For the next
thirteen days, everyone sang and danced in celebration.

The festivities were hosted by the Seven Fair Maidens of
Ling, all beautiful, and all with their hearts and minds so ten-
derly in the present moment that tears of recognition of the
preciousness and transience of human life came to all. As they
began to dance, Drukmo asked her cousin Ne'uchung to bring

her the golden cup filled with longevity wine and properly aged beer.

With both hands draped in a long white khata, Drukmo held up the auspicious cup, raising it and offering the nectar three times, and then sang a song extolling Gesar and his victory and ending with these last verses expressing her love and devotion.[44]

Lord Great Lion, the golden mountain of your presence
Is as though embraced by the youthful clouds of dawn.
Your armor and weapons are radiant,
And your authentic presence is unrivaled.
Lord Great Lion, like a blazing jewel,
You emanate a shower of benefit and well-being.
Please hold me inseparably.
At the tip of a pliant stem is a lovely blue lotus,
And like a hovering honeybee,
I offer myself to you, Lord Great Lion.
Beautiful to hear is the voice intoxicated by great bliss,
And with a song like that of the kalavinka bird,
I offer myself to you, Lord Great Lion.
The waves of wandering thoughts, when overcome by
    transcendent joy,
Are an ocean of amrita of bliss-emptiness, free from
    thought.
Partake of this, Lord Great Lion.
The jeweled ship of the wealth of Kyalo
Is guided by the oar of compassion.
Make it your own, Lord Great Lion.
From now until the heart of enlightenment,

44. See Song Appendix, Song #8 for the complete song.

Accomplish the great purpose of the teachings and of all
beings.
May I, like a body and its shadow,
Be inseparable from you, Lord Great Lion.
Gesar, hold this in your heart.

Following her song, other songs and scarves were offered,
and then Joru's antelope-head hat, his fringed calfskins, and
worn rawhide boots were buried underground for good luck.
Finally, it was Trothung's turn to offer prostrations and a khata.

Then as he had promised to do, Gesar returned to Trothung
all the things that he had taken in the guise of Joru, such as Trothung's materials for yogic activity, including his white willow
staff and his nine-edged prosperity sack, with the qualification
that Trothung would lend them back to him when the time
came to confront the enemies of Ling.

Trothung agreed, saying, "Yes, these magical implements
will be at your disposal whenever you have need of them."

The celebration was coming to a close. Gesar turned to
Drukmo, and together they left for the palace Sengdruk Tagtsé,
with their horses walking behind them and the crowds parting
as they passed.

Denza came over to her husband, Trothung, and said, "Well
then, now what do you make of the wager of the horse race that
was predicted by your Hayagriva? How about your precious
golden throne, not to mention your sweet and lovely Drukmo
and all that wealth? The other warriors are no doubt disappointed, but none were played as such a fool as you, the laughingstock of Ling."

Trothung, unable to dampen his tendency to self-
aggrandizement, replied, "Oh, Lady Denza, I was the one who
was given the prophecy by Hayagriva. I have been working
only for the good of the kingdom. I have not for one moment,

not for one thimbleful's worth of time, had the least concern for myself."

From the moment that Gesar was enthroned, just as a snake sheds its skin, the land of Ling and its inhabitants inclined toward the attitude of loving-kindness, steeped in the compassionate wisdom that is that most primordial and universal human aspiration, that to never wish harm to another.

And so it was that Gesar was born in a wondrous manner and, prevailing in the horse race, won the throne, King Kyalo's fortune, and the hand of Drukmo. In the years that follow, Gesar will bring glory to the Land of Snow.

Song Appendix

Song #1, Chapter 3

I am the guru Padmasambhava, the Lotus Born One.
I came from the continent of Chamara
For the benefit of beings of the three realms
And went to the land of the nagas
To save them from the suffering of disease.
They expressed their gratitude by offering me this nagini
   maiden,
And finally I came to Gog.
This, finally, is the singularity that unites these events.
This nagini is to be your stepdaughter,
This Turquoise Tent in Nine Partitions
Your prized treasure,
This *One Hundred Thousand Verse Wisdom Sutra*
Your object of devotion,
And this naga beast, a dri with turquoise horns,
Will crown the wealth of your livestock.
Receive these blessings.
Do not trade any of these treasures for profit.
Keep them well, and gradually realization will come to you.
This nagini maiden must not be betrothed.
Keep her as your cherished daughter.
Ralo Tonpa, you will rise in status,
And the district of Gog will expand and increase.
Son of noble family, whatever you desire will occur.
If you do not understand the song, there is nothing to explain.
Ralo Tonpa, keep this in your heart.

Song #2, Chapter 4

The song begins Ala Ala Ala.
Thala leads the melody.
If you do not recognize this place,
It is the flourishing valley of the land of Gog.
If you do not recognize me,
I am the daughter of the naga king Tsugna Rinchen
And the youngest of the three royal princesses,
Yelga Dzéden, now called Gogmo.
I was given by the great teacher Padmasambhava
To the royal family of Ralo of Gog,
Into their temporary care,
And told that, when the time was right, my destiny would
    arrive.
I have lived as Ralo's daughter for some time,
A time of great change for the people of Gog,
But now I do not know where the families have journeyed.
Perhaps they have gone north toward a snowy wasteland.
As for the dri, it was laden with the naga treasures,
Including the Nine-Partitioned Azure Tent
And the *One Hundred Thousand Verse Sutra*.
The Gog pack animals could not bear this burden,
And we barely managed to load these treasures onto the dri.
Like renegades fleeing a massacre, we traveled by night.
The dri turned back for home,
But only I noticed.
All that my father Tsugna had entrusted to Gog
I could not bear to give up, so I rode in quick pursuit.
I was catching up with the dri, and when I grew close,
I dismounted my steed and ran on foot.
Unable to capture her, I lost my way
And wandered after the dri until time itself seemed to stop.

Pain and pleasure, good and ill, your fortune, these three—
Aren't they designs drawn by your own karma?
Earlier this morning
In a state of foggy sleep, unbidden, a dream came to me:
A boy with a turquoise topknot
Who wore blue water-silk garments
Gave me a precious turquoise pail
Filled to the brim with milk to quench my thirst.
He told me not to abandon the dri, but to follow after her,
And the benefit foretold by Padma would be accomplished.
And so I did as the dream bade.
I come into your midst, unburdened and free.
If you understand these words, it is sweet to your ears.
If you do not, there is no way to explain it.
Cousins and uncles of Ling, bear this in mind.

Song #3, Chapter 6

Ala Ala Ala begins the song.
Thala leads the melody.
This is the manifest cannibal demon land belonging to Joru.
In case you do not recognize me,
I am Denma Jangtra, a humble minister of Ma.
Joru, listen, and I will tell you the way things are.
All that we perceive may be illusion.
Whether corpse, mirage, or rainbow,
If recognized, are neither good nor ill.
If not, then illusion will be held as real.
Representing the people of Ling,
I am here to beseech you, the child Joru.
But when I approached, you unleashed a torrent of illusion.
Then, clearing it away, my eyes are opened,

Not to be closed again.
Divine Joru, keep this in your mind.

SONG #4, CHAPTER 7

The song is Ala Ala Ala.
Thala leads the melody.
Guru Padma Uddiyana
And Auntie Manéné Nammen Karmo
Surrounded by one hundred thousand motherly dakinis,
Today come here to befriend me.
I am the one known as King Joru.
Outwardly, I am a beggar boy, a lonely vagrant.
Inwardly, I am the pillar that supports the drala.
Secretly, I am the embodiment of all the victorious ones.
Residents of the six provinces, listen to my song.
In this valley of Ma, the great snow lion's belly,
The west reaches to the land of India,
The east reaches to the land of China,
The north directly connects to Achen Hor,
While in the south, the land connects to Ati Rong.
Here the Ma River winds in three loops.
The first loop is the portion of land called Ling.
The remaining two are the inhospitable plains of the land
    of Hor.

In the highlands of Ma, the sky is like the eight spokes
    of a wheel,
And the land is beautifully arranged, like an eight-petaled
    lotus.
In between, the great mountains appear like the eight
    auspicious symbols.

Of all lands, it is by far the finest, a land for the most revered
    leader.
This portion of the land is to be given to Nyibum Daryag
    [Excellent Banner of One Hundred Thousand Suns]
Of the Elder Lineage of the eight Serpa brothers,
Together with the Go'jo and Achag tribes.
From Upper Ma to the thirteen mountains of Tsé-lha,
Take your seat, like the sun embracing the golden mountains.

The sunny side of the valley of Ma is like a lotus naturally
    blooming,
A land where great bucks frolic in play
And where the brown wild yaks butt their horns.
Because the grass is so abundant, the baby yaks get lost in it.
Because the trees are so dense, the deer hide there.
This is the land where the great ones should reside.
This portion of the land is to be given to Anu Paseng
    [Courageous Youthful Lion]
Of the Middle Lineage of the six provinces of Ombu,
Together with the three tribes, Ga, Dru, and Den.
From Middle Ma to the place where the nine high mountains
    unite,
Take your seat, like beautiful flowers in a meadow.

The land of Madro Lu-gu'i Khelkhung
Is a place where the winds pay taxes by scattering the grass
And the river pays its due by carrying logs downstream.
The backdrop of mountains resembles a drawn curtain
And the Ma River, a water offering.
This is the land where a chieftain of great power should
    reside.
This portion of land is to be given to Uncle Chipon Gyalpo
And his son Yutag.

On the great shady side of Ma, in the wealth valley of
    Drag-do [Lower Crag],
There is a fence of one hundred and eight stupas
And a thousand and two shrines with one hundred
    thousand tsa-tsas.
This is the land where the subterranean naginis constantly
    bow down
And the animals of the humans and nagas mingle.
It is a land where a sovereign leader should reside.
This portion of land should go to the great father, King
    Senglon,
And his son Gyatsha Zhal-lu of Bumpa.

In the six upper regions of Ma called Darlung Chugmo
    [Wealthy Silk Valley]
The plains resemble a perfectly arranged mandala,
With the herbs and flowers as the mounds arranged upon it.
The streams and rivers look like knotted silk scarves.
This is the land where a leader of great family lineage should
    reside.
This portion of land goes to Rinchen Darlu [Precious Silk
    Scarf]
Of the Lesser Lineage of the four districts of Muchang,
Together with the tribes of Kyalo and Tshazhang.
From Lower Ma up to Lu-gu,
Take your seats, like arrows placed perfectly in a quiver.

In Sidpa Kholmo Rogdzong [Black Bellow Fortress of
    Existence],
The snow falls throughout the summer just as in winter,
And autumn and spring are but a driving blizzard.
If a human cries out, a demoness will answer.

If a dog cries out, then a fox wails in response.
In this land, until a mare reaches nine years of age,
She cannot birth a foal,
Until a young dri meets a stud for nine seasons,
Her calf will not be born,
And until the white prosperity sheep reaches three years
    of age,
Her lamb cannot be born.
The narrow passageways are roads as thin as throats,
While the plains are as expansive as lotus flowers in bloom.
This is a land where a mighty man should abide.
This rocky land will be given to Uncle Trothung.

In great Upper Ma, on the highest snow-capped peak,
Stallion caribou reign over the three highest mountains.
Musk deer take the middle white crags to be their fortress.
The lower region flows with rivers teeming with undulating
    fish.
A stomach empty in the morning will be full by night.
During the three months of summer, its mountain peaks
    are cool.
In the three months of winter, the valleys hold their warmth.
This is the land where a warrior should reside.
This will be the portion of land of Nyatsha Aten [Stable
    Nephew Fish].

Alpine willows thrive on the great black crests of Ma's
    mountain ridges,
The land where the tigers show their six smiles
And the great tribes dwell both in summer and winter.
This is the land where unruly warriors should reside.
This portion of land is given to Tag-rong's Zigphen.

In the valley of Jang in Ma where nine turquoise manes are
    braided,
Each mountain has eighteen secluded valleys,
And each plain is an eighteen days' journey.
The men gaze over and over at this very sight.
This is the land where the mighty warriors should reside.
This portion is given to Sengtak Adom [Lion Tiger Youthful
    Bear].

In Nyima Lebchen Porog [Raven Great Sun Flats],
The three months of spring come early,
And the three months of winter are not so very cold.
In the early morning, the sun envelops the homes,
And at sunset, day turns instantly to night.
The only minor drawback is the presence of enemies;
If a man lacks a brave heart, this is not the place for him.
This portion of land is for Cholu Darphen.

In Ma, on Churi Lhathang Tramo [Rippling Colorful Divine
    Plain],
The white husks of grain are like flocks of driven sheep.
There the sorrel mules scatter like herds of wild yaks.
It is a playful land where the flowers seem to dance.
This place, where the bees sing their little songs,
Is a land where one who is wise should reside.
This portion of land is for Tshazhang Denma Jangtra.

Between the lower mountains of Ma at Padma Khyung
    Dzong [Padma Garuda Fortress]
And a mountain that looks like a poisonous snake slithering
    downward
Is the rocky crag that resembles the mouth of a red Yama.
It is the passageway of the eight classes of maras and tsen,

A place of evil magicians unwanted even by our sworn
    enemies.
It is a land where one of power should reside.
This portion of land is for Gadé Bernag.

In the center of the land of Ma rests the uppermost hill,
Tashi Tsel [Auspicious Vermillion Hill], endowed with
    prosperity.
It is a land where the white-ridged dri who calve each year
    roam,
Where the supreme mare births twin foals,
And the white prosperity sheep continue to multiply.
It is a land where a wealthy person should reside.
This portion of land is for Kyalo Tonpa.

At the vista of Dzachen Khujug in Ma
Where the Golden Yak Pass in Hor meets the summit,
Is the winding path where the Hor bandits roam.
In this land you can see them clearly from afar.
This land is only for one who is swift-footed.
This portion of land is for Dongtsen Nang-ngu Apel [Mighty
    Glory of the Tribe].

In the valley of Dzatri Ga'u-ser [Golden Amulet Crag Throne]
    in Ma,
The high mountains rise snow-covered and rocky
Above the fortress of the forest, the tether of the earth.
This is the land where one of high rank should reside.
This portion of land will go to Michen Gyalwé Lhundrub.

In Ma on the sunny side of Dragkar Gudril [United White
    Crag]
Is a vast plain spread out like a carpet

And a great mountain that seems as though it is summoning
   guests.
This is a place where one of great decisiveness should abide.
This portion of land is for Sergyi Argham.

In the upper valley of Ma called Darthang Chugmo [Wealthy
   Silken Plain],
At the highest point are some three great valleys,
And in the foothills, three broad plains unite.
Here is the land where, summer and winter, the myriarchies
   barter.
This is a land where one with a great following should reside.
This portion of land is for Tongpon Treltsé [Highest-Ranking
   Chieftain of a Thousand].

At Datra Lungpé Sumdo [Colorful Silk Conjunction of Three
   Valleys],
The mountains are forested, musk deer reign,
And the resounding call of the cuckoo can first be heard.
In its lowlands of interlaced lakes and plains,
The first blooms of summer flowers can be seen.
This portion of land is for the one who enjoys luxury.
This portion of land is for Yuyag Gonpo [Protector of
   Excellent Turquoise].

In Ma Dru-gu Gu-lung Tramo [Colorful Valleys of Ma],
There are nomadic lands of spacious valleys and open paths.
Here it is warm and close to the farmers,
And the earth and stones to build a home are already there.
This portion of land goes to Lingchen Tharpa.

In Ma, at Nachen Damgyi Gongwa [Collar of Marshes and
   Bogs],

Is the cushion of the dense earth.
Here at the headwaters of the Ma River
Is the land where fathers and uncles should abide.
This portion of land goes to Namkha Serzhal [Golden Face
of Space].

In Ma, in Nyikhog Padma Lung [Sunny Lotus Valley],
Is the route travelers take when they are upward bound,
And when they return, it is the gathering place of wealth.
It is a marketplace where judgments and reputations are
made.
This is the place where a handsome cavalier should abide.
This portion of land goes to the three Ngo-luk brothers:
Tsangpé Ngo-luk [Brahma] of Agé,
Dar-jam Ngo-luk [Gentle Scarf] of Mupa,
And Sintsha Ngo-luk [Raksha Maternal Nephew] of Tag-rong.

Tradong Sinpo [Falcon Face Raksha],
Dza-zelmo Gang [Spotted Crag Hill Spur] of Ma,
And the shaded valley Lung-do [Dark Lower Valley]
Are sacred grounds that meet in the Ma Valley.
Only one of great merit can reside here.
This portion of land should go to those endowed with
karmic power,
Those praised with the name Victory Banner:
Guru Gyaltsen of Denma,
Nyima Gyaltsen of Kar-ru,
And Tharpa Gyaltsen of Nag-ru.

Buyi Phentag of Abar [Drawn Tiger Boy of Abar]
And Cha-nag Ponpo Singsing [Chieftain Black Metal],
Please take your seat on the land and join the tribes of the
Greater Lineage.

Changtri Ngamchen [Great Awesome Myriad Jackal] of Ombu
And the hero Nyima Lhundrub [Spontaneous Sun],
Please take your seat on the land and join the tribes of the
    Middle Lineage.

Gung-gi Marleb [Upper Red Plain] of Rongtsa
And Shalkar Gyangdrag [White Crystal Far Famed]
    of Bumpa,
Please take your seat on the land and join the tribes
    of the Lesser Lineage.

Bu-yag Drug-gyé [Handsome Son Dragon] of Kyalo
And Tshazhang Kyalo Trikor [Nephews of the Kyalo Tribe]
Can have whatever portion of land makes them happiest.

In the colorful valleys of Lower Ma, arranged like astrological
    charts,
Are the naturally originating playing stones of the
    gods-demons.
This is a land where a great magician should abide.
This portion of land goes to Khaché Migmar [Big Mouth
    Red Eye].

In the rich valley of Ja-shingnag Markhu Yolwa [Rich
    Rainbow Forest],
Which is the central land of Upper and Lower Ma,
If you look up, you can see the source of the Ma River,
And if you look down, you can see the Turquoise Valley.
This is a land where one of great decisiveness should abide.
This portion of land goes to the great arbiter Zuchen Werma.

In Upper Ma at Di-yag Tagthang [Tiger Plain Knolls]
Is the place where the people of the great provinces convene

And the travelers from China and Tibet stop over to rest.
It is for one who is a guardian of the general wealth
As well as the one who arranges meetings and councils.
This is a land where one of great power should abide.
This portion of land goes to Wangpo Darphen [Powerful
    Unfurled Silk].

In Middle Ma at Lu-gu'i Tséra,
All the plants are healing,
And the animals scented by medicinal herbs.
This is a place where a doctor should reside.
This portion of land goes to Kunga Nyima [All-Joyful Sun].

Upon the colorful ridged mountains of Ma,
At the convergence of three great valleys
And the confluence of the fords of three great rivers,
Is the land where a diviner should reside.
This portion of land goes to Kunshé Thigpo.

That mountain over there is Ab Mountain [Mole Mountain],
And this mountain here is Ur Mountain [Bird Mountain].
Where Ab and Ur merge,
The scurrying groundhogs come close enough to kill,
And the neighboring grouse come close enough to be game.
This is a place where one who is poor should reside.
This portion of land goes to my old friend Khyishi Gu-ru.

At the lower valley of Ma, where three turquoise valleys
    merge,
Is a land where there are more moles than lice
And the most delicious wild yams are found.
The Chinese tea merchants go up the staircase,
And the Ladakhi merchants come back down.

If one is begging, this is where provisions for a journey will
    be acquired.
If one waits, then the marks of success will come.
This is a place where a beggar should reside.
This portion of land goes to me and to my mother, Gogmo.

Even though previously I was cast out of Ling,
Once again, I will stay in Lower Ma.
Rather than having a belly full of undigested food,
Do not eat; rather keep an empty stomach.
Rather than accepting wages to carry a backbreaking load,
Wander the kingdom begging and enjoying inexhaustible food.
Rather than fathers and uncles lacking in affection,
Take delight in travelers who are free from love and hate.
In the ranks of the great tribes of Ling,
I, a beggar boy, had no hope of staying.
However, I am part of the paternal lineage,
And my mind must turn toward my clan.
Those who are penniless but entangled with business
Have enslaved themselves to debt.
The beggar who is starving but still begs his relatives
Has sold out to their frank ridicule.
Even though I know this, I cannot let the situation go.

My welcoming gifts for the six provinces of Ling
Are these fortresses as well as a treasure trove
That must be shared as the general wealth of all.
For the citizens of Ling,
There are the dzo bearing excellent tea
And the land of Ma abounding in the six grains.
As for the ancestral castle of Chophen Nagpo,
It will be the fortress of the nine tiger cubs of the
    Greater Lineage

And be called Kukhar Tazhi Zilnon [Quells the Four
    Borders with Splendor].
For the eight warriors of the Middle Lineage,
There is Tsendzong Nyima Khyilwa [Shining Sun Secure
    Fortress].
And for the seven brothers of the Lesser Lineage of Bumpa,
There is Kukhar Khyugtrug Tagtsé [Garuda Chick Tiger
    Peak Fort].

Inwardly, support the dharma with statues, scriptures,
    and stupas.
Outwardly, maintain the local customs,
And display the golden spire.
All of this must be upheld from generation to generation.
Concerning Ngulchu-tro Dzong [Ormolu Fortress] of the
    Bumpa Clan,
Trakhar Namdzong [Vulture Sky Fortress] of Chipon,
Trothung's Be'u-tag Dzong [Tiger Gem Fortress], and others,
You must not squander their wealth.
From among the twelve myriarchies of Ling,
Here we will have fifty neighborhoods of a thousand
    families each.
The leaders will be the Thirty Brethren
Who include the Seven Super Warriors
And the Three Ultimate Warriors: Falcon, Eagle, and Wolf.
In their own districts, fortresses, political affairs, and so on,
They must have complete sovereignty as vast as the sky.
They must be as steadfast as the support of the earth.
When the bandits of Hor pass through here,
The people of the six provinces of Ling have no reason to
    confront them
As I am the owner of the land,
And the origins of the dispute stem from me.

I will stand up and face them.

If you understood this story, it is sweet to your ears.

If not, there is no way to explain it.

Ling, bear this in mind.

SONG #5, CHAPTER 9

The song is Ala Ala Ala.

Thala leads the melody.

Ever since I was born in my dearest mother's lap,

My beauty has stood out from the crowd.

Well, then, good sir, Divine Son Joru,

Listen here to some examples of how it is.

In the wealthy district of Kyalo,

I, the maiden Drukmo, was content in my own home.

The hordes of mighty warriors of Ling think I am just a
    plaything,

And you come here dancing around on horseback,

Joru, treating me with contempt.

This innocent maiden staying in her home,

How sad to think this is the way of karma.

The prayer flags hoisted on the mountain peaks are lovely
    from a distance,

But anchored on the mountain, they are powerless to leave

Yet unable to remain still, flapping constantly in the wind.

The mountain does not suffer; it is simply a mountain.

The icy wind does not suffer; it is merely being wind.

It is the innocent prayer flags that are punished.

I, Drukmo of Kyalo,

Compelled by my station, am powerless to leave

Yet unable to stay, manipulated by Joru.

But, regardless of station, Ling's men do not suffer;

For them it is just a horse race.
Joru, you do not suffer; to you it is all a game.
Suffering and punishment fall on Drukmo's shoulders.
As it is said that the boy Joru is mandated by heaven,
If dissension has been spread among the gods,
And if the nagas have been troubled, Drukmo confesses it.

SONG #6, CHAPTER 9

No matter how many songs I sing,
May they resound with the clear bell of truth.
Now then, Gogmo's wondrous son,
I have some things to tell you.
According to the worldly Tibetan proverbs,
If humans are ignorant of their ancestral lineage,
They are like wandering monkeys in an endless jungle.
Likewise, if you are ignorant of the hierarchy of your values,
You are like a stranger who has lost his way.
To begin, there are four classes of noble horses:
The Dowa, the Begto, the Mu-kheng, and the Gyiling steed.
The long-torsoed are the best of the Dowa breed,
The white Begto, the bulky Mu-kheng, and the light Gyiling
Are the superior ones of their breeds.
The largest noble steeds, like the rays of the sun,
Are perfectly proportioned,
The crossbreeds, like a taut silken thread,
Are supple but firm,
And the smaller noble steeds, like an iron flute,
Have fine coats and long bodies.
The frontlets of horses are ordered thus:
The superior horse must have a garuda frontlet,
The middling horse, that of a goat,

And the horse with the frontlet of a deer is inferior.
There are also three varieties of hocks:
The bull hock, deer hock, and goat hock,
Corresponding to superior, middling, and inferior horses.
There are seven types of horse teeth.
The kyang type is large and concave,
The bull type is like the pods of pennycress,
And the sheep type is small and pearly white.
These three are the best teeth of all.
Then there are teeth that are sharp, like a tiger's,
Those that hang down, like a camel's,
And those that are snaggle-toothed, like a pig's.
These are the three worst types of teeth.
Finally teeth with a small concavity are of intermediate
     quality.
There are five distinctive coats.
First, the long coarse hair that is like that of a deer
And, second, the short coarse hair, like that of a tiger,
Are the superior coats.
Then hair that is long and smooth, like that of a fox,
Or short and smooth, like that of a grizzly bear, are the
     inferior coats.
The donkey coat, neither smooth nor coarse,
Distinguishes horses of middling breed.
There are seven kinds of hooves.
A high and attractive hoof, like a fine cup made from rhino
     horn,
A hoof that is worn down with a rim like ridged copper
     petals,
A hoof that is short and straight, like iron fangs,
These are the three superior types of hooves.
Hooves drawn in with no cleft in the sole,
Those that are rounded with no edge,

And those that are flat and leave no clear print behind
Are the three worst types of hooves.
A hoof is middling that has no attributes, save not being
    crooked.
In general, a horse must have sturdy bones.
Its neck bones must resemble those of a tiger
And preferably be nicely rounded.
The backbone should be solid in the middle
And, without sagging, curve elegantly at its three main joints.
The lowest and most resilient bones are the hooves,
Which are best large, thick, and short.
The poll, just behind the ears,
Is best low rather than high.
Behind the tail are the haunches,
Where, conversely, high rather than low is best.
The muscles of the thigh should not bulge
Like a gravid belly, but are better flat.
The forelock should be thick and long.
The mane, long and flowing as silk,
And the horse's neck, akin to a stretched khata,
Is better long than short.
The ribcage, which cradles the lungs,
Is better well-proportioned than simply large.
The upper flank, where the kidneys rest,
Is better to be pulsating than to be weak,
And as it pulses, it is best if the ribs move in rhythm.
As the vessel for the breath, the lungs are best buoyant.
As the vessels for blood, the liver is best if compact
And the spleen if salubrious.
As the vessel for eaten grass, intestines are good if capacious.
Those are the four vessels of a great steed.
Just as a person adorns his head with a hat,
The horse's head and ears are its millinery.

A person in this rugged clime must have sturdy shoes.
Just so, a horse's hooves are best if they are substantial.
The rump above the tail must be able to hold a liter of grain.
Between the eyes and ears, there should be a clear cavity
And between the two nostrils a narrowing.
Between the forehead and the shoulders, there must be
     definition.
The four limbs must be solidly built
And the forelegs aligned with the shoulders.
There are five traits that enhance a horse's speed.
A horse with a falconlike breast can whip like a gale wind,
One with the mattocklike head of an autumn yak wields
     agility,
And one with the haunches of a stout-loined lion can outrun
     a doe.
Another with flaring nostrils and sharp eyes is fast as a rabbit
     on the run,
And one as rare as a hairless tiger has the speed of scudding
     clouds.
These five qualities endow racehorses with skill.
As if that were not enough,
On the head of an excellent horse
One finds seven features, named for seven animals:
The deep brow of a drong,
The downcast eyes of a tortoise,
The slit pupils of an angry snake,
The cavernous nostrils of a snow lion,
The fleshy mouth of a Bengal tigress,
Fine vulture-down ears,
And a deer-chin muzzle.
These are the fine features resembling those of seven animals,
And a superior horse is endowed with them all.
As if that were not enough,

On the body of an excellent horse,
One finds eighteen sets of rippling muscles.
At the forehead, muscles that interlock like a raven's crossed
neck-feathers,
And at the nape, muscles that overlap like those at a tigress'
neck.
The masseter muscles are bulky, prominent as a sheep's
full belly,
And the muscles of the throat are lithe and undulate like fish.
At the base of the neck, the trapezius muscle rises forward
like a saw,
And as it reaches posteriorly, it resembles the split shoulder
of a yak.
The pectoral muscles are compact and shaped like a frog,
The shoulder muscles bulge and rise like the full moon,
The muscles of the lower leg are taut as a golden chord,
And along the spine, the muscles are sinuous, like a slithering
snake.
As though it were the pitched spokes of a golden wheel,
The latissimus muscle supports the saddle,
And the intercostal muscles are penetrating,
Like a turquoise dragon entering its cave.
The croup muscles resemble a heap of wool,
The gastroc muscles look like piglets asleep in their sty,
The muscles of the loins are like a sack of barley,
The inner thigh muscles are like a tightly wound ball of yarn,
And the muscles of the barrel evoke the tributaries of a great
river.
Muscles that interlace like fingers are located at the base
of the tail.
These are the eighteen rippling muscles,
And a superior horse is endowed with them all.
As if that were not enough,

The domed cranium should be thick,
Fronted by prominent cheekbones.
The cranial cavity should be elevated three fingerbreadths,
Its poll like palms pressed together.
The head and the neck should be elegantly joined,
The withers thick,
And the scapulae, fine and wide.
The humeri should be short and relaxed,
And the fore-cannon bones, straight and supple.
Where the saddled is placed, the horse should be slightly
    broad,
And the three intervertebral joints should be flexible.
The ribs should spread like feathers,
The pelvis should be long,
The femur short and curved and the femoral head wide.
The hind-cannon bones should be straight,
The pastern bones just above the hooves should be long,
And the fetlocks are better to be short.
The root of the coccyx should be short and thick.
These are the twenty bones of a hero.
It is said that each superior horse has them.
All of these are complete within a superior horse.

Song #7, Chapter 11

The song is Ala Ala Ala.
Thala leads the melody.
May the guru, yidam, dakini, these three,
Remain inseparable as my crown ornament,
And may they grant their blessings.
Hail to my friends—

When we were youthful, we shared the job of caring for the
little lambs.
When we were even younger, we were flower-picking
companions.
Listen to Drukmo's song.

You cannot predict which horse will be the fastest,
But we will know it when the winning rider assumes the
throne.
You cannot say which boy is best,
But it will be obvious when one of them becomes king
of Ling.
As for knowing who will conquer the southern continent
Jambudvipa,
There is no need to bicker; we will know soon enough.
For today we view this spectacle,
This horse race of colorful Ling.
For everyone racing, from the highest chieftain
Down to the lowliest Gu-ru,
The main booty they say is Drukmo.
But I have my doubts.
More likely it is Kyalo's great wealth and the rule of the
kingdom.

These are the Thirty Brethren who are all hoping to win
this wager:
Nyibum Daryag of Serpa,
Anu Paseng of Ombu,
Rinchen Darlu of Muchang; those three
Are the Three Ultimate Warriors,
Known to the enemies as Falcon, Eagle, and Wolf,
The heart, eyes, and life force of Ling.

Then Gyatsha Zhalkar of Bumpa,
Unrivalled Sengtak Adom,
Tsagyal Denma Jangtra,
Chieftain Zigphen of Tag-rong,
Chokyong Bernag of Gadé,
Cholu Buyi Darphen,
And Nyatsha Aten of Tag-rong
Are the Seven Super Warriors.
They are the hammers that strike the head of the enemy
And are like parents who watch over vulnerable relatives.
They are the very foundation of Ling
And the leaders of its seven ten-thousand-strong armies.

Then Uncle King Chipon,
Lion Minister Senglon,
Mazhi Chieftain Trothung,
And Lhabu Namkha Sengzhal
Are the four elder statesmen of Ling,
Those with minds more vast than space
And deeper than the oceans.

Then Nangchung Yuyi Metog,
Gung-gi Marleb of Rongtsa,
Shelkar Gyangdrag of Mupa,
Changtri Ngamchen of Ombu,
Cho-nga Paser Dawa,
Gungpa Buyi Kyatra,
Chief Sengseng of Cha-nag,
Yuyag Gonpo Tongthub,
Dongtsen Nang-ngu Apel,
Godpo Nyima Lhundrub,
Bu-yag Drug-gyé of Kyalo,
Buchung Daryag of Serpa,

And Abar Buyi Phentag
Are the Thirteen Cherished Sons of Ling.
They are newest to the ranks of the warriors,
Like lions with the three skills perfected
And garuda chicks with fully developed wings.
Outwardly, they are as sharp as poison thorns,
And inwardly, they are as soft and gentle as a lambskin
  chuba.
Though lowest in rank,
As youth, they are the most treasured.

Michen Gyalwé Lhundrub and Lingchen Tharpa Sonam
Are the two men of karmic power,
And Gyapon Sergyi Argham and Tongpon Treltsé Shemchog
Are the two unrelenting warriors.
They stand firm as Mount Meru
But advance with the intensity of the sun.
They hold fast as the four stays that hoist the white tents
And are as strong as the four pillars on which a square house
  is built.
They are the chieftains of their four tribes.

Tonpa Gyaltsen of Kyalo,
Guru Gyaltsen of Denma,
Nyima Gyaltsen of Kar-ru,
And Tharpa Gyaltsen of Nag-ru
Are the four who carry the name Gyaltsen [Victory Banner].
They excel in attaining merit and virtue.
They are indifferent to hierarchy
And care not for their own glory or fame.

Tsangpé Ngo-luk of Agé,
Dar-jam Ngo-luk of Mupa,

And Sintsha Ngo-luk of Tag-rong
Are the three men who are called Sheep-a-peep Ngo-luk.
Their good looks are renowned among the masses,
And even sheep turn to glimpse their faces,
Thus they are called Sheep-a-peep.

The arbiter Werma Lhadar
And the judge Wangpo Darphen
Are the two arbiters of Ling,
Renowned for their broad-mindedness.
Over hundreds of meetings,
No one has overruled their authority
Nor reversed their decisions.

Those were the Thirty Brethren
Who are the reincarnations of the thirty great mahasiddhas
And now have the honor of being the Thirty Brethren.
They are the men who stroke the whiskers of tigers,
Who seize the horns of wild yak,
And who grab the turquoise mane of the snow lion.

The doctor Kunga Nyima,
The astrologer Lhabu Yangkar,
The diviner Kunshé Thigpo,
And the magician Khaché Migmar
Are the four minor warrior mentors—
One who cuts the lasso of the Lord of Death,
One who dispels the invisible spells of enemies and spirits,
One who directly reveals the future,
And lastly one who, as a last resort, can confuse the minds
    of the enemy.

Gu-ru, son of Khyishi
And Gogmo's son, Joru,
Are the two beggars of Ling,
Yet by birth they are of the ancestral lineage of the
    mighty warriors.

Those Three Ultimate Warriors—Falcon, Eagle, and Wolf—
Are as exalted as the sun, moon, and stars.
If one of them were to win the wager, the treasure should go
    to all three.
Set like jewels in the azure firmament,
May their sovereignty be as all encompassing as the sky.

Those seven sublime Super Warriors,
Resembling the seven golden mountains,
Should unite to become the ornaments of the world.
May their fervor be as staunch as the earth.

Those thirteen little cherished sons,
Like the thirteen ancient arrows of existence,
May they share equally the tiger-skin quiver.
Until the time comes to tame the enemy,
May they continue to grace the ground of Ling.
If the buddha activity of the auspicious connection does not
    go astray,
They will come to be the weapons that tame the four maras.
May the ancient arrows be not scattered.

Those four very wise mentors

Are like the four great rivers that flow from the mouths
    of four animals.[45]
May they merge together as the ornament of the great ocean.
They will come to subdue the world with their power.
May they flow without interruption.

Those four wise tribal chieftains
Are like the four pillars that support a square house.
Let them unite to adorn the noble ancestral castle.
May they be immovable.

Those four men who have earned the name Gyaltsen
Are like the four claws of the proud white lion.
May they unite to adorn the white snow mountains.
They will come to splendidly subdue their enemies.
May they never age or decline.

Those three men who have earned the name Sheep-a-peep
    Ngo-luk
Are ornaments of the perfect beauty of the world.
May they mature as tigers in their prime,
And may their youth never decline.

The two arbiters of Ling
Are the two eyes that distinguish good and bad karma.
May they unite to become a repository of skillful means and
    wisdom
And utter only what is exactly right.
May their karma be untainted.

---

45. This is a reference to four great rivers, given as the Ganges, the Indus, the
Pakyu, and the Sidha, considered to arise from the mouth of an elephant, peacock, horse, and lion, respectively. We were unable to identify the Pakyu and
the Sidha as current-day rivers.

Joru is perky, ever so perky.
Gu-ru is crooked, ever so crooked.
Although it is hard for them to unite,
Today, I, Drukmo, will bring them together.
The straight arrow prefers to go.
The curved bow is happy to stay.
Although their actions and forms are dissimilar,
When they collaborate, the enemy's life is cut off at the root.
Therefore, the clean and the filthy should be complementary.
Although manure is not part of the food,
It is the best companion for the growth of beans and grains.
Just as the irrigated paddies are the ornament of China
And the stalks of grain bring benefit to Tibet,
Joru and Gu-ru should have a pact to join together.
May the difference between good and bad be discerned.
No matter who wins the wager,
May it become the general wealth of the tribes.
May it not become grounds for dispute.

Well then, now the spectacle begins.
From the Ma Kali middle path of the gods,
The man dressed in white
Who seems to be led by a celestial army
Is Dongtsen Nang-ngu Apel
Astride the swift steed Turquoise Bird.
The horse seems not to be running, but flying.
Flying, it seems to traverse the path of the birds.
After that comes the supreme Tharpa Gyaltsen
Astride the swift steed Tshal-lu Tshamshé [Sorrel Dancer].
Then comes Chief Zigphen of Tag-rong
Astride the steed Porog Tongcham [Raven One Thousand
    Dances].
Then comes Nyatsha Aten

Astride the steed Gang-ri Dingshé [Snow Mountain Jumper].
Then comes Trogyal, the son of Gungwa
Astride the steed Nag-tra Phurshé [Black-Spotted Flyer].
Then comes Sintsha Ngo-luk of Tag-rong
Astride the steed Kyungnag Phurshé [Black Garuda Flyer].
After him is Chief Sengseng of Chagnag
Astride the steed Lung-gi Trulkhor [Magic Wheel of Wind].
After him is Mazhi Chief Trothung
Astride the steed Pharwa Nga-nag [Jackal Black Tail].
Those are the eight men and horses of Tag-rong.
They are like a lineage of great and majestic tigresses.
Fearless, they run through the sandalwood forest,
Snapping the trees into bundles of twigs.

Further on, from the Greater Lineage,
That swarthy man with conch-white teeth
Is Nyibum Daryag of the royal lineage of the Mukpo Clan,
The chief of the Serpa of Upper Ling
And the head of the Three Ultimate Warriors,
Atop his swift mount Serdang Nyima Trulkhor [Golden Sun
    Magic Wheel].
Next comes Cholu Buyi Darphen
Astride the steed Mug-gu Dingshé [Maroon Flyer].
Next comes Michen Gyalwé Lhundrub
Astride the steed Gapa Trijam [Blaze Gentle Seat].
Next comes the great Tharpa Sonam
Astride the steed Khyung-nag Dingshé [Soaring Black
    Garuda].
Next to come is Phentag, son of Abar,
Astride the steed Meri Tsubshé [Turbulent Volcano].
Next to come is Sergyi Argham
Astride the steed Gya-gyug Serja [Racing Golden Bird].
Next to come is Sotra Yami [Unrivaled Sparkling Teeth]

Astride the steed Tong-gyug Phenpo [Swift Racer].

Finally comes Tsangpé Ngo-luk of Agé

Riding Gang-ri Odden [Radiant Snow Mountain].

These are the eight men and horses of the Greater Lineage.

The Greater Lineage is like a glacier,

The eight men are like statuesque lions,

And the eight horses like their lavish turquoise manes.

The Greater Lineage roams the snow-capped mountains.

You can see their trail on the glaciers right now.

Further on comes the center beam that established the Middle
Lineage,

A boy as vigorous as a turquoise-maned lion.

He is Anu Paseng of Ombu,

The middle of the Three Ultimate Warriors

And one of the four heirs.

He rides the swift-winged horse Marpo Lung-shog [Red
Wings of Wind].

After him comes the warrior Sengtak Adom

Astride the steed Tong-ri Rag-kar [Thousand-Mountain
Palomino].

After him comes Chokyong Bernag of Gadé

Astride the steed Lung-nag Jeichod [Captures the Black
Wind].

After him comes Dzongpon Lha-lu [Divine Naga] of the
sunny side of Ma

Astride the steed Maja Tshal-lu [Vermillion Peacock].

After him comes Nyima Lhundrub of Godpo

Astride the steed Mug-gu Tongcham [Sorrel Dancer].

After him comes Gonpo Tongthub of Yuyag

Astride the turquoise horse Norbu Lungdzin [Jewel Catches
the Wind].

After him comes the only son Drug-gyé of Kyalo

Astride the great steed Gugya Rachig [Select Unicorn].
After him comes Mikar Lhabu Samdrub of Dru
Astride the steed Ngangkar Dro-kyid [White Swan Happy
    Gait].
They are the eight men and horses of the Middle Lineage,
Men like turquoise dragons rising from their lair
Astride horses like massing southerly clouds.
The Middle Lineage is racing in the colorful Crag Mountain.
Look, you can see that the rocks are notched with their trails.

Next, the man who you see coming is Chipon Rongtsa Tragen,
Riding the steed Sha-kyang Drelgo [Ochre Mule Head].
Next comes Senglon Gala Rigshé [Knowing Awareness]
Riding the steed Gangkar Gyengchen [Great Haughty
    Mountain].
Next comes Lama Gyaltsen of Gojo
Riding the steed Tringyi Shugchen [Great Strength of the
    Clouds].
They are the three brethren of the Lesser Lineage.

Now you see coming, swooping like a black eagle for prey,
The son who is like a garuda chick with fully developed
    wings,
Rinchen Darlu of Muchang,
One of the Three Ultimate Warriors
And the youngest of the four heirs.
He is the rope ladder that leads to the sky.
The swift mount that he rides is Yuja Triphel [Turquoise Bird
    Increasing Myriad].
Next comes the unrivaled Gyatsha Zhalkar,
An emanation of the divine king of the swans,
One of the four heirs,
And the grandson of the king of China.

He is preferable to seven hundred thousand warriors in battle
And is the leader of the Seven Super Warriors of Ling.
He rides the swift and noble steed Gyaja Sogkar [Pheasant
    White Shoulder].
Next comes Denma Jangtra of Tshazhang
Riding the steed Ngultrug Dempa.
Next comes Rongtsa Norbu Lhadar
Riding the steed Maja Trikar [White Throne Peacock].
Next comes Dar-jam Ngo-luk of Mupa,
Riding the steed Dzamling Rabkar [Glittering White World].
Next comes Darphen Nagpo of Mupa
Riding the steed Serdang Ya-med [Incomparable Golden
    Radiance].
Next comes Chipon's son, Nangchung Yutag,
Who is the support of the life essence of the Thirty Brethren
    of Ling,
The one who uplifts the spirit of every human being.
He rides the steed Maja Trichen [Great Peacock Throne].
Next comes Cho-nga Paser Dawa
Riding the steed Dungja Yu-ngog [Conch Bird Turquoise
    Mane].
Those are the eight men and horses of the Lesser Lineage,
Men like great soaring garudas
With eight horses like the fully extended wings.
The Lesser Lineage is racing in the hilltops,
And you can see that the grassy hills are already beaten
    down.

Farther along you see that fair man with golden ornaments,
Tonpa Gyaltsen of Kyalo
Astride the steed Gugya Rachig [Select Unicorn].
Then comes Lhabu Namkha Sengzhal
Astride the steed Norbu Chamshé [Jewel Dancer].

Then comes Nyima Gyaltsen of Kar-ru
Astride the steed Log-mar Khyugshé [Red Lightening Bolt].
Then comes the great arbiter Werma Lhadar
Astride the steed Ngangpa Tselden [Agile Swan].
Then comes the judge Wangpo Darphen
Astride the steed Serden Phurshé [Golden Flyer].
Then comes the doctor Kunga Nyima
Astride the steed Sernya Rag-kar [Golden Fish Palomino].
Then comes the diviner Kunshé Thigpo
Astride the steed Tshal-lu Tingkar [Vermillion Fetlocks].
Then comes the astrologer Lhabu Yangkar
Astride the steed Dung-dog Chamshé [Conch-Colored
    Dancer].
Then comes the skillful magician Khaché Migmar
Astride the steed Gapa Droden [Blaze Prancer].
Then comes the Tibetan youth Michung Khadé
Astride the steed Khamhya Chukar [Palamino White
    Muzzle].
Then comes the handyman Gochod Yogpo Pagyal
Astride the steed Nag-tra Yak-gying [Spotted Haughty Yak].
Then comes the minister Akhod Tharpa Zorna
Astride the steed Gawa Géring [Old Long Life].
Those are the general public servants of Ling,

The three knowledgeable mighty warriors
And the four mentors who are minor warriors,
Down to the servants, beggars, and dogs.
Not only does each of these fools think his the fastest horse,
Not a one of them thinks himself unable to prevail.
Joru and Gu-ru have fallen behind,
And Dongtsen has taken off in front.
The rest are somewhere in between.

We have no way of knowing how things will turn out.
Which steed is taking the deepest breaths
Or which rider's windhorse is strongest
Are not things that I can know.

At the last comes the man bent as though carrying a great
    heavy load,
Yet he has never dropped it to the ground.
He actually has nothing, but pretends to have it all,
And he wears an unusual lead pouch hanging from
    his side.
His name is Khyishi Buyi Gu-ru,
And his horse is Gapa Trikyid [Blaze Happy To Be Led].
Following him is Gogmo's cherished son, Joru,
Riding his white-muzzled steed, Wild Kyang.
It doesn't look as if he is even racing, but rather just
    staying put—
Staying and chatting, yet still preparing to win the wager.
Who can know, but he sure looks like Joru
And the horse looks like my friend Kyang.
Where the ofttime fool Joru really is, no one can know,
And where the steed Wild Kyang rides, no one can tell.
Those two beggars of Ling,
Whether they are rich or poor, I do not know.
All the noble steeds of colorful Ling
Are running like banking fog up the mountain pass,
Running straight out like falcons flying,
And running downhill, tumbling like an avalanche.
No one can gain merit through theft.
No one can block previous karma with his or her own hand.
If you have understood this, it is sweet to your ears.
If not, there is no way to explain it.

SONG #8, CHAPTER 12

The beginning of Drukmo's final song:
The song is Ala Ala Ala.
Thala leads the melody.
In Tara's buddhafield, the pure land of Turquoise Leaf Array,
White Tara, know me
And be this maiden's friend and companion.
If you do not recognize this place,
It is the excellent land of Mönlam La [Aspiration Mountain
    Pass].
If you do not recognize me,
I am Kyalo Sengcham Drukmo.
They call me the fairest maiden in Jambudvipa
And the heart essence of the country of Ling.
I am the daughter of Kyalo Tonpa.
Today by tossing the flower,[46] I have chosen you.
I greet you now with thirteen offering scarves
As well as the long-stemmed auspicious cup
Filled with Queen of Siddhis longevity wine.
The grape wine of the land of India,
Rice liquor from the land of China,
And fresh barley beer from Tibet
Are the drinks that please the drala,
The select offerings that please the werma,
And the longevity nectars that extend life expectancy.
Please partake of these drinks that uplift one's spirit.

---

46. This is a reference to the tradition within tantric practices of tossing a
flower onto a mandala plate. Drukmo is using this analogously, but most commonly it is part of a ritual in which the spot on the mandala where the flower
lands denotes an auspicious connection with a particular tutelary deity or
buddha family.

The Queen of Siddhis longevity scarf
And the three activity scarves of lha, lu, and nyen,
The treasure scarf of the queen of China,
The divine cloth of the land of India,
A pearly scarf from an oyster's mouth,
A water scarf from the nagas, and so forth,
Are the thirteen offering scarves.
Today they are offered to greet you Great Lion.

This golden throne that quells the three realms with
    splendor,
I thought the highest ornament of Ling.
Yet today it does not touch the ground
Even though the white lions are not hoisting it up.
The silk umbrella Rinchen Pungpa [Heap of Jewels],
I thought the highest ornament adorning the golden throne.
Yet today, even without the pole-bearers holding it aloft,
It reaches into the sky, turning and spinning.
The drum of the law Selwé Odden [Brilliantly Shining],
The conch of the law Karmo Gyangdrag [White Lady
    Furlong],
And the cymbal Nyima Drug-drag [Sun Dragon Voice],
Today, without being sounded or struck,
Their melodious sounds spontaneously resonate.
Isn't this delightful, Lord Great Lion?
Isn't this joyous, people of Ling?
And not only that,
The wealth of the treasury of Crystal Crag
And the self-existing weapons of the drala
Today have come together to ornament this great being.

This lord of helmets Gyalwa Thodkar [Victorious White Skull]
Is offered to adorn your crown chakra of great bliss.

The silk pennon Nyima Rangshar [Self-Arising Sun],
The victory banner Tashi Gu-tseg [Auspicious Many-Tiered],
The garuda pennon Godkyi Ulu [Vulture Down],
The colorful studded gems in the front, like five-colored
    silks,
And the helm ornament Lhayi Sopa [Divine Sentry]
All unite as ornaments of this white helmet.
May its glory surpass the heavens.

Along with the king of armor, Tro-nag Zilpa [Resplendent
    Bronze],
The billowing of the longevity knots on the black belt Drala
    Tsedud [Drala Longevity Knot],
And the shield Ba-mar Lingzab [Red Cane Deep Backing],
With massing rainbow clouds of werma,
Unite to ornament this great being.
May his life force be as solid as a rock.

From the longevity clothing Tongden Jigme [Fearless One
    Thousand],
The amulet Mamo Lado [Life Essence Stone of the Mamos],
And the sash, the karmic scarf of the dakinis,
Blessings abound like scudding clouds of mist, so amazing.
A drumming rain of siddhis
Unites to adorn the three nadis (avadhuti, rasana, and
    lalana).
May his lifespan be longer than a river,
Firm and stable, without aging or infirmity.

Mongolian boots, which quell the eight classes with splendor,
Along with the knee covering that protects from all harm,
Unite to adorn the feet of this great being.
May he suppress and reverse the classes of demons.

The tiger quiver Drala Dzongchen [Great Fortress of
the Drala]
And the leopard case Werma Lané [Werma's Life Essence
Source]
Naturally unite to ornament his weapons.
May his wisdom and means be indivisible.
The sword Tabpa Lenmé [Strikes without Reposte]
Sparkles with local guardians,
The lance Khamsum Dradul [Subjugates Enemies of the
Three Realms]
Shoots the poison flames of the nyen,
The lasso Drulnag Domgu [Nine-Fathomed Black Snake]
Makes the panting sound of naga demons,
And the bow Ragod Khyilpa [Curving Wild Horn]
Chokes the air with the poison vapor of Rahu demons.
The divine arrow that knows human language
Is the thick glottal click of the drala.
The slingshot Chumig Gu-Dril [Braided Nine Eyes]
Blows the black winds of the mamos.
The life essence stone that attracts the oath-bound
guardians
Is a lightning-born meteorite
That radiates the light of the te'urang.
The ax Drag-ri Harshag [Crag Mountain Rock Splitter]
Sends out the sparks of king demons,
And the razor knife Shelgyi Drichung [Crystal Razor]
Causes the Nyentag to descend like lightning.
Unite today in the hands of this great being.

May he be the yoke upon the Hor and Dud
And bind naga and tsen to the oath.
May he annihilate Shingtri,
Turn Sadam to the dharma,

Bind the four maras by oath,
And turn the four borderland countries to the dharma.

Just as when the moon arises from the mountain peak
To blossom the jasmine flowers in the gardens and swell the
    milky lakes,
Lord Great Lion, when your lotus feet place a yoke upon the
    haughty ones
The doctrine of goodness and decency will flourish.

Lord Great Lion, the golden mountain of your presence
Is as though embraced by the youthful clouds of dawn.
Your armor and weapons are radiant,
And your authentic presence is unrivaled.
Lord Great Lion, like a blazing jewel,
You emanate a shower of benefit and well-being.
Please hold me inseparably.

At the tip of a pliant stem is a lovely blue lotus,
And like a hovering honeybee,
I offer myself to you, Lord Great Lion.
Beautiful to hear is the voice intoxicated by great bliss,
And with a song like that of the kalavinka bird,
I offer myself to you, Lord Great Lion.
The waves of wandering thoughts when overcome by
    transcendent joy
Are an ocean of amrita of bliss-emptiness, free from thought.
Partake of this, Lord Great Lion.

The jeweled ship of the wealth of Kyalo
Is guided by the oar of compassion.
Make it your own, Lord Great Lion.
From now until the heart of enlightenment,

Accomplish the great purpose of the teachings and of all
  beings.
May I, like a body and its shadow,
Be inseparable from you, Lord Great Lion.
Gesar, hold this in your heart.

Glossary of Places and Terms

abhisheka. A ceremony of empowerment, common to Buddhism, Hinduism, and Jainism.

bodhisattva. One who aspires to attain enlightenment but only for the benefit of all other sentient beings, always placing the needs of others before themselves.

bodhicitta. Mind directed toward clarity and compassion. An inherent quality of all beings.

chakra. Literally means "wheel." Generally refers to a network of centers within the body.

Chamara. An island southwest of Jambudvipa inhabited by demons.

daka, dakini. A male or female deity or energy spirit. Generally wrathful or semi-wrathful, though the female dakinis are often portrayed as helpful in one's spiritual path.

dharma. Refers to the spiritual teachings of Buddhism as well as worldly dharmas, which denote the way that things work or a more secular notion of truth.

doha. Spiritual hymn or yogic song, commonly recited spontaneously.

drala. Spiritual protective energies, often symbolically represented as armed figures on horseback, or as animals, or nature spirits such as moutains or rivers. Interchangeable with the term *werma*.

drong. Wild yak. Larger and more powerful and aggressive than domesticated yaks.

Dud. A country of demons and bandits north of Ling that figures prominently in a subsequent tale, *The Battle of Dud and Ling*, generally regarded as the greatest battle saga of the epic.

dri. A female yak.

dzo. A male beast of burden resulting from the cross between a yak and a cow.

dzomo. A female dzo. Dzomo are fertile whereas the dzo are sterile.

empowerment. See *abhisheka*.

garuda. A large mythic bird. In Hinduism, it is Vishnu's mount, and in Buddhism, it is the king of the birds representing the warriors' vastness, strength, and power.

Gog. The country bordering Ling, home of Ralo Tonpa Gyaltsen. Gesar's mother was brought there after leaving her naga kingdom and thereafter was called Gogmo, or "woman from Gog."

Hor. A kingdom to the north and east of Ling, ruled by demons and populated by bandits. Raiding parties came from Hor into Ling particularly to prey on traveling merchants. A later tale relates the story of war between Hor and Ling.

Jambudvipa. The southern continent in Buddhist cosmology referring to the world of humans and equivalent to the planet earth in Western cosmological systems.

kaya. The Tibetan honorific term for the body.

khata. A ceremonial scarf.

khatvanga. A tantric scepter. An ornamental three-pronged spear adorned at the top with three human heads.

kyang. Also spelled kiang. A Tibetan wild ass. A very powerful and noble creature that to this day roams the high plains of Tibet.

Ladakh. A region in far western Tibet. Now on the northern border of India and Tibet.

Lake Manasarovar. One of the world's largest high-altitude freshwater lakes at 15,000-foot elevation with a surface area of 160 square miles and maximum depth of 300 feet. It is spectacular to behold, deep blue in color with the holy mountain of Kailash visible to the north. It lies in southern Tibet approximately 600 miles west of Lhasa. The lake is sacred to Hindus and Jains as well as to Buddhists.

Ling. A large ancient kingdom in eastern Tibet, presumably in Amdo Province.

Ma Chu River. The river in northeastern Tibet that flows into China, where it becomes the Yellow River. Sixth-largest river in the world.

Ma Valley. Large valley in Ling in the area of the headwaters of the Ma Chu River.

Magyal Pomra. A mountain range in northeastern Tibet and also the name of the mountain spirit, or zodor, associated with it.

major and minor marks. The thirty-two major marks and the eighty minor marks that describe the physical attributes of a buddha.

mara. Usually translated as "demon." A class of native malevolent beings that can cause obstruction. When capitalized, refers to the tempters of Shakyamuni Buddha who appear just prior to his enlightenment.

Mount Kailash. A mountain in southwestern Tibet. It has 21,770 feet of elevation and is sacred to Hindus, Buddhists, Jains, and Bon. In Buddhist cosmology, it is known as Mount Meru and is often pictured as the center of the universe.

myriarchies. A community comprised of approximately 10,000 households.

nadi. Literally "channel." Subtle body channels found within the physical body. They are said to number 72,000 with three main channels: the avadhuti, lalana, and rasana.

naga, nagini. A class of beings associated with water. Water serpents that are iconographically represented as having human torsos and blue-skinned, serpentlike lower bodies. The female naginis have turquoise hair.

nirvana. The state of enlightenment beyond confusion where suffering due to the clinging to fixation, aggression, confusion, and desire has been overcome.

nyen. Spirits of mountain ranges. In between the celestial gods and the underground spirits. Nyen Gedzo also went by the zodor name Magyal Pomra.

Nyida Khatrod. A meeting place meaning "Conjoined Sun and Moon."

rakshasa. Cannibal demon. Shape-shifting monster.

samsara. The confused cyclic existence of this world, in contrast to nirvana.

sangha. The community of Buddhist practitioners.

Seven Super Warriors. A group of superior warriors consisting of Gyatsha, Zigphen, Denma, Nyatsha, Sengtak, Gadé, and Darphen.

stupa. Ornamental tower-shaped monument usually containing the relics of meditation masters.

Tag-rong. One of the districts of Ling, and home to Trothung.

Ten Virtues.

1. to renounce killing and instead protect life
2. to renounce taking what is not given and instead practice generosity
3. to renounce sexual misconduct and instead follow the rules of discipline
4. to renounce lying and instead tell the truth
5. to give up sowing discord and instead reconcile disputes
6. to abandon harsh speech and instead speak pleasantly
7. to renounce worthless chatter and instead recite prayers
8. to renounce covetousness and instead learn to be generous
9. to give up wishing harm to others and instead cultivate the desire to help them
10. to put an end to wrong views and instead establish in yourself the true and authentic

Thirty Mighty Warriors. A group of superior Ling warriors, some of whom also belong to the ranks of the Seven Super Warriors and the Three Ultimate Warriors.

Three Rare and Supreme Ones. The three Buddhist objects of refuge: the Buddha as example, the Dharma as teaching, and the Sangha as inspiration and companions.

Three Ultimate Warriors. Falcon, Eagle, and Wolf were respectively Nyibum Daryag, Anu Paseng, and Rinchen Darlu. Great warriors and leaders of Ling.

torma. Figures made usually of barley flour and butter that are used as ritual offerings in Buddhist ceremonies.

tsa-tsa. Small clay icons, often made from a mold as a meditation practice. Commonly consecrated and placed on a shrine or within a stupa.

tsen. Malevolent nonhuman earth spirits.

werma. See *drala*.

yak. The main beast of burden in Tibet. The female yak, a dri, is prized for her milk. Both the yak and dri are important sources of food, and their is fur used is for clothing and in tent construction.

yaksha. Nature spirit, usually benevolent.

zodor. A class of worldly spirit deities originally part of the Bon pantheon and attached to a place, often a mountain. The main zodor in the epic is Magyal Pomra, the name both for the mountain as well as the zodor.

Name Glossary

Amitabha. Buddha of the Sukhavati, the land of bliss, the pure land, the western buddhafield.

Amnyé Gompa Raja. An evil Bon sorcerer who attempts to kill Joru as an infant.

Avalokiteshvara. A bodhisattva, the embodiment of compassion, and one of the three principal protectors of this world, the other two being Manjushri and Vajrapani.

Chipon Rongtsa Tragen. Brother to Trothung and Senglon, uncle to Gesar, and elder of Ling. The chieftain of the Lesser Lineage of Mukpo. His son Lenpa Chogyal is killed in a raid on Gog.

Darphen. One of the Seven Mighty Warriors, and one of the elder leaders of Ling who has an important role in the later stories of the epic.

Demkar Lhamo. Naga queen wife of Tsugna Rinchen and mother to Gogmo.

Denma. Chief minister of Gesar, clever strategist, and tactical planner. Also known for his archery skills and as a great and loyal warrior.

Denza. Trothung's wife.

Dongtsen Apel. A leader of the Lesser Lineage of Ling and younger son of Trothung.

Dorje Ngangkar. The renowned diviner, and friend to the nagas.

Drukmo. Daughter of Tonpa Gyaltsen of Kyalo, the wise and beautiful girl who marries Gesar. Her hand is won in the horse race. Also known as Sengcham Drukmo, with Sengcham meaning "lion" and Drukmo meaning "sister dragon."

Dungkhyung Karpo. One of Gesar's drala brothers and one of his personal bodyguards. Co-born with Gesar.

Gesar. Known by many names at different times in the epic. *Dondrub* and *Topa Gawa* were names given to the mind stream prior to Gesar's birth. *Joru* was the name given to him shortly after birth by his half-brother Gyatsha. *Gesar* and *Norbu Dradul* were each his names after he wins the horse race and is enthroned as king. Also known as *Sengcham Gyalpo*, meaning Great Lion King.

Gogmo. The woman from Gog, Gesar's mother. A nagini and daughter of the naga king Tsugna Rinchen. Metok Lhadzé and Lenyu Khatam Do-to were her names prior to her leaving the naga lands with Padmasambhava.

Gyatsha. Elder half-brother of Gesar and grandson to the emperor of China. Becomes second-in-command to Gesar in further exploits of the epic.

Gyaza. Daughter to the Chinese emperor, primary wife of Senglon, and mother of Gyatsha.

Hayagriva. Horse-headed deity in the Buddhist and Hindu pantheon. Attendant to Avalokiteshvara.

Kunshé Thigpo. Literally "All Knowing Accurate One." A diviner.

Khyishi Buyi Gu-ru. Khyishi, which literally means "dead dog," is the lowliest clan of beggars and warriors. He was a companion to Joru at the beginning of the horse race.

Kunga Nyima. Literally "All Joyful Sun." A doctor in Ling who Gesar meets up with during the horse race.

Kyalo Tonpa Gyaltsen. Wealthy leader and father of Drukmo. Said to be the wealthiest man in Ling.

Lady Demkar Lhamo. Gogmo's mother and wife of the naga king Tsugna Rinchen.

Lenpa Chogyal. Son of Chipon. Killed in a battle with Gog.

Lhundrub. Also known as Gyalwé Lhundrub, he was an important chieftain of one of the six districts of Middle Ling and an elder warrior. A wealthy man who was a model of the noble respected leader.

Ludrul Odchung. One of Gesar's three drala siblings and guardian for Gesar.

Manéné. See *Nammen Karmo.*

Nammen Karmo. Also known as Manéné. Gesar's aunt and protector. Seen to be the feminine manifestation or aspect of Gesar's wisdom. Throughout the many stories of the epic, she provides important council to him and appears to him at dramatic times, sometimes as a bee or or other times as a dakini, often riding a horse or a lion.

Padmasambhava. A major figure in Tibetan Buddhism, historically felt to have come from India in the ninth century. When in Tibet he had many manifestations including *Padma Totreng, Lotus Born One, Guru Padma,* and *Zilnon Padma Drakpo,* as well as *Guru Rinpoche.*

Ralo Tonpa. King of Gog who received Yelga Dzéden, the nagini princess who will become Gogmo, Gesar's mother.

Senglon. Brother to Chipon and Trothung and husband to Gyaza, father of Gyatsha and Gesar.

Sengtak. A leader of Ling and one of the Seven Super Warriors, one of the most famous warriors of his clan.

Sheep-a-peep Ngo-luk. Warrior of Ling famed for his physical beauty. Gesar meets up with him during the horse race.

Thalé Odkar. Drala sister and protector of Gesar, co-born with him.

Thangtong Gyalpo. A spiritual advisor to the Mukpo tribe, a great Buddhist lama who serves as a major priest for Ling.

Topa Gawa. See *Gesar.*

Trothung. Brother to Chipon and Senglon. Uncle to Gesar. Chieftain to the Tag-rong province, an area in what is present-day Golok. Mischievous and slandering. Often at odds with Gesar.

Tsugna Rinchen. Naga king and father to Gogmo. Maternal grandfather to Gesar.

Werma Lhadar. One of the great arbiters of Ling. Often called upon to make judgments in important court cases and for mediation.

Zigphen. A chieftain of the Tag-rong tribe. Trothung's son, and one of the Thirty Mighty Warriors. Important warrior in the later stories of the epic.

The text of this book is set Linotype Palatino 10/15.
Designed by Hermann Zapf in 1948, and named after
16th-century Italian calligraphy master Giambattista Palatino,
Palatino is based on humanist fonts of the Italian Renaissance,
which mirror the letters formed by a broadnib pen,
giving the text a calligraphic grace.